I0629352

IN THE LIFE EVER AFTER

AN ELLIE KENT MYSTERY

ALICE K. BOATWRIGHT

Firefly Ink
BOOKS

For information, email Firefly Ink Books at FireflyInkBooks@gmail.com
or write to:
Firefly Ink Books
Box 351 20126 Ballinger Way NE
Shoreline, WA 98155-1117

ISBN: 979-8-9864344-7-6 (Print)
979-8-9864344-8-3 (Ebook)

Printed in the United States of America

Cover design by Karen Phillips
Book design by Sue Trowbridge

ALSO BY ALICE K. BOATWRIGHT

Ellie Kent mysteries
Under an English Heaven
What Child Is This?

Other fiction
Collateral Damage
Sea, Sky, Islands
Mrs. Potts Finds Thanksgiving

For Jim, my partner in crime and all things,
with love always

Learn what you are and be such.
—Pindar (ca. 518–ca. 438 BC)

An empty tomb precedes a resurrected life.
—Richard B. Pilgrim

CHAPTER ONE

Friday, February 23
Near Cherbourg, France

The fog became thicker and thicker as the road wound closer to the cliffs overhanging the English Channel. It was like driving straight into a void, and Clio Matthews found herself clutching the steering wheel of her little Renault, as if a tighter grip could help her see the way. She didn't enjoy driving even at the best of times, and this was definitely not one of those. A trickle of sweat ran down her spine.

She had ended up on this narrow cliff road by mistake, because she missed a turn when she thought she recognized the driver behind her as Edmund Danton. Not that this was likely. She had emailed him about her decision not to return to Paris, but to go straight on to England after her meeting about an upcoming exhibit at Galerie d'Artisanat in Trouville. He had cheered her on and said he'd be thinking of her, but he never suggested he would try to join her.

"Maybe you'll finally find those beautiful coins while you're there," he'd added in a postscript.

This was something of a joke between them, because he couldn't believe that, until recently, she had assumed her father's collection of Greek and Roman coins—missing for more than 15 years—would never be found. In his view, she had been passing up the chance for a treasure hunt with a million-pound pot of gold at the end; but, to her, the very thought of those coins only brought back family history she had done her best to forget.

Edmund didn't understand that it was only since she happened to meet him through her Paris gallery a few weeks before that she had talked much about her past with anyone. In his gentle, quirky way, he had cajoled her into revisiting memories and feelings she'd kept firmly locked away.

From that perspective, it was thanks to him that she'd finally written to Corinna and decided she was ready to let go of Oak Cottage and fully embrace her life in France. Still, as she drove on through the fog, she felt her confidence falter. Her last-minute decision meant the only ferry she could take was from Cherbourg. And she could have waited. Gone back to Paris. Corinna had not yet responded to her letter, no doubt because she had her own mixed feelings about going back to Little Beecham. To their meeting again. Now or ever.

The future was as impenetrable as the fog swirling around her. A pea-souper, she thought, which reminded her suddenly of childhood: Mrs. Murphy giving them pea soup for tea, and Pindar calling it "sea poop," which Corinna said was rude, but Clio laughed until she choked. She could almost imagine that was the scene she would find at Oak Cottage now. Not the silent house that had stood empty since her last visit more than a month ago.

The car she thought looked familiar had now been

following her for several miles. Clio glanced in her rearview mirror and wondered how she could have been so mistaken. The aggressiveness of this driver—the way he stayed close enough to make her go faster than she would have liked and never slowed even when she tapped her brakes—reminded her of someone, but it was certainly not Edmund.

She was thinking of his warm, friendly smile as she rounded a curve and headlights suddenly loomed out of the fog. On the narrow road, the oncoming car appeared to be heading straight for her; and, at the same time, the driver behind drew closer. Dazzled by their lights, she lost all sense of where she was on the road and turned the wheel too sharply in hopes of avoiding a collision.

A small misjudgment, but a fatal one.

In the next instant, she was off the road, airborne and helpless, as the ground fell away to the sea-washed rocks far below.

CHAPTER TWO

March 5 to 8
From England to France and back

Ellie Kent watched the rain-drenched English countryside flash by the train windows, surprised at the relief and excitement she felt to be leaving Little Beecham even for a few days. The train from Kingbrook to London hurtled along the tracks through villages and towns, past fields where new lambs pressed against their mothers for shelter, and through stretches of woods, where patches of yellow coltsfoot and celandine promised that spring was on its way.

In the seat facing her, her husband Graham was reading *The Guardian*, and she decided that, in his tweed suit, he could pass for a character out of one of those classic English movies from the 1940s. If they had been in a compartment, she would be the beautiful young woman in trouble, and he, the handsome stranger with whom she would exchange barbed, witty remarks. By the time the train reached its destination, they would have solved a mystery and fallen in love.

In real life, they were on the one-hour journey to London, where they would pick up the Eurostar to Paris. Neither train offered compartments, but that didn't matter, because they had already fallen in love. This was the next chapter, where the young woman is on holiday with the man of her dreams. Ellie smiled to herself, pleased that her own life had found its way to a happy ever after.

Of course, Graham didn't know what she was thinking. He read on, absorbed and relaxed, as if going to Paris were an everyday event in his life. But now and then, Ellie could catch him looking at her with an expression that showed he was as pleased as she was.

When he paused to shake and refold the pages of the paper, she tapped his knee with her toe.

"What do you want to see first?" she asked.

He smiled and said, "You drinking espresso in a Paris café."

"Ditto," she said, and they both laughed.

This trip had been Graham's idea. He thought they should celebrate their six-month anniversary, since they had been unable to take a honeymoon at the time of their marriage. Then they had been too busy preparing for her move from San Francisco to his home in England. But now, with Christmas behind them, and Easter still a few weeks off, he said they could get away.

Ellie was more than ready for a break from the long, dark winter in the Cotswolds. Even if the weather in Paris turned out to be every bit as cold and rainy as it had been in Little Beecham, it would still offer lights, color, people, and that enduring aura of romance.

She was not used to thinking of Europe as a place you could pop over to for a couple of days, but it was. Between breakfast and tea, they traveled from the vicarage to a flat overlooking the medieval streets of the Marais, and, in no time, they were ensconced in their own neighborhood café.

Ellie was happy to find that they quickly fell into the habits of their early relationship in California. For four whole days, Graham never had to don his clerical collar, and she was able to trot out her favorite city clothes. When they weren't meandering through museums and shops, or strolling along the banks of the Seine, they spent hours in cafés all over the city, people-watching and talking.

They also devoted a good deal of time to being alone at the flat, with no phone calls that had to be answered. No parishioners needing help, solace, or advice. And no wardrobe required. Graham read her poetry in his mellifluous French, while she soaked in the deep, narrow bathtub, and, in return, she used the special trick she had with her thumbs to massage the kinks out of his back.

On their last day, Ellie was debating what scarf to wear with her midnight-blue sweater and black slacks, when she heard Graham's phone chirp, announcing he had a message. The sender, she saw, was Charles Bell, the warden for Little Beecham's Church of St. Michael and All Angels, where Graham was the vicar. Usually, such messages had nothing to do with her, so Ellie was surprised to see her name.

The text said: *Corinna Matthews has been released. Heard she came looking for Mrs. Kent. Thought you ought to know.*

A quick scan of the people she'd met since she moved to England, as well as family, friends, university colleagues, and former students in the US produced no memory of anyone named Corinna Matthews. Aside from that, Ellie couldn't imagine why someone looking for her should concern Graham or be any business at all of Mr. Bell's. She did find the word "released" intriguing, though.

A moment later, when Graham emerged from the shower,

toweling off his lanky body and thick, gingery hair, she said, "You have a text from Mr. Bell."

"Has something happened?" he asked.

"I don't know. It beats me what it's all about."

In the mirror, she saw him pick up the phone as she doubled a long blue-black-and-silver silk scarf, wrapped it around her neck, and pulled the ends through, French style. As she watched, his expression darkened from surprise to displeasure, but he quickly turned off the phone and said, "It's nothing, love." Then he smiled, as if to underline his point.

"Nothing," she said, as she sat down on a chair to pull on her black leather boots. "As in nothing to worry about? Nothing to do? Or nothing you're going to tell me?"

"All of the above," he said firmly. "We're in Paris on holiday, remember?"

"I do, and I can't imagine any place I'd rather be or anyone I would rather be with. But I can tell you know who this person is who was looking for me, and I don't, so I wish you'd tell me."

"The only thing you need to know about Corinna Matthews is that it wasn't you she was looking for. She's someone who's been away for years and must not have heard about Louise's passing."

"Seriously?" It gave Ellie a little jolt to realize that the Mrs. Kent in the message referred to Graham's first wife, who had died more than three years ago. "And this event was such a big deal that Mr. Bell had to text you about it?"

"Well," he said, dismissively. "You know Charles. He fancies himself as the watchdog when we're away and then needs to remind me that our holiday puts an extra burden on him."

"Hmm," she agreed, although Graham's eagerness to drop the subject made her think there must be more to the story.

Nevertheless, when he pulled on his tweed jacket, threw a

wool scarf around his neck, and said, *"On y va,"* she decided to let it go. Instead, she put on a dash of lipstick, fluffed up the artfully casual Parisian haircut she'd had the day before, and followed him out the door.

He was right. Nothing going on in Little Beecham mattered today. They were in Paris together, and the sun had come out.

The darkening landscape of France had disappeared, and they were in the tunnel under the English Channel before Ellie thought again about Mr. Bell's text. As she peered through the window, she could see only blackness, the flash of tunnel lights, and her own reflection, but the gravitational pull of England and home had already begun to draw her away from the holiday.

It still unsettled her to be confused with Louise, although this was inevitable in a village where people commonly addressed one another by their surnames only. Louise had been all that Ellie was not—or so it sometimes seemed—English, for one thing; a tall, blue-eyed blond; and a kind, much-beloved vicar's wife for the parish. Finding her own way to be Mrs. Kent continued to be a challenge. She also wondered about the contexts in which you would use the word "released" and why it mattered that Corinna Matthews had returned to Little Beecham.

Next to her, Graham snored softly over Camus's *L'Étranger*, which he had bought that day at a used-book stall by the Seine. When the book began to slide off his lap, she reached out to catch it, and her movement woke him, as she hoped it would.

"Enjoying this?" she teased, handing him the book.

He yawned and slipped it into the pocket on the back of

the seat in front of him. "I'm sure I was, if I could only remember what I was reading. Where are we?"

"Nearly out of the tunnel, I think. I can feel the pressure changing. Literally and figuratively."

He nodded, suddenly more awake, and pulled out his phone for the first time since the morning. There was no service in the tunnel, but he could see the messages that had been sent during the day. "Bloody hell," he said, frowning, and held out the phone for Ellie to see that Mr. Bell had been busy:

14:00 *Numerous calls from people upset about CM's return.*
16:00 *Stephens threatening to sell Odyssey House if CM stays at Oak Cottage.*
18:00 *Rumors are there will be a campaign to protest.*

"A campaign to protest?" asked Ellie. "I think it's time you told me who this Corinna Matthews is and why she's getting everyone's knickers in a twist."

Graham ran his fingers through his hair, sighed, and said: "The short version is she was a brilliant, beautiful girl who threw her life away with one rash act and has spent the past fifteen years in prison."

Ellie raised her eyebrows at the brilliant and beautiful, but confined her response to the obvious: "What did she do?"

"She killed her brother."

"Killed?" she repeated, as if she had misheard. "As in murdered? And these were people you knew?"

He nodded. "Everyone knew them. Her father was a distinguished classics don at Oxford, and the family lived at Odyssey House—that neoclassical pile on the B road heading towards Chadstone."

"So, what happened?"

He shrugged in an irritated way. "That's just it. No one has ever really known."

"It wasn't obvious?"

"That Pindar died, and that Corinna had killed him, yes. But she claimed to be in an alcoholic blackout, and consequently didn't remember a thing. Her inability to explain what happened or why shocked people as much as, if not more than, the murder itself. Pindar was a ne'er-do-well, but public opinion turned very much against her."

"Why do you think she came back, then? I would have thought Little Beecham would be the last place she'd want to be."

"It probably is, but, unfortunately, her sister has now died too—quite recently—in a car crash. That means Corinna owns Oak Cottage—which was formerly part of the Odyssey House estate."

"Hence the unhappy neighbor."

"Quite." He stared at the window as if memories were rushing by like their reflections. Then he turned to Ellie and said, "The thing is, the idea that a murder could happen in that family was hard for people to accept, but they had to then, and they'll have to accept this new situation now."

"Meaning . . . ," Ellie prompted.

"Corinna confessed, she was convicted, and she's taken her punishment. Now the law says she has the right to a fresh start."

Ellie nodded in agreement, though judging from his tone and Mr. Bell's texts, she wanted to say, "Just not in Little Beecham." But Graham had opened his book again and begun to read with fierce concentration.

That may have closed the subject from his point of view, but Ellie's curiosity was now aroused, and she knew that, even if Graham were reluctant to talk about this bit of village history, other people would be more than happy to fill her in on every detail.

She was also aware that there was another issue at hand. He seemed to have forgotten that Corinna had come looking for Mrs. Kent. And while Louise might no longer be available to extend a hand, Ellie made up her mind there and then that Mrs. Kent still could and would.

CHAPTER THREE

Friday, March 9
Little Beecham, Oxfordshire

The morning after their return from France, rain poured down with a vengeance, and, as Ellie cleaned up after breakfast, she watched their rough-coated Jack Russell, Hector, joyfully tear around the churchyard. Like a true Brit, he was never fazed by rain, and she knew he would not be persuaded to come in until he was thoroughly soaked.

Graham had already retreated to his study after a hurried bowl of porridge. He wanted to get a start on his sermon for Sunday before anyone arrived demanding his attention.

"I've already had a message from Charles saying he wants to come over with Geoff Stephens to consult with me," he'd told her.

"About what?" asked Ellie.

"They seem to think I can influence Corinna and her plans."

"Can you?"

"No," he said, then brushed her cheek with a kiss.

"No? Just like that?" she asked, catching hold of his arm before he could slip away.

"Yes. Believe me. I know of whom I speak," he said, and then he was gone.

Interesting, thought Ellie, who imagined that Graham's quiet powers of persuasion could overcome anyone. She looked forward to finding out more about this Corinna Matthews, but, in the meantime, she was in no rush to leave the kitchen made toasty by the steady heat of the Aga to go up to her own study on the third floor of the rambling Georgian vicarage. Instead, she read the paper, drank her tea, then cleaned up Hector, who finally came to the door when he was satisfied that he could not be any more wet or muddy.

She had just finished putting the soggy towels into the washing machine when the housekeeper, Doris Finch, arrived carrying a pressed apron. She offered her usual tersely polite "Good morning" as she tied the apron around her ample body and surveyed the domain that she had ruled over for 30 years.

This morning Ellie caught the look of surprise at her Parisian haircut, which she could tell the older woman judged to be both too casual and too sophisticated for an English village vicar's wife. Which is to say, exactly the sort of misstep she had come to expect from the young, divorced foreigner her current vicar had chosen to marry.

For her part, when she married Graham, Ellie had not quite grasped what the setup at the vicarage would be like, in that the housekeeper was more permanent than the people living there. When she first arrived, this made it all too easy for her to feel like something out of place. Nevertheless, since then she and Mrs. Finch had made an effort to "rub along"; and Ellie's idea of taking soup to sick or needy parishioners during the flu season had given them a joint project that created at least a patch of common ground.

That morning, as soon as the housekeeper had poured herself some tea, they sat down at the long farmhouse table to go over the plans for the day. Then Ellie picked up her mug and nodded to Hector, who'd been watching them from his bed by the Aga. They both knew to vacate the kitchen before the whirlwind of cleaning, cooking, and baking began.

Ellie's study under the eaves was furnished with things she had shipped from home—not only her books and memorabilia, but also an old oak schoolmaster's desk and a colorful wool braided rug made by her grandmother. She loved the privacy and the view, which looked out on St. Michael's with its square Norman tower, the churchyard, and the woods beyond. The only drawback was that, while heat might rise, little ever seemed to make it this far. With each fresh gust of wind and rain, the old panes of glass rattled, and Ellie shivered, pushing her feet closer to the space heater and Hector, both under her desk.

In her previous life (as she now thought of it), she had been a professor of English literature, specializing in 18th-century British women writers. That's why *Women's Voices*, an international literary journal, had asked her to write a review of *Walsingham*, a 1797 bestseller with a cross-dressing heroine written by Mary Robinson, who was better remembered for her colorful sex life than her writing. Ellie was delighted to see this "bad girl" author get some recognition, but, as she stared out the window at the worn gravestones with their rain-battered flowers, she found it hard to focus. Her thoughts continually turned from past fictions to present-day facts, and she finally gave up.

It was hopeless to try to write about literature, when what

she really wanted to do was search the internet for information about Corinna Matthews who, like herself, was a professor's daughter. Who, like herself, had been accused of murder. Although, in Corinna's case, she had been guilty and gone to prison, while Ellie had been innocent and managed to prove it.

Her first search turned up the recent news about Clio Matthews, 36, killed in a car accident in Normandy. She was described as a native of Little Beecham, who was an artist and lived in Paris. The item also noted that she was predeceased by her parents and brother, but did not mention a sister still living.

When Ellie added "murder" to the search, it quickly became clear that Pindar Matthews' death had generated widespread coverage. The crime, committed in a stately home in the Cotswolds, made for a juicy story, with the added spice that it involved a distinguished Oxford don's family with a duke in the branches of the family tree. There was nothing the British media and public loved better. Ellie drank two more mugs of tea before she thought she had the whole story.

It had begun on the morning of the Spring Bank Holiday at the end of May, nearly 16 years before, when the Thames Valley Police were summoned to Odyssey House, home of the late Professor Cleve and Lady Anne Matthews of Little Beecham, by their 21-year-old daughter, Clio.

Clio Matthews said she had arrived home after being away overnight with friends in Oxford and found a trail of blood leading from the kitchen door to the library. There she discovered the writing desk overturned, papers and other objects scattered across the floor, and a letter opener lying in a pool of blood. Frantically, she had called to her older sister and brother, who did not reply; and when she searched the house, she found

Corinna, 27, unconscious on her bedroom floor. But, of Pindar, 29, there was no sign at all.

By the time the police officers arrived, the younger Miss Matthews was going into shock, while the elder was groggy and dazed, but uninjured.

Corinna Matthews told them she had been at home all evening, but had heard nothing of the violent fight that obviously took place in the library. When asked for an explanation, she said she had been upstairs in her room, as usual listening to music with headphones on.

She had last seen her brother in the early evening and freely admitted they had not parted on good terms. "All our conversations have devolved into arguments about money since our father died," she was quoted as saying. "The way he left his estate made Pindar feel very hard done by." Of his movements after he left—where he went, with whom, and what might have happened between them—she said she had no idea.

The police immediately initiated a search for Pindar and anyone who had seen him the night before, as well as anyone who had turned up at one of the area hospitals or surgeries with a stab wound. When the SOCOs determined that the amount of blood at the scene indicated someone had died there, the focus of the investigation shifted from assault to murder.

Although Corinna continued to insist that she knew nothing about what occurred, it didn't take long for the evidence to begin painting a picture contradicting her claim that she had remained in her room all evening. There were no fingerprints or physical evidence showing anyone outside the family, except the housekeeper, had been in the library. Corinna's fingerprints were found on the leather handle of the bloody letter opener; and the clothes she'd been wearing the previous day were located, stained with blood, in a laundry hamper upstairs. The trail of blood Clio saw on the floor could be traced from the kitchen door to the parking area where Corinna's car stood, and, in its boot, there was a heavily bloodstained tarp.

When DNA testing proved all the blood at the scene was from one person, and a comparison with hair samples found in Pindar's room proved that it was his blood, Corinna was taken into the Chipping Martin Police Station for questioning under caution.

"Did She Kill Him?" headlines were followed by a recap of the more lurid details and photos from the crime scene. These contrasted with a photo of Corinna, showing a pretty, dark-eyed brunette in a cap and gown, looking exultant as she graduated with a first-class degree from Cambridge. One of her tutors remarked that he was terribly shocked and saddened by the news of the murder. "She was one of the finest students I've ever had," he said, as if she were the one now dead.

The media described her as coldhearted, but Ellie thought the photo of her getting out of the police car at the station showed someone terrified, but desperately determined to keep her emotions in check.

No matter what her solicitor—or even the police—advised, Corinna terminated her interview almost immediately by confessing that she had been drinking heavily all evening and must have blacked out. That's why she had no memory of the quarrel leading to the murder or what happened afterward. Nonetheless, she was adamant that she was the one who killed her brother, and the subsequent headlines trumpeted the news: "She Did It!"

With no evidence of Pindar being alive after he was seen leaving the local pub, the media interest shifted to the search for his body. This involved not only local police, but also groups of volunteers who scoured the area around Little Beecham until it was revealed that tests on Corinna's clothes showed traces of salt water.

The police then conducted a wider study of CCTV footage, and her car was identified heading toward the coast near Weston-super-Mare during the night of the murder. This led to the supposition that she had found a place where, unseen by CCTV cameras, she could push Pindar's body into the Severn Estuary, and its powerful tide would have taken him out to sea within hours. That a young woman could do that to a member of her family generated loud public outrage.

But still no explanation was offered for what took place. Beyond repeating her original story about what she saw when she returned home that morning, Clio Matthews refused to say anything either. The silence of the two sisters provoked speculation, but the only motive that emerged was provided by a young woman who called herself Pindar's fiancée.

Lila Ashton, a barmaid at The Three Lambs in Little Beecham, read a victim statement to the court, claiming that she and Pindar had been in a relationship, and that, in high spirits that last evening, he had proposed, and she had accepted. "If you're wondering what the motive was, I can tell you. It was hateful jealousy of our happiness and nothing more."

Photos of the young blond sobbing as she told her story appeared over and over again in the media, playing up the difference between her and the shuttered face of the defendant, who was quickly found guilty of murder and received her 15-year minimum life sentence without a word.

Corinna Matthews had no history of violence or a criminal record, but the judge cited the use of the letter opener as a weapon and her lack of remorse in setting her sentence. Public opinion was divided over whether justice had been duly served. There was considerable skepticism about whether she really could have carried out the murder and disposal of the body in a blackout; and some people thought her treatment of the victim was indefensible no matter what led to the murder. Ellie shivered when she read that one unidentified resident of Little Beecham declared, "A public hanging on the village green would be more fitting for the likes of her."

A number of old photos accompanied the news stories, and they gave Ellie heartbreakingly different perspectives on the family. One showed the imposing Odyssey House, which the caption described as inspired by the famous neoclassical Cairness House in Scotland. Another showed the Matthews family on a visit to the Parthenon in Greece. In this one, the stout, bearded, and bespectacled Cleve Matthews was pointing out some detail of the architecture to an arrestingly beautiful young Corinna. At her feet crouched a little girl, who was playing with a stick; and a blond woman, presumably Lady Anne Matthews, sat on the crumbling marble stairs, looking elegantly bored as she talked with a sulky boy in a striped T-shirt.

More recent photos included a snapshot of Pindar, handsome and grinning in cricket whites, with his arm around a young teen identified as Clio; more lurid photos of the library with its bloodstained Persian carpet; and a mug shot of Corinna in which lank, dark hair framed a face wiped of all expression.

Again and again, Ellie returned to the photo of the Matthews family at the Parthenon and was reminded what a good thing it is that no one knows the future.

After all she'd read, she wondered what Corinna would be like now, 15 years later. The two murderers Ellie had encountered in the past had never faced up to their crimes, but Corinna had, right from the start. Would that mean she'd come to terms with what she did? Ellie couldn't quite imagine how you could move on after taking someone's life, no matter what the law said about fresh starts.

The story of the murder had so absorbed her, she half expected her thoughts to have summoned Corinna back to their door, but they didn't. By the time she and Hector clambered down the stairs at 11 o'clock, she had decided the next best thing was to take matters into her own hands. She would go by Oak Cottage with one of her hot meals and introduce herself.

In the kitchen she found Mrs. Finch had already set out the insulated lunch boxes Ellie used for what she called The Soup Car; and, as they filled them with containers of hot chicken soup and packets of fresh homemade bread, butter, cheese, chocolate biscuits, and fruit, Ellie said, "I suppose you've heard that Corinna Matthews has returned to the village."

Few things raised a smile on Mrs. Finch's face, but her naturally dour expression turned even more sour as she said, "Everyone at the shop was talking about that this morning, and not one person had a good thing to say about her." She snapped shut the lids on the filled boxes.

"I guess that's not surprising," said Ellie, as she served herself a bowl of soup from the pot on the Aga and sat down to eat her own lunch. "But some people must remember her from before the murder. Doesn't anything else you ever did count, once you've done such a terrible thing?"

Mrs. Finch's mouth worked as if she were trying to get rid of something stuck between her teeth. "She had a nice way with Isabelle, I'll give her that, but I never took to her myself."

Ellie looked up from buttering a slice of wholemeal bread. "Isabelle?"

Mrs. Finch nodded. "Oh, yes. Miss Matthews sometimes minded Isabelle, and the two of them became very thick. I remember them sitting right there where you are, laughing over some kind of counting game when Isabelle was just a little bit of a girl."

"No kidding," said Ellie, trying to square this new image with the glowing graduate and the grim mug shot she'd seen on the internet. To imagine Corinna in this very kitchen playing with Graham and Louise's daughter. "That's exactly what I meant. Isn't that still part of who she is?"

Mrs. Finch shrugged, as if she regretted sharing the memory. "Perhaps. But there was something off about that whole family," she said and began to work flour and lard together with quick, light fingers. Some of the soup stock, chicken, and vegetables had already been turned into a creamy filling, and now she was making a pie crust. "Everyone always said Miss Matthews was brilliant, like her father. But to kill her brother and go to prison, all the while claiming she didn't remember a thing—well, that's just daft."

"It happens, though," said Ellie. "Alcohol can cause black-outs, and you have no memory of what happened—which is not the same as not remembering, you know. There are no memories formed in the brain to remember. But I'd be willing to guess, she knew why it happened."

"Perhaps, but if she did, she was that dark about it. Even with Mrs. Kent, who was dead certain there had to be some mistake."

"You mean Louise thought Corinna didn't do it?"

"It's not for me to say what she thought," said Mrs. Finch, pursing her lips.

"What about Graham? Did he agree?" Ellie asked, but it was clear from the housekeeper's expression that she would not say anything further.

"No matter what, the whole business must have been trau-matic for everyone," said Ellie, trying a new tack.

"You have the right of it there. We've had plenty of deaths, but never like that. Here today, gone tomorrow, with no body and no explanation. The whole village turned out to search for him, until the police decided she must have pushed him into the Severn. That broke their young sister's heart, and I've heard she drove off that cliff because Miss Matthews was coming out of prison."

"People think Clio Matthews committed suicide?" asked Ellie. "After all these years?"

Mrs. Finch shrugged and pronounced: "That's what they're saying." She slapped the soft dough down onto a floured board and deftly rolled it into a circle.

Ellie felt the inarguable authority of "they" in her reply, but ventured to say, "The news account I read said it was ruled an accident."

"Well, if there could be room for doubt, that's what it would say, isn't it? But I wouldn't be surprised if she couldn't bear the thought of her brother's killer going free." Carefully she placed her crust on top of the filling, pinched the edge all around to make a border, and pricked the middle with a fork. Her hands were as gentle as her words were harsh. "From the talk in the village, I reckon if Miss Matthews is as brilliant as they used to say, she'll show it now by selling that cottage sharpish and leaving us in peace."

"You're probably right, but maybe we can help her in the meanwhile, no matter what happens next."

"I'm sure the vicar will know what's best," said Mrs. Finch, with a look that suggested she had not forgotten Ellie's ways of helping people had sometimes been more dangerous than delivering soup.

Mrs. Finch's version of the Corinna Matthews story made it clear to Ellie that she had been far more important than just someone "everyone knew," as Graham had described her. She was a family friend and babysitter, whose role in her brother's death may even have been a source of disagreement between Graham and Louise. Why he hadn't told her all this from the start?

But when she went to ask him, she found his study door closed, and the pleasant clatter of his typewriter replaced by the rise and fall of strained voices. Among them, she recognized Graham and Charles Bell and presumed the other must be Corinna's unhappy neighbor, Geoff Stephens.

"The sale-and-purchase agreement was all ready to sign. The deal was set," she heard him say in a loud, resentful voice.

"Surely, Corinna knows no one wants her here and she will act accordingly," said Charles.

"Have you ever met Corinna?" asked Graham, in a tone that made it clear the question was the answer.

"No, and that's just the reason we need you to act. To explain. To get her to see where her responsibility to the village lies," said Charles urgently, and Geoff Stephens jumped in, adding, "There will be trouble, if you don't!"

"What kind of trouble did you have in mind?" Graham asked mildly, and the two men began to talk over each other, both backing away from and reiterating what sounded like a threat. Whether against Graham or Corinna was not entirely clear, but, obviously, Ellie's questions would have to wait until she returned.

The rain had let up, but a cold wind whipped at her anorak as she loaded the lunch boxes into the back of their blue Mini Cooper and prepared to set off. In addition to getting to know more people away from church, The Soup Car project had required Ellie to learn her way around the countryside on her own. Today's rounds would take her to the villages of Ledfield, Upper Shortfield, and Parson's Corner; and, after that, she could swing by Oak Cottage on her way home.

The sky remained quilted, low, and gray, and the landscape looked wintry, except for the wild yellow primroses that splashed the verges with color. For Ellie, driving on single-track roads took as much concentration as driving on a California freeway at rush hour. She was quite used to driving on "the wrong side" now, but, even when she didn't have to deal with an oncoming car, she had to watch carefully for the white fingerposts pointing the way, so she didn't become lost.

Twice she nearly missed a turn, because her thoughts had drifted from the road to what was known about the night Pindar Matthews died. She wondered whether anyone else had shared Louise's doubts about what happened and looked forward to whatever she might learn on her rounds that day.

The answer was: not much. Most people, whether they had known Corinna before or not, accepted her guilt and were satisfied to conclude that her presence was a most unwelcome reminder that you could never know what darkness lurked in the heart of your neighbors. "A person like that . . . she's not the sort you expect to find in a nice village" was the general sentiment.

But when Ellie reached the Parson's Corner cottage of George Pinkerton, a widowed sheep farmer in his 8os, she began to see that, while she might want to understand the past, dealing with the present could prove to be the bigger challenge.

As she set out the lunch in George's tiny kitchen, they chatted about the news of the day, which naturally included the return of the native murderer. She was about to try him out on whether he ever doubted Corinna was guilty when his next words silenced her.

"The law may say she's paid the full tariff, but there are

those who don't agree. It's not just that she killed the bloke. She pushed him into the sea, so he'd never be found. Never rest. That makes people wonder. Why killing him wasn't enough."

Ellie gulped and set aside the idea of mentioning fresh starts. In fact, she realized that she'd imagined herself assuming Louise's role as Corinna's champion when she really had no idea what she'd be getting into.

"I expect she won't be here long," he added, "but there will be trouble anyway."

"Trouble?" said Ellie. The repetition of this word was disturbing. "I've heard there might be some sort of protest. Is that what you mean?"

He paused from eating his chicken soup to tear off bits of bread for his three aging sheepdogs, who were clustered around his feet, waiting patiently for treats.

"Some folk are still determined to have their say," he told her. "I know, because my great-niece Lila is such a one. She testified at the parole hearing about what she calls 'the trauma' she still suffers, and she was that mad when her words made no difference. They still released her."

"Is that Lila Ashton . . . the one who said she and Pindar were engaged?"

He nodded. "Aye. She was just a silly lass then. Thought that bloke was her Prince Charming, so his murder came as a terrible shock. She's done all right for herself since, but she's never married, and there's a bitterness in her. So, you can imagine Corinna Matthews, free as a bird and the last survivor to collect the family loot, is not a prodigal daughter, home at last. There will be no one laying out a feast for her."

Ellie bit her lip, remembering the photos she'd seen online of the young woman who sobbed as she read her victim statement at the trial. "Of course," she said and sighed.

Murder, she knew, always left ripples of pain for everyone

connected to it, like a rock dropped into a pond. And she could see how Corinna's silence about that night would have only intensified the anger against her. To say nothing of the missing body.

"I do understand that. But won't trouble only make life worse for everyone?"

George looked at her askance, then bent down to rub first one dog's ears, then each of the others, as they pushed forward for equal treatment. When he finally turned back to her, he said, "You know the saying . . . an eye for an eye. There are those who choose to take that literally, so it's hard to guess what might happen."

On that ominous note, Ellie packed up, said goodbye, and dashed out to her car through the rain, which had begun again. It was only three o'clock, but the dark, stormy sky and watery light made it seem later as she drove back down the B road toward Little Beecham with her windshield wipers flailing.

She watched closely for the stone pillars and gate that marked the drive to Odyssey House and resolutely tried not to think about the advisability of what she was doing. Why she had decided she should defend a confessed murderer whom she had never met, in face of the hostility and justifiable anger of her neighbors. Was it really because of Louise, who believed there must have been a mistake? Or was it because of herself? She was attracted by such an unlikely mission, demonstrating the trait her father used to call the spirit of contradiction.

All I am doing today is bringing soup, she told herself, as she drove through the open wrought iron gates. She hadn't committed herself to anything else, and whatever came next remained to be seen.

The gravel drive was unlit and lined with towering rhododendrons, so even though she drove slowly, in the pelting rain, Ellie missed the turnoff to Oak Cottage and suddenly found herself in front of the main house. Odyssey House was the kind of place she always thought was much too imposing to feel like a home, and, at the moment, only scattered lights were lit in the ranks of pedimented windows. Despite the broad front steps and pillared portico, the house, with its border guard of well-pruned shrubs, looked unwelcoming. Untouched, it appeared, by the tumultuous events in the lives of its former inhabitants, and arrogant like the current owner. Without pausing, she swung around the graveled circle and headed back down the drive.

This time she spotted the narrow offshoot that ended in front of a large cottage built from the same honey-colored stone as the main house and framed by sprawling oaks. There was a car parked there, indicating someone was at home, but no other sign of life.

She turned off her engine and listened to the pounding of the rain on the roof of the Mini. Then, taking a deep breath, she pulled up the hood of her anorak, grabbed the last lunch box, and climbed out.

The baying started as soon as she rang the doorbell. A loud, mournful sound of warning that seemed to come from the second story. As Ellie stepped back to look up, the hound's jowly face appeared between the curtains, and then she saw a woman join him. It was only a glimpse, but she was sure she recognized the intense eyes and dark hair of Corinna Matthews. She seemed at first to be staring at the Mini, but when she caught sight of Ellie, she snapped the curtains shut.

And that was that. Although Ellie waited, no one came to the door, and there was silence from within. She debated whether to leave the lunch box on the stoop anyway, but concluded the message was clear enough: she and whatever she had come to offer were not wanted.

"I guess I won't be applying for a job with Welcome Wagon," said Ellie to Graham, as she took mugs of tea into the sitting room, where a fire burned brightly. The drapes were drawn, closing out the rain and gathering darkness.

"The what?" he asked.

"Never mind. It's an American thing. Let's just say I tried to deliver one of our meals to Corinna Matthews, and it was a mistake."

"Why?" he asked, coming to sit beside her on the old leather sofa.

"She saw me from the window, but she wouldn't answer the door."

He grimaced. "I could have warned you that might happen."

"Could you? Then why didn't you?"

"First of all, because I didn't know what you were planning, and, second, because I only learned more about what's going on today."

"Oh. Right. I would have told you, but you were busy, and it was an impulse thing. Mr. Bell did say she came looking for Louise, and I just wanted her to know I would be glad to help. You know, even though Louise can't."

"I'm sure she would have appreciated your motives had she known." He smiled and patted her knee.

"Don't tease," she said, pushing his hand away. "Tell me what you found out."

"The gist of it is, you are a stranger, and she probably assumed your mission was not friendly. The campaign against her is already underway with a petition to the Parole Board, hate mail, and posts on social media designed to rile up the masses."

"Even though no one knows how long she's planning to stay?"

He nodded. "According to Charles, some people initially hoped to be able to overturn the Parole Board decision to release her. An idea that only demonstrates a lack of knowledge about the system. The Parole Board is like the court. You might not like the decision of the judge and jury, but they aren't going to change their minds because of your opinion."

"And petitions are going around anyway?"

"Apparently. After all, not all concerned citizens express their opinions on social media. Charles blustered on about the reputation of the village, the way he always does, but Geoff Stephens really cares only about buying Oak Cottage. He's wanted it ever since he bought Odyssey House, and Clio had finally indicated she was ready to sell. Now he's at the mercy of whatever Corinna wants to do."

"Nonetheless, I can't imagine those two involving themselves in a campaign of protest."

"No, that's not their style. They were pushing for me to be their emissary, and I said no chance. It was not a pleasant meeting."

"I can imagine," said Ellie. "You know, I heard today that Lila Ashton is planning to make trouble."

Graham shook his head ruefully. "I suppose that was predictable. In fact, she's probably the one organizing the campaign. She's not a barmaid anymore. She runs a PR firm based in Chipping Martin and has the reputation for being very good at her job."

"Ouch," said Ellie. "Considering all that, it does seem as if Corinna would have been better off hiring someone to clear out the cottage and put it on the market. Sell it to Geoff Stephens and be done with it."

"Her advisers may well have wanted her to do that, and obviously, she didn't." His expression reminded Ellie of when he told her Corinna had thrown her life away with one rash act. But he surprised her by going on to say, "You know, I don't think going there today was a mistake. You treated Corinna the way you would any new neighbor, and I think that's the way we need to go forward."

"Really? Okay, that sounds like a plan," said Ellie, who was so pleased, she was content to leave the subject there and not tax him about all he had not told her.

They did not revert to the subjects of Corinna or the campaign until after they'd eaten Mrs. Finch's chicken pie; taken Hector for a walk, while the rain paused; then dried themselves by the sitting room fire because the rain had started again while they were out, and they all got wet; thoroughly discussed his sermon on loving your neighbor and her review of *Walsingham*; and gotten ready for bed.

Ellie always felt as if she'd arrived home—the home at the center of home—when she climbed into bed next to Graham, but she knew she wouldn't sleep well if she didn't bring up that question from the morning about whether he, like Louise, had doubted Corinna's role in the murder.

"You know," she said, turning on her side to face him, "there is something I need to ask you about our new neighbor. Yesterday you described Corinna as someone everyone in the village knew, so I didn't understand that she was really a family friend. I also didn't get that Louise refused to believe she committed the murder, but that you, perhaps, were not so sanguine."

Graham turned to her with a smile and plumped up the pillows under his head. "Let me guess, Mrs. Finch has been stirring you up. But there's no mystery there, Ellie. Corinna was a friend of Louise's, and she minded Isabelle sometimes, but the reason Louise and I had different opinions about the murder is no secret. It stemmed from the fact that I had a history with the family, and Louise didn't. Cleve Matthews was one of my tutors when I was at Oxford."

"You knew them all back then?"

He nodded. "Cleve enjoyed impressing his favorite students by inviting them to dinners at Odyssey House, where we all had to speak Latin or sometimes Greek. Whichever he commanded."

"Good Lord. That must have made for lively conversation. And was Corinna involved with that?"

"She was. Only eighteen, a sixth-former . . . but well cast in the role of Circe."

"Meaning she used her charms to turn all you boys into swine, wolves, and lions?"

"She could and did. We all thought she was devastatingly attractive and clever, in part because Cleve had taught her more Latin and Greek than all of us knew put together. She was also his daughter, and some mistakenly thought getting involved with her might be the first step toward a successful academic future."

"I'll bet that was a slippery slope. What about Pindar? Was he there too?"

"He was. He'd already been sent down from Oxford, so he was hanging about, seething with resentment towards us and the attention lavished on his sister. Did you know the Greek poets Pindar and Corinna were bitter rivals, fond of trading insults? It seems Cleve set them up to be at loggerheads from the moment he named them. The antagonism between them was painful even back then."

"I suppose Clio must have been just a child."

"Like a fairy floating around in a white chiffon dress."

"Did she speak Latin too?"

"No. She spoke her own made-up language. And very convincing about it she was too."

Ellie laughed. "I would have liked to hear that. And where was the beautiful Lady Anne on these occasions?"

"Absent, due to ill health, which I later understood meant intoxicated. Oh, it was quite the scene, and Cleve played all of us like a puppet master."

"Did you dance?"

"I tried for a while, but I wasn't very good at it."

"You didn't fall under brilliant and beautiful Circe's spell?"

"Only briefly."

Ellie raised her eyebrows. "How brief is briefly?"

"Just long enough for me to discover that, even at eighteen, Corinna had inherited her father's brains and strong will, but her mother's looks and weaknesses."

"I see. I guess. So how did she and Louise become friends, then? That seems a rather unlikely fit."

"Not really. By the time I took the living here at Saint Michael's, Lady Anne had passed away. Pindar was still around playing Jack the Lad, but the girls were both at university. They came back when Cleve died unexpectedly, and Corinna found herself named a trustee of his discretionary trust.

"Pindar was furious that he did not receive his inheritance outright and did everything he could to undermine her. At first, I think Louise felt sorry for Corinna. She was a young woman in a tough position. But they ended up having some very good times together."

"Hmm . . . ," said Ellie. "And you, I guess, were busy with other things."

He laughed. "Precisely. I admit, I tended to keep my distance."

"Well, I'm not sure I see a future as friends for us. From the way she looked down at me today, I could more easily imagine her turning me into something. A toad. Or a puff of smoke."

Graham laughed and pulled her toward him. "That I sincerely doubt. She may have had us lads in the palm of her hand back in the day, but I don't think she could do that to my Ellie."

"Why, thank you," she said and gave him a kiss.

After Graham was asleep, though, Ellie lay awake. The rain had stopped, leaving behind a loud silence. She got up and went to a window that overlooked the quiet high street. The stars were shining brightly in an indigo sky, and trees stirred in the breeze.

She was about to return to bed when she saw a slight figure in a long overcoat and felt hat, accompanied by a hound nearly half her height, coming down the high. Corinna.

As Ellie watched, they made their way through the churchyard and past the church, then paused in front of the vicarage. She wondered what Corinna could be looking at, then remembered the two Minis parked in the drive. Blue and red.

Perhaps she was realizing who had visited her that day. Or perhaps she had seen those cars before and thought it was Graham who had come to see her. Ellie suspected, if that had been the case, she would not have reacted the same way.

Ellie was still watching when she noticed something else. Another person—a man, she guessed—who kept to the shadows, but followed Corinna as she continued on down the high street, and seemed very intent on not letting her out of his sight.

This reminded Ellie of what George Pinkerton said about some people taking "an eye for eye" literally. She had not taken him literally, but, if stalking were part of the campaign against Corinna, she could only hope it was not a prelude to anything worse.

CHAPTER FOUR

Saturday, March 10

"I've been thinking about what you said yesterday," Ellie told Graham, as she buttered a pile of toast the next morning. She was still in her pajamas and robe, but he was already in "uniform"—his black suit and clerical collar—to go to Kingbrook Hospital and give Holy Communion to an elderly parishioner who'd had surgery. "It sounds like you'd been aware of Corinna's drinking problem for a long time—but maybe Louise wasn't, so she was less able to accept that as an explanation for the murder."

"Maybe," he said, adding Marmite to his toast. "Corinna certainly took care to be sober when she was minding Isabelle or going about with Louise. But you know, Ellie, there's no need for you to get too wrapped up in this story. I'm sure Corinna will leave Little Beecham as soon as she has sorted out what's in the cottage and put it up for sale."

"Even so, I'm curious. It seems so out of character."

"For Corinna to commit murder?"

"No, well, yes, but I meant for Louise to doubt the confession. I've always thought of Louise as empathetic, but also very sensible."

Graham smiled, but his tone was skeptical. "You mean it's the psychology that intrigues you, not the crime."

Ellie blushed. "As you've told me more than once, there's no mystery about the facts of the crime."

"Very true. But I hope you also know I didn't immediately jump to the conclusion Corinna was guilty. It wasn't unthinkable that someone would kill Pindar—he was a manipulative bastard—but I was as shocked as everyone else when it turned out Corinna was involved. To be honest, I felt guilty—and angry—that she never asked either of us for help before the situation got so out of hand."

"But you did believe it when she confessed."

"For sure, because I couldn't imagine why she would do that, unless she believed it was the truth."

"Maybe she was covering for someone else."

He shook his head. "There wasn't anyone else, and, you know, Louise eventually did change her mind, so you shouldn't get stuck on her initial reaction. Hardly anyone believes someone they know and like is capable of murder even in extreme circumstances."

"I suppose you're right."

"I am right, and you won't be able to help Corinna unless you accept her past for what it is, as she must."

"Yes, I can see that," Ellie conceded, but, in her mind, accepting what happened was not quite the same as believing the whole story was either fully known or understood.

Up in her study, she sat down in front of her computer, while Hector stretched out on the braided rug. She opened the file for her review of *Walsingham*, determined to finish it, but once again she couldn't concentrate on Mary Robinson. After an hour of putting words in and deleting them again, she decided to take a Twitter break and discovered #justiceforpindar was trending. Her hope that this referred to something esoteric about greater appreciation for the classical Greek poet lasted only as long as it took her to click on the link.

Tweets from someone called SplashwithLAshton.org harped on the theme that Pindar Matthews' killer had been freed. Many focused on the injustice of a life sentence being only 15 years, which, when Ellie thought about it, did seem short, compared with the sentences doled out in the US.

Would Pindar come back to life now? the tweeters asked.

When would his "sentence" end?

These questions had been amplified endlessly by the retweeters of the world in what was obviously another part of Lila Ashton's campaign.

It didn't take long before Ellie reached her saturation point and shut down her computer altogether. As if that made a difference. When she stood up with a sigh and stretched, Hector leapt to his feet with eyes full of hope. In his opinion, all of life's problems could be solved by one of five options: eat, walk, play, cuddle, or sleep. She decided that today's answer was "walk." And she knew where she wanted to go.

Morag MacDonald had been Louise Kent's closest friend, and she'd taken Ellie under her wing when she arrived in the village. They hit it off well, in part because Morag was at a similar point in life: an inheritance had allowed her to leave her longtime teaching job at Little Beecham's village school. Ellie admired the adventurous spirit with which she had been trying out new professions, the latest being interior decoration, and she told herself she just wanted to find out how it was going. If she learned Morag's opinion on the murder and Louise's reaction to it, that would be nice too.

With Hector happily at her heels, Ellie bundled up in an anorak and knitted cap, put him on his leash, and together they set out. The sky that morning was a surprising blue, but the still, cold air hinted that there would be frost when the sun went down. Saturday morning shoppers were out on the high street, encouraged by the sun that turned the stone cottages and shops a pale gold and illuminated the grass on the verges. John Tiddington's butcher-shop window bore a sign reminding customers to put in their orders for Easter lamb; and the village shop offered a new window display of garden tools and a basket full of seed packets.

The MacDonalds lived in Blackthorn Cottage on Crooked Lane, which was narrow enough to trap the cold, but when Ellie went around to their sunny backyard, she found Morag and her 14-year-old son, Seamus, working in their garden. They were raking up the detritus of winter that had gathered around the new growth sprouting out of the ground. Their cheeks were pink with the cold, and they both looked up with pleasure at the sight of Ellie and Hector.

"Finally," said Seamus, leaning on his rake. "Now we can stop for tea."

Morag smiled, pulled off her gloves, and pushed her damp, dark curls off her forehead. "Good idea," she said, her dark eyes twinkling. "But you can finish raking up that muck and pile it on the compost while we put on the kettle."

Seamus made a face, but went back to work as Ellie followed Morag through the back door into the kitchen. This was a pleasant, cozy room with a small green Aga and green-and-white-striped curtains on the windows overlooking the garden.

Morag made the tea, while Ellie sat at the table to cut up a lemon drizzle cake and arrange the slices on a plate.

"It's only Marks and Sparks, not homemade like you get at the vicarage," said Morag, as she poured their tea and passed the milk and sugar.

"Personally, I love anything I don't have to bake myself," said Ellie, as she took a bite of the sweet, tangy cake. "Is this a sign the new career is flourishing?" she asked, tapping the stack of interior design magazines on the table.

"Not on your nelly. I've already discovered I have no patience whatsoever with people obsessed about the perfect fittings for their loo. I'm looking to buy a new sofa for us, though."

Ellie grinned. "At least you're decisive. I wish I were equally clearheaded about what I want to do."

Morag lifted an eyebrow, and Ellie knew she was probably thinking some people would suppose she already had a new career as the vicar's wife. But Morag said only, "The answer will come for both of us, I'm sure. Meanwhile, how was the holiday?"

"Wonderful. It was great to have Graham all to myself, if you know what I mean."

"I do. And the new haircut is brilliant," said Morag, ruffling her own mop of curls again. "However, if your goal is to fit in here, you should have gone to Cherie at Fab Nails and Hair in the village. She would have given you her 'Vicar's Wife Special'—a nice bob for ten pounds and no travel costs."

Ellie grimaced. "I'm sure she would have, but I couldn't resist the opportunity. And anyway, there has to be a limit to the sacrifices one makes in the interest of blending in."

"On your head be it," said Morag, and they both laughed.

"Needless to say, the holiday bubble broke even before we got home, thanks to Charles Bell. He sent Graham a string of texts that made it sound as if the whole village were up in arms over Corinna Matthews' return."

"Ah, the murderer in our midst. I saw the petition when I was returning books to the library this morning. It already had quite a few signatures."

"Oh, Lord. What does it say?"

"It informs the Parole Board that allowing Corinna to return to the village is an insult to our community and renews the trauma of our unhealed wounds."

Ellie shook her head. "According to Graham, the Parole Board is done and dusted with that decision."

"Well, I think the principal goal is really to give Lila Ashton a chance to churn up everyone and relive her grief—or grievances—depending on your point of view."

"What do you mean?"

"I'm sure her grief has always been real enough, but I've also heard she tried to sue the family as a victim of the crime and got nowhere, so grievance might be the sharper emotion all these years later. She's certainly been hard at it on Twitter and Facebook today. The outrage experienced by people from New Zealand to California is truly remarkable."

Ellie laughed.

"You laugh now, but she's just getting started. One of Lila's specialisms is finding ways to get the media to turn out."

"The media? Is there a new case?" asked Seamus, who was just coming in from the garden. His goal in life was to be a private detective, and he was very clever at ferreting out information from all kinds of sources.

"Not for you there isn't," said Morag. "This case was closed before you were born."

"Then I guess you're talking about the gone-but-not-forgotten Odyssey House murder," he said.

"Don't you start," she warned, so he smiled sweetly, took

the cake and tea she handed him, and, with a sketched salute to both, went off to his room.

"That boy is becoming a magnet for trouble. Or is it trouble that is a magnet for him? Regardless, I have the same advice for both of you. Steer clear of the whole business. Let Corinna clean out the cottage and leave. You're not obliged to become involved."

"Aren't I? In a way, I feel I am, because the first thing Corinna did when she was released was to come looking for Louise."

Morag frowned. "Are you sure about that?"

Ellie shrugged. "That's what Charles Bell told us, and I have no reason to question it. Graham said she must not have heard about Louise's passing."

"I suppose that's possible. But it is surprising. When Corinna first went to prison, Louise was the only person to visit her, and after a while she told her flat out to stop coming. She claimed seeing her was making it harder to accept her situation."

"Really. Do you think that was because Louise didn't believe her confession?"

Morag fiddled with her cake crumbs, pressing them together with her fork. "You've heard that already?"

Ellie nodded. "Yes, although, according to Graham, it was only her initial reaction."

Morag looked as if she were debating what to say, and Ellie waited. As the pause lengthened, she knew there must be more coming.

"It wasn't just that. I didn't live here then, and I've never met Corinna, so I'm only passing on what Louise told me."

"Which was . . . ," said Ellie.

"She liked Corinna a lot. She was smart, well educated, and funny. When they were together, Louise didn't have to be the vicar's wife, and she loved that. I am sure you know what I mean. She was aware that Corinna drank too much, but she didn't realize how much or how it had already caused problems in the past.

"She was shocked when she heard about the murder, but even more shocked by Corinna's confession. In her opinion, the whole story didn't add up."

Ellie felt a little chill go down her spine. "What do you mean?"

"Louise and Corinna had spent Saturday afternoon together, and Corinna's mood was hopeful for the first time since her father's death. You know the discretionary trust that Cleve Matthews left was specifically designed to prevent Pindar from squandering the assets, and they'd been fighting about it bitterly. But, on that day, Corinna said she thought they may have worked out a plan Pindar could live with. She hoped she'd be able to resume her graduate studies at Cambridge, and she was even planning to attend a party with some uni friends on the bank holiday."

"So, in other words, murder was not on her mind."

Morag nodded. "On top of that, Louise was at Odyssey House that Sunday night. Corinna had left a sweater in Louise's car the day before, and she asked Louise to drop it by so she could wear it to that party. Louise said she would, and Corinna told her to come any time. Even if she had gone to bed early, she said the kitchen door would be unlocked until Pindar got in."

"What time did Louise get there?"

"Nearly ten o'clock. Both Pindar's and Corinna's cars were in the drive, but the kitchen door was open. When she went in, Louise told me she was struck by how peaceful the house felt. Clean and tidy and quiet. She assumed Corinna was in bed and Pindar not home yet, so she left the sweater and that was that.

"When she heard the news about what happened there later, she simply couldn't believe it. It was like a lightning strike out of a blue sky."

Ellie sighed. She had hoped for something more concrete. "I can see that, but all it really meant was the murder happened after ten o'clock," she said. "An hour later, Pindar could have come home from the pub drunk and awakened Corinna to start a fresh row."

"That's what the police said too. Although the people who were with him at the pub reported he was drinking, but had seemed in good spirits when he left."

"According to Lila, he proposed that night," said Ellie. "So, her version was probably that he came home from the pub, woke Corinna to tell her the good news, and she decided to kill him."

"I know," said Morag. "I've read that too. That the motive was jealousy over their happiness. But the fact is, no one knows what lit the fuse. Those two certainly had lifelong grievances because their father had always favored Corinna over Pindar. Louise thought dodgy stuff went on that Corinna never spoke about."

"I've wondered about that," said Ellie. "Whether Corinna used the idea of a blackout to avoid breaking her silence. Unfortunately, though, it sounds as if the only thing Louise's testimony did was shorten the timeline. How long does it take to drive from here to Weston-super-Mare?"

"Less than two hours."

"That means the murder could have taken place as late as midnight, and Corinna could still conceivably have gotten home before sunrise."

"I've never thought about that," said Morag. "And never

wanted to! If I never have to hear about another murder as long as I live, that would be fine with me.

"There was one other thing that Louise said, though, which I've always remembered: that the whole scenario seemed wrong. Pindar had always been in trouble of one kind or another, and Corinna had always tried so hard to be good. To meet her father's expectations."

Ellie stretched and rubbed her eyes, as if that could wipe out the past. Then she said, "It happens like that, though, doesn't it? The woman who's been beaten for years finally lashes out, kills the man, and then spends the rest of her life in prison."

Morag looked somber. "But that wasn't the story. In fact, no story was ever offered, other than the quarrels about money—and Lila's claim that Corinna was jealous. Neither of those issues seems significant enough to warrant murder, much less what she did with the body. I mean, even Louise, who was as staunch a friend as you could have, had difficulty with that. After all, it's not as if she hid the evidence of the crime so he would seem to have disappeared."

"I think all that had to be linked to the real motive. Whatever it was."

Morag stood up and turned on the kettle again. "Exactly. And whatever that was, it never came out, and I doubt Lila's campaign will pry any new answers out of Corinna at this point. Nor can I imagine there's any sort of apology she could offer that would make people feel better about how it went down then."

"Did anyone from the police take note of Louise's story?"

"I think one detective did, but once Corinna confessed, apparently everything happened quite quickly. I mean, the evidence showed that she was the only person who could have done it."

"And no one suspected she was covering for someone else?"

Morag shook her head. "That could only have been Clio, and her friends swore up and down she was with them all night."

"I'm always suspicious when people swear up and down. Whatever that means."

"Oh, Ellie. I hope you're not imagining you can pick up Louise's flag after all this time. I must say the whole story makes me grateful that my main problem in life is how to persuade a sweet fourteen-year-old to do his homework and steer him toward a career that will not continually embroil him in crime."

"No chance," said Seamus, reappearing in the doorway with his empty plate and mug. "I'm not really that sweet, Mum, and this is my vocation. And you know, I've been thinking. The murder may be a closed case, but there's still the professor's missing coin collection."

"Where did you hear about that?" asked Morag.

Seamus grinned. "Everyone knows about that. It's bog-standard schoolroom talk."

"I don't know about it," said Ellie.

"Professor Matthews had a fabulous collection of Greek and Roman coins supposedly worth millions, but he died suddenly without telling anyone where he had hidden it."

"Not millions," said Morag.

"Well, at least one," claimed Seamus.

Ellie looked from one to the other with affection. With their dark hair and eyes, fair skin and pink cheeks, there was no mistaking they were mother and son. "And let me guess," she said, turning to the boy. "You're hoping to be the one to find this missing treasure? After all these years?"

"Why not? Someone has to. And I wouldn't even want a reward."

"That story is only a village myth, I'm sure," said Morag.

"You know, Seamus, the family has never been obliged to announce that the collection was found, so who's to say it's still missing?"

"Good point," said Ellie.

But later, when she and Hector were on their way home, Seamus caught up with her on the high street. "You know, Guv," he said, using the title he liked to give Ellie when they worked together on a 'case', "Mum might be right about the coins, but she could be wrong too. And I'm in a very special position to find out."

"What do you mean?"

"I've become friends with Simon Stephens, who lives at Odyssey House, right where the coins were most likely hidden, so we've decided to search for them."

"Seamus—"

"There's no danger in that. And it's not like we'd try to claim them or anything. We'd turn them straight over to Ms. Matthews."

Ellie laughed. "I can see you've planned this all out. But don't forget they might not even belong to Corinna anymore. Don't you have a law in this country about buried treasure belonging to the government?"

"Yes, but I think that mostly has to do with digging up old bones and stuff in your garden. It all depends on what it is . . . and it doesn't make any difference unless it's found. We believe we have to at least try, what with Simon living right there, and now we're friends, and I'm a professional detective."

"So that's all there is to it—a treasure hunt. It has nothing to do with Corinna or the murder."

His dark eyes sparkled. "Cross my heart. Although I must say I think Simon has a thing for her."

Ellie raised an eyebrow. "Has he met her?"

"Not yet, but he's printed out all the photos from the internet."

She nodded. "He might find being in prison for fifteen years has changed her a bit. Regardless, I hope you both know his father is not happy to have her living next door, so you can imagine how he'd feel if he thought his son was infatuated with her. Much less tearing up floorboards to look for missing coins. As for you, you'd better be sure to do enough at home to keep your mother happy."

"Oh, I will. I know how to handle Mum. And I promise to keep you informed of all developments."

She knew she should underscore that there was nothing to keep her informed about, but instead she found herself saying, "Okay, good."

Back at home, Ellie made tuna sandwiches for lunch, but, when Graham didn't return, she wrapped his up and ate by herself. It occurred to her that she was sitting at the table right where Mrs. Finch had seen Corinna play a counting game with Isabelle. Back then, Corinna had been 27 years old and a Cambridge graduate student who returned to Little Beecham only to deal with her father's estate after his unexpected death. A painful duty, but surely, no one could have anticipated that it would change her life forever.

In the silent house, Ellie felt the presence of those past days and years in the Kent family's history that she could never share. She would always have to rely on other people's interpretations of what happened. Or would she? Suddenly she remembered that there was another, firsthand, source of information.

. . .

When she opened Isabelle's bedroom door, Ellie tried to suppress the feeling that she was an intruder. The room had the atmosphere that comes when a place is unoccupied, but Mrs. Finch obviously had it clean and ready for the girl who would be home soon for the break between terms at Cambridge, where she was now at uni. Everything was freshly dusted and tidy.

Ellie opened the cupboard door and peered past the row of shoes and boots, seeking the cardboard box she remembered. It was still there in a back corner: Louise's diaries and datebooks from her years in Little Beecham.

Carefully, she removed the heavy box and carried it up to her study where she could examine the contents at her leisure. She knew from previous experience that Louise's diaries were not reflective: she was someone who could be counted on to keep not only other people's secrets, but also her own. Still there might be some notations that would bring Ellie closer to what her feelings had been.

When she found the datebook for the year of the murder, she opened it to May. There, in Louise's neat handwriting, she saw that Graham had two dentist appointments and Isabelle's playgroup met on Wednesdays. During the week before the murder, Graham and Louise were invited to a dinner party, and Corinna's name and a time were written underneath, which made it clear she was scheduled to take care of Isabelle that evening. All very ordinary—and it was painful to imagine that march of days toward disaster.

On the day before the murder, Louise and Corinna had gone to Stratford for a Saturday matinee performance of *King Lear*. This must have been when Corinna left her sweater in Louise's car.

On Sunday, the family had gone for a walk in the Blenheim Palace gardens in Woodstock in the afternoon, and, in the evening, Louise had gone to something noted as "film society." But, the next day—the Spring Bank Holiday—had been left blank, except for a note in pencil: "C!!! What happened??!!!!!"

In the corresponding diary, she had written nothing at all about the day of the murder and the weeks that immediately followed, as if the events had rendered her speechless. But Ellie did find a slip of paper with a phone number that took her completely by surprise because she recognized it. The initials "DM" confirmed she was not mistaken.

This was a number that appeared in her own contacts: the mobile number for Derek Mullane, now a detective inspector with the Thames Valley Police. The very person who had pursued her as a murder suspect when Ellie discovered a body in the churchyard soon after her arrival in Little Beecham. If he had been the one to listen sympathetically to Louise, he must have been a greener detective and softer person back then.

She flipped forward to see whether there were any further notations that might refer to the murder, but all she found was that the initials "CM" began to appear regularly in the date-books on the same day of each month.

Ellie checked the following years and saw the notations continued for about a year and then stopped. She found no other information related to the murder, but at least she had a next step. These days she was on better terms with DI Derek Mullane, and she would ask him whether Louise had called him and what he remembered about what she said.

As she came downstairs, Ellie realized Graham must have returned. From the study, she heard the sound of his voice and a woman answering. For a moment, she thought Isabelle must have come home and felt embarrassed about her recent foray into her stepdaughter's closet.

But when Graham said, "It's very good to see you. I'm glad you came," she knew he was not speaking to his daughter.

The study door was slightly ajar, but Ellie knocked and waited until she heard Graham say, "Is that you, Ellie?" Then she opened the door and saw his visitor: the very same slender, dark-haired woman she had been thinking about so much.

Corinna's dark eyes flashed, seeming to take in every detail of Ellie's appearance, and Graham looked uncomfortably from one to the other. "I'm glad you're here. I wasn't sure if you were home," he said. "This is Corinna Matthews, who's come to see us about some trouble at Oak Cottage. Corinna, this is my wife, Ellie."

The space between them vibrated with indecision, as Corinna stood with her hands shoved deep into the pockets of an old, oversize tweed coat.

"How do you do," said Ellie, holding out her own hand. "I've been looking forward to meeting you."

Corinna seemed taken aback, but she took Ellie's proffered hand and remained standing until both Ellie and Graham were seated. Then she perched on the edge of the sofa, crossed her arms, and looked around the book-lined study, which must have once been a familiar place, as if she had never seen it before.

It was obvious to Ellie that Corinna had not bargained on having to discuss her trouble with anyone other than Graham. But what struck her more than their visitor's belligerent discomfort was the fact that, in her mid-40s, after 15 years in prison, Corinna Matthews was still a beautiful woman. Of course, she was paler than was healthy and slender as a sketch, as well as past her early youth. But far from detracting from her beauty, the tiny lines she'd developed gave her fine-boned face the dignity of experience, and her eyes were as dark and knowing as in the old photos.

When Ellie saw Graham begin fiddling with his fountain

pen under Corinna's intense scrutiny, she was suddenly reminded of Morag's surprise and the way she'd said, "Are you sure Corinna was looking for *Louise*?"

"What kind of trouble have you had?" asked Ellie, as the moment of silence lengthened.

"Someone has been breaking into Oak Cottage," said Graham, setting down his pen.

"Not exactly breaking in," said Corinna. "Coming in. Whoever it is has a key and comes and goes at will when I'm not there."

"That's creepy," said Ellie. "Do you know who else has keys?"

"The caretakers. Probably the owner of Odyssey House. But aside from them—and I am certain it is not them—I have no idea."

"Has anything been stolen?"

She shrugged. "I don't think so, but it's impossible for me to know what is supposed to be there. The person is searching for something and doesn't care whether I know it. In fact, he wants me to know about his visits. He—or she, I guess I should say— leaves little messages."

"Messages? What do they say?" asked Ellie.

"They suggest that I may be the last survivor of my family, but they are all still with me. Hardly an original thought, but disconcerting."

Ellie had been expecting anything but this, and Graham asked, "How is this expressed?"

Corinna gave a wry smile. "It's not spirit writing on the walls or ghostly footsteps, but yesterday I came back from a walk to find a cup of tea, still warm, and a half-eaten Pim's biscuit on the kitchen table. Whoever left that knew Pim's were my sister's favorite. And possibly also that I hate them."

"That's bizarre. So, it must be someone you know," said Graham.

"One might think so, but I don't know anyone here anymore, except you."

She looked pleased at the telltale reddening of Graham's ears. A sure sign that he was embarrassed. The former Circe apparently still enjoyed exercising her skills, Ellie thought, and jumped in to ask, "What else has happened?"

"Today an old lap rug that belonged to my mother was on the sofa in the sitting room, thrown aside, as if someone had just gotten up from a nap. I know that was in the box room two days ago, because I saw it there in a trunk of old clothes."

"And these things always happen when you're away from home?"

"Yes. I have a dog. A bloodhound, in fact. He would let me know if anyone tried to get in when we were there."

"Can he pick up a scent? Give any clue to where this person goes?"

"Not so far. We tracked the intruder across the garden and into the woods, but that was it. Toby is a dear old fellow, but he, like me, has spent his recent life in a cage. We're both rather rusty at dealing with the world."

Ellie tried not to gulp at the images the comparison brought up. "You said the person has been searching for something. Do you think your father's coin collection is the attraction?"

Corinna shook her head. "I would never even have considered that a possibility if I hadn't received this today." She pulled an envelope out of her pocket and handed it to Graham. The letter bore a French stamp and a return address in Paris. It had been sent to Corinna's prison address and forwarded to Little Beecham.

Graham opened the letter and held it so Ellie could see the

message too. It was from Clio Matthews and had been written two days before her death.

Dear Corinna,

I haven't heard from you, so I am writing again to be certain that you received my invitation to use Oak Cottage. It has been my base in England, but my life is really in France, and recent events have made me see that I am ready to live here full time. If you wish to keep the cottage, I hope you will buy me out or, alternatively, we can jointly sell it to a third party. The current owner of Odyssey House is very keen.

I plan to remove my personal things this week, but I will leave the furnishings, etc., in case there is something you want or need. There's nothing posh, but it's rather cosy and private. While I'm there I also plan to follow up on a new theory I have about what Cleve did with his coin collection! Imagine that. If the trail leads anywhere, I will let you know.

I do not wish you ill, Corinna, and I am sorry if you have thought I did. We should have talked long before this, but I hope we will soon.

Clio

"That's a nice letter," said Graham, folding it carefully back into the envelope.

"Nicer than you would have expected?" said Corinna.

"That's not for me to judge, but well done on Clio's part, I think. Did you not receive the first one?"

"No, but it wasn't unusual for prison mail to go astray. I would have answered, and I did hope to see her again."

They all fell silent for a moment, remembering the reason this would never happen now, then Ellie asked, "Do you have any idea what she meant by her new theory?"

"None. I would have said those coins were a lost cause

years ago. Pindar searched the entire property obsessively after my father died and never found them. By now, they could be anywhere in the world."

"But Clio might have discussed her idea with a friend—someone who also had a key and might think it was worth taking a look."

"I suppose. I mean, why not? My sister's friends have no love for me. They believed I ruined her life and maybe, with her untimely death, they're angry all over again and want to upset me. Frighten me. Which is ridiculous considering where I've been.

"I know there are also people in the village who can't wait to see the back of me—and they will—but it won't be until I'm ready. Until I've had time to see what's in that cottage myself. It's all that's left of my family, after all."

"That's perfectly sound," said Graham, "but I do think the police should be informed about this intruder."

"No! I am getting new locks and that's it. I do not want the police involved. I've only told you because I hope I can give you a set of the new keys. There's no one else here I trust."

"Of course," he said. "We'd be glad to keep your spares, and hopefully whoever is watching to see when you go out will soon give up this game."

That reminded Ellie of the man she'd seen the night before. "By the way, have you ever had the feeling you were being followed?"

Both Corinna and Graham looked surprised. "Why do you ask?" he said.

"Last night I couldn't sleep, so I got up and went to the window. I saw Corinna and her dog walking through the village, and I also saw a man watching and following them. He kept close to the shadows and did not act like just another person out for a walk."

"You didn't mention that to me," said Graham. "What did he look like?"

"A man. A shadow."

"Corinna, I really think you must report all this to the police."

"No," she said again, glaring at him. "I am out on license, so I do not want to do anything to draw the attention of the police, even if it's something that's not my fault or my doing."

"Then is there anything else we can do to help?" asked Ellie, hoping to cool down the atmosphere, which had so suddenly heated up.

Corinna turned her intense gaze on Ellie and said, "Actually, there is, and Michael-John Parker thought you might be willing to give it a go."

"He did?" Michael-John Parker was the owner of the local antiques shop, The Chestnut Tree, and one of her other good friends in the village. He was a very kind person, but he was certainly ahead of the pack if he had already befriended Corinna. "What is it?"

"I was very glad to receive Clio's letter, but I know nothing about her life. Why she was in France. Why she wanted to leave the cottage. And I don't know who else to ask except her old friends, but I am persona non grata with them. Michael-John thought you might be able to get them to talk to you."

"I can try—and meanwhile suss out whether any of them has gone in for a bit of haunting?" said Ellie, as she reached out to take a slip of paper on which Corinna had written the names and phone numbers.

Corinna responded with a faint smile.

"I still wish you had more support," said Graham. "You may remember Lila Ashton as a young, infatuated girl, but she's grown up now, and she is apparently intent on making trouble for you."

"I'm not concerned about her," said Corinna, dismissively. "I don't think anyone here has any idea what life is like in prison, but they'll find it takes a great deal more than hate mail and social media posts to rattle me." Then she stood up abruptly and added, "I thank you, though, for listening and for offering to help."

"Any time. Always," said Graham, jumping to his feet and holding out his hand. As Corinna took it, Ellie thought the emotion that passed between them was practically visible.

"Per aspera ad astra," said Corinna with another wry smile. Then she turned to Ellie with a brief handshake and left.

When they were alone again, Ellie didn't know what to say. What tone to take. So, she busied herself with opening a box of ginger biscuits and arranging them on a plate, while Graham filled the electric kettle.

At last, she said, "She doesn't seem to have lost Circe's touch after all these years. And I must say I can't quite picture her and Louise as bosom friends, but you two are an even more puzzling combination. I think you mentioned a brief fling? Or was it a brief spell?"

Graham smiled, but his ears were pink again. "Either will do to describe something that happened when we were both very young. I admit I found it disconcerting to see her again. But that is all.

"She's an old, old friend," he said, as he spooned tea into the china teapot, poured in boiling water, and popped on a tea cozy. "Now she's alone, facing the difficult task of trying to find her way back to herself . . . her past and her future . . . so, she needs our support."

"You know, sweetheart, you don't need to worry that it's *me* she's trying to get back to. She dumped me without a backward look, and I was lucky enough to meet Louise soon after."

Ellie laughed. "You are a man of mystery. How did I never hear that story before?"

"We have to save something for our old age," he said. "Or at least the second year of marriage."

"Really, I didn't know that. You mean you're not supposed to spill everything before the contract is signed?"

"I prefer to look forward to a lifelong process of discovery."

"Very eloquent. I like that. But to get back to Circe. If she's not trying to spin you into a new web, what's the deal with the secret society send-off?"

"That was definitely a flashback. 'Per aspera ad astra' was the motto Cleve had carved over his office door. The way he liked to think of his own rise from a middle-class grammar schoolboy to the heights of academia. It means 'Through adversity to the stars.' When I was a student, we used to say it before we sat our exams."

"So, she did want to remind you of when she had you under her spell."

He poured her a mug of tea and patted the space on the kitchen bench beside him. "As I said, for me, that's one of those memories that makes you glad you're not young anymore. I think you know the kind I mean."

"I do," said Ellie, who regarded him, with his kind, twinkly blue eyes and inviting smile, and swore to herself that she would be mad ever to allow jealousy to seep into her thoughts about him.

But she couldn't help putting herself in Corinna's place too. In the long, lonely years, she would have had plenty of time for regrets about things done and undone and may well have entertained the hope that some chapters of her history might still be rewritten.

CHAPTER FIVE

Sunday, March 11

On Sunday morning, the sun was out, melting the frost that silvered the pebbled path from the vicarage through the churchyard to St. Michael's. Ellie and Graham walked over to the church together, parting, as usual, at the vestry door.

Not many people had come to the service, and Ellie had observed that, on the whole, the 40-day season of Lent, with its emphasis on penance, had a dampening effect on church attendance. How much nicer to spend an extra hour feeling grateful to God for your warm bed than to get up and hear about your shortcomings.

This morning, the icy air in the church added to the penitential atmosphere. But, when the organ began to play—rallying the shivering members of the congregation to stand and open their hymnals—Ellie rose to sing with them, and that invariably lifted her spirits.

Her project for her first Lent in England was to read

William James' *Varieties of Religious Experience*—something she thought would contribute more to her spiritual development than giving up her favorite red licorice sticks—and she was finding it enlightening, although she wasn't even close to finished with only two weeks to go until Easter.

She particularly liked the way James' made a clear distinction between spirituality and organized religions. She expected she would never cease to be resistant about being told what to believe and how to express it. Nonetheless, she had come to love St. Michael's for the refuge and inspiration it had offered to anyone who sought them since long before Shakespeare picked up his quill. She also enjoyed the fact that she now lived in the midst of this centuries-long history, and her role as the vicar's wife, trivial as some aspects of it could be, gave her at least a walk-on part in the story.

After tea the night before, she'd gone up to her study to finish and send off her *Walsingham* review, while Graham, freshly provoked by their meeting with Corinna and the campaign against her, revised his sermon yet again in a fury of typing.

Messages about loving your neighbor were nothing new, and Ellie had often observed that Graham's words rolled over the congregation, a comforting sound, like the twitter of birds or the wind in the trees.

But this morning, people perked up when he stood before them, paused, and announced that his topic for the day was the word "as."

"Such a small word," he said, "so seemingly insignificant that it deserves close attention."

"For example, how are we to love our neighbors, whom we so frequently find irritating and in the way? The Bible tells us. We are to love them *as* we love ourselves. It's an equation. And a very specific contract.

"The same contract we're offered in the Lord's Prayer, which we recite so often," he continued. "How will we be forgiven for all our missteps and wrongdoing? *As* we forgive those who trespass against us. As and only as.

"God alone loves and forgives unreservedly. We need guidance, and it is provided: in all our relationships love and forgiveness will be ours only to the extent, and in equal measure, to the love and forgiveness we give others."

Ellie found it hard to keep from beaming at what she thought was a brilliant message, and quite a few people seemed to have heard, not only what he said, but also the underlying admonition. Regrettably, Charles and Mary Bell were not among them. They sat side by side in the warden's pew, nodding self-righteously like bobblehead dolls. Ellie thought they probably believed what Graham said didn't apply to Corinna, since everyone knew that you were not supposed to commit murder. That was a commandment.

When the organist, Mr. Dunn, had finished his postlude, it was the custom at St. Michael's to gather at the back of the nave for refreshments—Communion, part two. Ellie worked her way to the tea table with smiles and "Good mornings," but she had no sooner received her own tea and cake than she found herself accosted by her across-the-street neighbor, Mrs. Geraldine Bigelow.

"I suppose the vicar chose to lecture us on neighborly love and forgiveness today because of our reaction to that murderer's return," she said, pulling her purple wool shawl more tightly around her ample body. Mrs. Bigelow claimed to be a retired opera singer, though Ellie had found no evidence of her career online. She was nonetheless perfectly operatic in size and self-importance, and looking out her front window to see what was happening at the vicarage was currently one of her primary occupations.

"*Our* reaction?" asked Ellie.

"You must know practically everyone in the village has signed that petition to the Parole Board demanding that she be removed."

"No, I didn't know that, and I'm not sure I know what 'practically everyone' means either. Not everyone, I assume, and how many remains undefined."

Mrs. Bigelow smirked. "Another fine point of language, I'm sure, but I expect you'll know soon enough that everyone wants to see the back of her. Of course, the vicar must feel compelled to offer the other cheek, but I would have thought, under the circumstances, you'd be more than happy to see her gone."

Ellie stared at Mrs. Bigelow's smug face, making a concerted effort to keep her own expressionless. She supposed it was not very much of a stretch to guess that Lila Ashton had known about Corinna and Graham's long-ago fling, liaison, whatever it was—but the idea that she would circulate this as gossip to spice up her campaign was infuriating, to say the least.

Ellie, for one, intended to add no additional spice to the brew. So, she said only: "What makes me happy is my own concern, but I can assure you that a disruptive and unpleasant campaign against anyone in this village is not on the list." Then she smiled, said "Good morning," and turned her back, only to have her attention drawn to a vaguely familiar-looking woman in a red suit and black silk blouse, who had drawn around her a flock of parishioners listening avidly to what she said. Ellie had never seen this woman at church before, but she was clearly well known to others.

When she pulled a clipboard out of her black leather tote bag, and the butcher's wife, Mrs. Elsie Tiddington, leaned in to take a pen, Ellie realized why she looked familiar: she had seen her online. She'd been much younger then, but this was undoubtedly the pretty blond former fiancée of Pindar Matthews: Lila Ashton. Ms. SplashwithLAshton.org herself.

Ellie had to admit she had grown into an attractive woman with a confident manner. But her mores as a PR person left a lot to be desired, and openly soliciting signatures for her petition to oust Corinna, in the church, and only minutes after Graham's sermon, was beyond the pale. She was about to march over and tell her so, when she saw Graham, still in his vestments, glide serenely toward the group himself. In an instant, the clipboard vanished into the leather bag, and the parishioners fluttered away to whisper among themselves, while Lila stood her ground to take him on.

Ellie couldn't hear what Graham said, but his pleasant manner and expression never changed. Lila, on the other hand, flushed angrily, before announcing in a loud voice: "Biblical platitudes can't stop people knowing right from wrong. And believe me, we do! And we intend to act on it!" Then she stalked out, her high-heeled shoes clacking on the stone floor.

When the heavy church door had banged shut, there was an uneasy silence, until Graham smiled at everyone and said, "No one has ever suggested that loving your neighbor is easy," and the tension broke.

Several people gathered around to assure him that his sermon had been excellent, jolly well put. Ellie had been moving to join them, when Miss Priscilla Worthy appeared at her elbow.

"Wouldn't it be grand if we really did know the difference between right and wrong," she said, and Ellie suppressed the urge to laugh. As a best-selling author of romantic suspense novels, neatly disguised as an elderly lady clad in layers of sweaters and tweed, Miss Worthy had made a fortune off her characters' inability to distinguish between the two.

"Don't look at me," Ellie said, smiling.

"Nor me. And I'm not judging, but that poor girl, who seems to have carried a torch for a ne'er-do-well all these years, is the last person who should be lecturing Graham."

"Oh, well. He can take it."

"Yes, and I am sure Corinna has dealt with far worse than Lila's campaign where she's been. I am glad she has you and Graham as allies, though, because I expect she'll dismiss Lila's efforts out of hand, and that would not be wise."

"What makes you say I'm her ally?" asked Ellie. "I've barely met her."

Miss Worthy's blue eyes twinkled. "My dear Mrs. Kent, you must be aware by now that modern CCTV cameras aren't a patch on a village's traditional surveillance system. Everyone knows who goes where and when.

"I think, when you get to know her, you'll find Corinna a very interesting person. She survived her father's peculiar ideas about her upbringing—all those hours of studying Latin and Greek—and I expect she survived prison with equal fortitude."

"That's the closest thing to a compliment I've heard from anyone so far."

"Are you surprised? Intelligent women always make people uneasy, even when they haven't committed murder. But I'm certain you'll keep an open mind about her. You have no history here. That alone is a great asset.

"I never really knew the children, but I liked and admired Cleve very much, so please count on me to assist, if I can. Perhaps you could come and tell me how you're getting on. At teatime on Tuesday?"

"Thank you. I would love that," said Ellie, who had always found Miss Worthy very well informed about the village and its history. She was also curious to learn more about Cleve Matthews, whose peculiar ideas had ended up causing so many problems for his children.

"Splendid. And, by the way, the new hairstyle is most becoming."

When Miss Worthy left, Ellie turned to help Mrs. Bell clean up the tea things and complimented her on the homemade pink-and-yellow-checkerboard Battenberg cake she'd brought that day, but the older woman's replies were curtly monosyllabic. They had boxed up the last of the dirty dishes, before she cleared her throat portentously and came out with what was on her mind.

"You know, Mrs. Kent, in a village, everyone has an opinion, and being new here, and a foreigner, you may find it hard to know whose opinions are valid and what advice to follow. Of course, I know you will always let yourself be guided by the vicar. But sometimes the perspective of an older woman with experience can be invaluable."

The look on her face made it clear that she saw herself in this virtuous role, and Ellie wondered whether Mrs. Bell had noticed her talking with Miss Worthy. She knew the recent revelation that the seemingly meek spinster was also best-selling author Ramona Blaisdell-Scott had upended the former friendship between the two women. Long based on Mary Bell's unshakable superiority as the warden's wife and owner of the gracious Castor House, the relationship had not yet recovered from this blow. If it ever would.

Of course, Ellie knew better than to let on she knew all this. Instead, she said, "That's a very good point, and I will keep it in mind." She smiled sweetly and considered it a measure of her progress in her new role that she no longer felt honor bound to mention that she was perfectly capable of thinking for herself and did not need Graham, much less Mrs. Bell, to tell her what to do.

. . .

It was their custom to go out to Sunday lunch at The Bull in Kingbrook. The old pub was usually crowded, but not with people they knew, so it offered a chance to be on their own and relax. Afterward, Graham dropped Ellie off at home and went to follow up on parishioners who were sick or in the hospital. She needed to work off her roast-beef-and-three-veg meal, so she changed her clothes and took Hector for a run and then a ramble along the footpaths through the fields and woods surrounding the village.

Eventually, they ended up at her favorite spot for ruminating on life and its mysteries: the hillside overlooking the ruins of Beech Hall. Built of the local stone, in its heyday, Beech Hall had been a classic Elizabethan manor, with two wings and a central porch, surrounded by manicured gardens and woods, but a fire in the 1930s had destroyed all but one wing of the house, and nature had reclaimed the grounds.

A family named Rutherford had owned Beech Hall for hundreds of years, but the last member of the family had died a few months before. In Ellie's brief experience with them, she had discovered how passionate families can be about holding on to their secrets. No doubt every family had this instinct to some extent, but she wondered whether more than a quarrel about money lay behind the violent denouement in the life of the Matthews family.

The elements she'd learned of so far—control of a trust, a quarrel over inheritance, a missing coin collection—might surely have caused legal battles and a fruitless search that could make people miserable for generations, but it was harder to picture them leading to a physical fight to the death. That would be motivated by some other kind of secret, wouldn't it? Something deeper and more unbearable that a person would go to prison to avoid revealing.

But what was it? She went back over the story in her mind

until the seat of her pants was damp and the cold had begun to seep into her bones. Definite signs that it was time to get up and start home.

Hector had run off, and she was scanning the hillside for him, when she saw Michael-John Parker appear out of the gaping hole that had once been the entrance to the hall. She hadn't even noticed him arrive, but Hector had spotted his golden retriever, Whistler, and was already running down the hill to greet him, so Ellie followed.

As usual, Michael-John was dressed in immaculate country-gentleman style and greeted her as if he were welcoming her to his own home, although he was actually a former London financier who'd never lived in the country until he retired at 35 to Little Beecham and opened his antiques shop.

"I wondered whether you were ever going to notice me," he said, with a smile. "I could tell you were daydreaming without a care in the world, while I slaved away collecting the latest rubbish left behind by who-knows-whom." He held up a bulging bin bag for her inspection. "It amazes me what a tip this place becomes when I'm away for a few days. But your holiday obviously agreed with you. I love the new look."

Ellie laughed. Aside from her new haircut, which made any outfit look stylish, she was wearing exactly she what always wore when she went out running: old sweatpants and sweatshirt, a hand-me-down anorak, and running shoes. "Thanks, and did you enjoy your time in London?"

"I did. But I came home to a pleasant surprise."

"That being?"

"Our new neighbor. Whom I quite like, despite the lurid tales about her past. She adds some much-needed depth to the flavor of our little community."

"You mean Corinna. I heard you'd met, but not how."

"It was quite embarrassing, as a matter of fact. I went to

Oak Cottage expecting to see Clio, only to learn about her car crash. I hadn't heard, and I had no idea who Corinna was."

"Ouch. Were you and Clio friends?"

"Not exactly. But I have a couple of her marionettes in the shop, and I'd promised her that I would talk to the blokes I know with London galleries who might be interested. And they were. Too late, unfortunately."

"Marionettes?"

"Yes. Although marionette isn't exactly the right word to describe what she made. They're more like kinetic sculptures. Made from antique doll parts. Arms, legs, faces. You should come and see them."

"I will. Was Corinna very taken aback when you turned up?"

"She was at first, but she was pleased to meet someone who'd known her sister and appreciated her. She knew nothing about her work and was very interested. We ended up having a nice chat. That cottage is quite pleasant, you know—the rooms are less poky than in most cottages. She said Clio had kept it the way it was when they were children and the Odyssey House caretakers lived there—complete with pine furniture, rag rugs, and twenty-year-old jars of jam. But there's a rather nice landscape over the mantel that I'd swear is by Walter Sickert. She said it came from her mother's family, and, if I'm right, it's worth a tidy sum."

"Sounds like you covered a lot of ground in one visit," said Ellie.

He grinned. "Well, you know how it is. Aside from my professional interest, we outsiders have to band together. I don't care what she did in a blackout a million years ago. Lord knows, I wouldn't want to be judged by that myself. The crimes of the present are enough for me."

She was about to ask whether he knew about the campaign

against Corinna, when another man—a stranger—emerged from Beech Hall.

"I'll bet you could easily put twenty condos within the original footprint," he was saying, as he studied the screen on his cell phone.

Michael-John glanced at Ellie, embarrassed. "I never said anything about condos, Kidder. We don't do condos in these parts," he told the man, who looked up, surprised to see Ellie.

He was in his mid-40s, very good looking, but with the spray-tanned skin and pseudo-streaky blond hair that pegged him as being from Southern California, even if you didn't hear his voice. Ellie thought the fact that he also wore brand-new English country clothes only made his foreignness more obvious. "Why not?" he asked. "Were you imagining you'd live here alone?"

Michael-John cleared his throat. "Not at all, old man. Just dreaming. Dreams are free and require no building permissions. But, without further ado . . . let me introduce to you to our local American, Mrs. Kent."

"How do you do," he said, stowing his cell phone in his jacket pocket and holding out his hand. "Jeremy Kidder." His handshake was firm, professional, and practiced. He smiled with perfect American capped teeth and said, "I have the distinct feeling I have put my foot in what you call here a cowpat."

"You have indeed," said Michael-John. "The mere mention of housing developments is enough to cause mass hysteria in Little Beecham." To Ellie, he added, "I brought Kidder over to see the ruins, so he might understand my infatuation."

"Which I interpreted to mean it was a business opportunity. My bad."

"It's all right. You couldn't know. But if there will be any development here, it won't be any time soon," said Ellie. "This property was left to a trust controlled by the Church of England."

"What a shame," he said, showing those teeth again. "It would be a lovely spot to live."

"Yes, we all agree on that. Are you looking for property here?" asked Ellie.

He affected a casual laugh. "Not me. I'm just nosing around. On holiday. I lost my way and ended up on Parker's doorstep. He has kindly taken me in hand."

"Will you be staying in the area long?" Ellie looked from one to the other, trying to suss out the nature of their relationship, if there was one. Jeremy Kidder did not seem to her like Michael-John's type, but what did she know?

Jeremy apparently thought he was, because he glanced at Michael-John with a coy smile and said, "Perhaps."

"In that case, I will no doubt see you around, but now I must be on my way. I'll come by the shop soon, Michael-John, and it was very nice to meet you," she added to Jeremy, then whistled for Hector.

When she arrived at home, Ellie found two paper bags full of mail addressed to Corinna on the kitchen table.

"What's all this?" she asked Graham, who was making a salad for their tea to go with the leftover chicken pie.

"A present for you. From Corinna. She got the idea from something Parker said about your interests. Abilities."

"Seriously?" Ellie lifted out a handful of the letters. Most were in the same kind of envelope. She opened one and saw it was written in block letters with a marker: "GO BACK WHERE YOU BELONG!" The words were surrounded with a crude drawing of a barred window. "Very creative," said Ellie, wrinkling up her nose.

"You are interested, though, aren't you? She did ask if I thought she should throw them straight into the bin, but I told her I thought you'd be willing to take a look first."

Ellie moved the bags to the floor. "So, I presume this activity falls under supporting thy neighbor, but not getting too interested in old crimes."

He grinned and set the salad on the table. "Something like that."

"When was Corinna here?" Ellie asked, noticing the two tea cups and plates in the dish drainer.

"About four o'clock."

"Has the intruder returned?"

"No. She said she stayed home all day looking through the boxes of family papers and things that Clio saved. The locks will be changed tomorrow, so after that, there shouldn't be any more problems," he said confidently, as if locks could be the solution to all Corinna's problems.

"Per aspera ad astra," said Ellie, and Graham laughed.

She doubted things would go that smoothly, though, especially after she had plowed through the bags of hate mail. She'd curled up on the sofa in the sitting room with Hector beside her. He at least thought the letters flying into a bin bag were a great game. She was increasingly disgusted.

A lot of work had gone into this project of Lila's. The letters and social media posts. The petitions. The gossip. And maybe even a stalker.

Most of the hate letters were along the lines of "Get out of town" and "We don't want murderers here." The few words were written with markers or cut out of newspapers and magazines, then pasted on white A4 paper. From the similarities, Ellie imagined Lila inviting members of the Women's Institute over for a hate-mail writing party, complete with tea and biscuits.

A handful of them were different, though. They were written on different kinds of paper and with different pens, but when she laid them out together, Ellie thought those differences had been carefully chosen to make it appear they were written by different people. She was no expert on handwriting, but they looked to her as if they might be by someone attempting to alter the style from letter to letter. All were postmarked from Chipping Martin or Kingbrook, but that was no clue to their origin because mail dropped off at the various village shops all went on to those larger post offices.

"Graham," she said, interrupting his work on the crossword puzzle. "Come and look at these five letters. I want to know what you think."

He set aside the newspaper and joined her on the sofa to study the letters she'd spread out on the coffee table before them:

"You will never escape your past!"

"You'll never have a moment's peace, no matter where you go."

"Your evil act will follow you all the days of your life."

"Why should you live when he didn't?"

"Murder begets murder. Your turn will come."

Graham looked taken aback. "These are serious threats. I thought from what Corinna said the letters were more of a joke."

"Most of them are very generic. I'm no authority, but, as hate mail goes, I would call them innocuous. But these seem like they're from the same person, and the rhetoric gets more violent as the sequence continues."

He nodded. "Were they open? Had she read them?"

"No. I opened them. They were sent, one each day, starting

last week. Before Corinna even arrived!"

"Well, I think you should put them back without touching them further, if you can. I'm going to tell Corinna that the police really do need to know about this."

"Good luck with that," said Ellie, picking up the letters and envelopes with the tail of her shirt over her fingers and dropping them into a bag on their own. "I agree the police should be told . . . but don't you think they need to know the whole context? I mean, the break-ins and everything. Who knows whether or not one person is behind all of it?"

"Under the circumstances, I am most concerned about those letters. The intruder isn't harming Corinna—while this letter writer is increasingly threatening. Did the letters really come in that sequence?"

"They did. I was careful to look at the postmarks."

He frowned. "I do understand Corinna's desire not to be involved with the police ever again, but I don't think she can ignore this."

Ellie agreed and wondered whether these letters might be from Lila Ashton herself. Whether the public campaign could be a smoke screen for her private desire for vengeance. And if it weren't Lila, who else was involved?

CHAPTER SIX

Monday, March 12

When she arrived on Monday, Mrs. Finch informed Ellie that it was time for the vicarage's annual spring cleaning, which she always did before Holy Week. She would begin that day in the attic, she said, and would be finished by Friday week. Ellie gulped, offered to help, and was happy to be turned down, except for taking over more of the shopping.

That agreed, Mrs. Finch gave her a list, and she set off for the village shop, opening the door with its tinkling bell, just as Lila Ashton was leaving with a handful of signed petitions. She held them in a way that made visible the fact that every line bore a signature.

"Good morning. It's Ellie, isn't it?" she said, barring the way forward. Ellie thought it was remarkable that being addressed by her first name could sound so aggressive.

"Yes. Good morning, Lila," she replied, dodging a bit to her left so she could get by the other woman, but without success.

Lila intended to talk, and Ellie thought she was trying to

even up the score after her unsuccessful encounter with Graham at church the day before. She also noted her very professional on-the-job-look: perfectly coiffed long blond locks, subtle makeup, smart navy all-weather coat, and expensive gray wool slacks. All of which made Ellie deeply wish she had not grabbed the oldest anorak in the Kent family collection of old anoraks hanging in the entryway off the kitchen. This one was notable for the fact that Hector had chewed off the cuffs in his long-ago puppyhood, but it had seemed fine for a quick run to the shop. Unfortunately, Lila's smile made it clear she had noticed.

"I don't see your name on our petition, Ellie," she said brightly, "but it's not too late. I've left some fresh ones with Mrs. Wiggins."

Ellie stared at her, before saying, "I have no intention of signing today or any other day."

Lila's smile moved quickly from falsely pleasant to chilly. "Well, you might want to give that another think. I'm sure you don't want everyone saying the church doesn't acknowledge the village's concerns."

There was that word again: everyone. As if the more you repeated it, the more true it would become. Lila then sashayed past Ellie and out to her British-racing-green BMW parked outside. Obviously, the girl who had once imagined Pindar Matthews was her ticket to a good life had done very well on her own. As Ellie watched her speed off down the high street, she wondered why Lila hadn't left Little Beecham and its bad memories in the dust long ago.

Usually, she enjoyed going to the village shop to poke around its narrow aisles stocked with everything from home-made bread and fresh milk to umbrellas, toys, and garden tools, but this morning she wanted to avoid any more social encoun-ters, so she hurried through Mrs. Finch's list.

When she had found all the items the housekeeper needed, she put a handful of red licorice sticks into the basket for herself, and took it to the counter. There the proprietor, Mrs. Wiggins, looked up from *Hello!* magazine to greet her with a broad smile.

"Our Lila's quite the pushy one, isn't she?" she said. "She's always been dead set on getting what she wants, but it was more amusing when she was a youngster. These days she seems to think if she pushes hard enough, we'll all sign on as extras in the film of her life."

Ellie laughed and said, "Well, I'm fully booked." She noticed there were blank petitions on the counter, but Mrs. Wiggins had mixed them in with a flyer for the annual village Easter Egg Hunt, an offer of free kittens, and a promotion for 10 percent off on a manicure at Cherie's Fab Nails and Hair. "You don't seem to be giving her campaign pride of place."

"I never take sides. The shop is for everyone. I must say, though, people do enjoy a petition," said the shopkeeper, shrugging her heavy shoulders. "Signing makes them feel as if they're doing something. Taking part in the community. That said, I could count on one hand those I've had here that came to anything."

"I guess I'm glad to hear that," said Ellie.

"Of course, you can be sure our Lila also knows the limits of a petition, and she'll have other arrows in her quiver. Sharp ones, too. She means to make her point that the law might say Corinna has paid for what she did, but there are those who are not satisfied. Besides, she needs to keep her client sweet."

"Her client?" asked Ellie.

Mrs. Wiggins looked at Ellie over the top of her glasses. "You don't think she got the dosh for that fancy car by working for nothing, do you?"

"No, but I was under the impression this was something of a personal crusade."

"I'd describe it as a meeting of the minds, and one willing to put money on it."

"And whose minds would that be?"

The shopkeeper licked her finger and turned the page of her magazine. "Now, Mrs. Kent. I'm sure you can suss that out for yourself. No need for me to be telling tales."

Just then the doorbell tinkled, and a woman Ellie didn't know holding a small child by the hand came in. Mrs. Wiggins greeted them and nodded to Ellie, clearly her cue to leave.

She picked up her bag of purchases and started for home with plenty to think about.

It had never occurred to her that there might be someone financing the effort to force Corinna out. That being the case, one name came immediately to mind: Geoff Stephens. But would a successful Harley Street consultant stoop to such a thing? Just to buy out a neighbor and get control of a cottage? She had no idea, but she was certainly going to try to find out.

She also wondered again to what lengths Lila and her campaign would go, and, halfway home, curiosity made her set down her bag of groceries on the sidewalk to check Twitter. There she found that the tweeters had moved on from the issue of Corinna's return to the village. Now the focus was on what happened to Pindar and the injustice of her never revealing what she did with his body. Photos of woods, ditches, quarries, and the sea were all tagged "#whereisPindar."

Ellie sighed. If the body hadn't gone out to sea, surely it would have been found long before this, wouldn't it? She took a quick look at Facebook and saw the posts there were similar. For all this grassroots activity online, though, it didn't appear Lila had anything very new or substantial to work with. And, assuming Graham was right, zero hope of impressing the Parole Board, so what was point?

At least the ominous tone of the more threatening letters had not become part of the social media chatter. Ellie put her phone away on this positive thought, if it could be called that.

Mrs. Finch had proposed the Soup Car lunch use beef barley soup from the freezer that day, since she was too busy cleaning to make a fresh batch. As Ellie waited for it to heat on the Aga, she made phone calls to the people on Corinna's list and left a message for DI Mullane to please call her.

It had rained during the night, but the storm had blown out, bringing a clear morning with a mild breeze that carried the sound of birdsong. Ellie's first two visits were to homes on the outskirts of Little Beecham. Mrs. Jane Davenport was a retired librarian with emphysema, and Miss Honoria Pierce-Wilson had lived most of her life as a missionary in Malawi before chronic malaria brought her home. Both reported they had seen Lila's petition, but declined to sign it. "Why should I want to harass someone who owned up to what she did wrong and paid the penalty for it?" said Miss Pierce-Wilson. "If anything, the world needs more people like that."

So much for the "everyone" claim, Ellie said to herself, and this gave her hope she was right. Lila's campaign would come to nothing. Social media interest would die out, as it always did; the Parole Board would decline to respond to the petition; and Corinna would be left in peace to decide what to do with the cottage and her life. This would spell the end of any other interest or threats, too.

She managed to hold on to these feelings of optimism until she reached the brick row house of Mrs. Penelope Whittaker in Kingbrook. Pen, as she liked to be called, had been a faithful member of St. Michael's when she lived in the village and continued to come to church when she could, but, at 80 years old, that was not often.

"I work in my garden, and that's my church these days," she liked to say. Unfortunately, she had begun her outdoor work when it was too cold and developed bronchitis that turned into a nasty bout of pneumonia. After a week in the hospital, she was back at home again, where, it seemed to Ellie, she spent all her time in bed poring over garden catalogs with her big gray tiger cat, Barney, at her side.

Usually, she liked to talk about the gardens she'd had over the years, and her enthusiasm made her stories vivid, even when the details of plant varieties and Latin names went over Ellie's head. But when she wasn't feeling well, Ellie would read to her, as she lay quietly stroking Barney. Pen said she had never had much time for fiction before, but they were both engrossed in a Ramona Blaisdell-Scott novel, *The Buried Heart*, which Ellie had chosen because the heroine was a keen gardener, who falls in love with a blind man.

She had been hoping they might continue the story that day, but, when she entered Pen's room with her tray of lunch, she found the older woman sprawled across the bed in her nightgown, as if she had tripped and fallen there. Her outdoor clothes and copies of several gardening magazines were scattered on the floor. In case Ellie missed the point that things had gone very wrong, Barney sat crouched on the bookcase, meowing indignantly as if to say it was about time she got there to help.

"Pen? What's happened? Are you all right?" she asked, setting down the tray.

The older woman started at the sound of Ellie's voice and lifted herself up, but her blue eyes looked blank. When she said, "Who are you?" grabbing the duvet to pull over her legs, Ellie felt her heart lurch.

"I'm Ellie Kent," she said, trying to sound calm and friendly. "I've brought your lunch."

"Did you let him in too?" Pen demanded.

"No. It's only me, but Graham would be happy to visit if you wish. I've just brought your lunch," she said again.

Slowly, awareness seeped back into the ashen face, but she still looked disoriented and frightened. She abruptly refused any help with getting back under her covers, so Ellie took the opportunity to pick up the clothes and magazines on the floor.

"It looks like you went out this morning," she said, trying to act as if nothing unusual had happened.

"I went to pick up my magazines," said Pen, in a belligerent tone. "I never dreamed *he* would be there. How could I?"

"Someone you knew was at the newsagent's shop?"

She jerked her head in a way that might have been a nod.

"Was that nice?"

"No, I tried to hide, but he knew me, and the look he gave me made my blood run cold."

Ellie had been about to set the tray of food in front of her, but the older woman shrank down under the duvet and closed her eyes tightly. "I'm sure he followed me home, so now he knows where I live. Are you certain you didn't let him in?"

"I am, and I didn't see anyone around. That was probably me you heard downstairs."

She opened her eyes again and said, "Are you sure?" And she looked so frightened that Ellie went back downstairs to check.

"There is absolutely no one else here," she reported when she returned to the bedroom. "Only you, Barney, and me. And the doors are locked."

"Jock never would believe that what I saw meant anything. He told me to say nothing, and now look what's happened."

Ellie wanted to ask what she meant, but tears had begun to leak from the corners of Pen's eyes, and she turned away, curling up tightly. Barney, at least, took this as a sign that some sort of order had been restored, so he leapt onto the bed to take up his usual spot by her side.

Ellie waited a few minutes, hoping Pen might say something more. Or want to eat. Or do something. But she didn't stir for so long, she seemed to have fallen asleep.

Perhaps that was what she most needed, Ellie thought as she picked up the lunch tray and took it back down to the kitchen. There she put the food away and left a note for the visiting nurse, who would come later. Still, she felt upset by the way her own visit had turned out, so she called the nurse to ask whether there was anything else she could or should do.

"Mrs. Whittaker had an encounter in the newsagent's shop with someone who upset her, and she has asked me repeatedly whether he had gotten into the house," Ellie told her.

Much to her surprise, the nurse was unconcerned. "I wouldn't worry about it, love. I'll be there shortly and see to everything. A lot of my older ladies and gents get confused when they're on those strong antibiotics, and you'd be amazed at what they come out with. She'll be right as rain the next time you come."

Ellie thanked her and hoped she was right. Then, whether she was reassuring herself or the sleeping woman upstairs she couldn't say, but, before she left, she checked every door and window again to be certain they were all locked.

Back at the vicarage, the noises coming from the attic sounded as if Mrs. Finch might be tearing the house down, so Ellie bundled up again and went out for a walk. Clouds had gathered, and the broody atmosphere suited her mood. She was worried about Pen, who had always seemed so busy and confident, even as she was recovering from her illness. The lost, confused person she'd met that day was someone else entirely, and Ellie could still feel the intense fear that radiated from her.

The beeping of her phone broke into her thoughts, and she received calls in quick succession from Geordie Murphy and Melissa Engelthorpe. Both suggested she come the next day and she agreed, before realizing she didn't know who they were or what Corinna wanted from them.

When Corinna didn't answer her phone, she decided to stop by the cottage anyway. Her first surprise visit had failed miserably, but now they had met—and if Corinna could drop in unexpectedly on Graham, surely Ellie could exercise the same neighborly privilege.

As she walked down the drive, she could see why Michael-John admired the graceful stone cottage with its two tall chimneys. But the sprawling oaks surrounding it reminded Ellie of a fairy tale, and not one of the nice ones.

Once again, no one answered her knock at the door, but she heard barking from behind the cottage, so she followed the flagstone path around to a large fenced garden carved out from the woods. There she was met by Toby, Corinna's big red bloodhound, who stood guard over her, as she sat on the back steps, smoking a cigarette.

When Corinna saw Ellie, she nodded a greeting and put her hand on the dog, who lay down at her feet. Today she was wearing more borrowed clothes: battered khaki pants and a much-darned sweater that had clearly belonged to someone taller and heavier. But her face had picked up some needed color, and her knees and hands were dirty, as if she had been pottering in the garden.

Ellie could tell her arrival had interrupted a moment of contentment, and she felt the embarrassment of poor timing. "I'm sorry to come without warning," she said. "I did call, but there was no answer, so I thought I'd just stop by on my walk. Geordie Murphy and Melissa Engelthorpe both want to see me tomorrow, so I need to know more about who they are and what you hope to learn."

"Sure," said Corinna. "That's good news." She got to her feet, but Ellie thought she looked reluctant. No matter how many years had gone by, they were like two angles of a triangle, and it wasn't Louise who connected them, as she had first imagined. It was Graham.

After a last look around the garden, Corinna said, "Would you like some tea?" and Ellie said thank you.

They went in through the back door, which opened into a boot room that doubled as a garden shed, and then through another door into the kitchen. Entering the cottage was like going back several decades. The cherry-sprig wallpaper and red curtains in the kitchen were faded, but the old-fashioned gas stove was clean, and everything was very neat.

Ellie sat down at an old pine table while Corinna washed up, then filled a kettle with water, and set it on to boil. Looking around at the rows of souvenir china on the dresser and the converted kerosene lamp on the table, Ellie thought this might actually be the perfect place to recuperate from years in prison. Nothing about it signaled that life had gone ahead without you.

After Corinna had poured boiling water over the loose tea, she placed an old-fashioned Brown Betty teapot on the table with a pitcher of milk, a bowl of sugar, and a plate of McVitie's digestive biscuits. She performed these everyday tasks in such a careful, concentrated way, it was almost as if she were doing them for the first time. Toby followed her every move with his eyes, thumped to the floor beside her when she sat down, and laid his head against her knee, with an adoring look.

"You asked what I hope for, and I can't tell you how strange that sounds to me." She rubbed the dog's long, velvety ears thoughtfully. "Toby and I aren't very used to getting what we hope for, are we, Tob? But we're starting to learn," she said, as she handed him a biscuit. It disappeared instantly and she laughed, giving Ellie a glimpse of the beautiful girl who had once beguiled her father's students.

"You'll find the Murphys and Melissa are challenging in different ways, but they were all very devoted to my sister. Geordie and Ruby were the gardener and housekeeper for Odyssey House and a constant presence in our lives. I found these clothes hanging in the mudroom, so I assume Geordie has continued to work for Clio up to the present. I expect she would have been lost without them in many ways, but the truth is they were never very fond of me or Pindar. We were older and less needful of Ruby's hovering care.

"Melissa is Clio's executor, and I am sure she meant well, but I believe she was instrumental in the plan to whisk Clio away from home as soon as I was taken for questioning and to keep her away until I was locked in prison. I understood she needed a safe place and time to take in what happened, but I never imagined we wouldn't speak again."

Ellie was too surprised not to be blunt. "You never spoke to Clio? In all these years? That letter you received this week was the first communication?"

Corinna nodded. "It's my fault. I did try to write to her. Quite a few times. But there are some things that simply can't be put into writing."

"And she never visited?"

"No. I didn't want her to, and, anyway, a prison visiting

area is no place to talk. So, in keeping with family tradition, I said nothing. And neither did she."

Ellie sipped her tea, remembering her earlier reflections on the motive for the murder. Once again, she felt convinced that money was only the surface issue—surely not a subject that was so sensitive it could never be written or talked about. But she saw the flash of defensiveness in Corinna's expression and knew enough to drop the subject.

"That's very sad, as it turned out," said Ellie. "It seems unlikely that either the Murphys or Melissa will confide in a stranger, so why don't I stick to asking them about Clio's life in general and the house keys in particular? I can also try to get a feeling for whether they have any idea who your intruder might be."

"That sounds fine. You may be a stranger, but I'm sure you'll receive a warmer welcome than I would. Anything they tell you is more than I know now, but I am particularly curious about why Clio said she was ready to move, because this cottage feels like her cocoon. Her way of connecting to her life before. If you know what I mean.

"That person who comes in has no idea how much I feel like I'm the intruder myself. But, as I said the other day, what's here is all that's left of my family, so I want to see what it is and try to piece together what it tells me—if anything—before I leave."

"Have you had any further thoughts about what he might be searching for?"

"No. I've been looking through the family papers in the box room, and there's certainly nothing valuable there. But he has been back."

"Again?"

She nodded. "Yesterday. When I took those letters over to the vicarage."

"Really? He must be observing your movements very closely to know when you leave the house. What happened this time?"

"I'd been reading a book my father wrote on the evolution of Greek mythology, and, when I came back, it was all torn up. The pages scattered on the floor."

Ellie was taken aback, but Corinna's expression remained impassive.

"Does that mean anything to you? You said you thought the other things he did were messages about your family still being with you. This sounds angry. Even violent."

She shrugged and looked down at Toby. "Yes, so I guess this time the message was supposed to be from Pindar. He hated my father. And me."

Ellie felt a chill go down her spine, and Toby stood up, leaned in, and reassuringly licked Corinna's face with his long, pink tongue. She smiled and hugged him.

Ellie poured them both some more tea. "You know I did glance through those letters you received, and most of them were harmless junk, but a few were directly threatening."

"Were you shocked by that?" she asked. "I've received many nasty threats over the years, so I don't give them a thought."

"But then you were in prison. Aren't you more vulnerable now? One of the letters said 'Murder begets murder.'"

"As in someone wants to kill me?" Corinna still looked unconcerned, although Ellie had the impression that she was pleased to have someone else worry about her. Particularly if that someone else were Graham.

"How would I know?" said Ellie, feeling annoyed. "You must have a better sense of what your risks are than I do."

"I'm sorry. I don't mean to be so flippant. I know it's hard to understand my perspective, and it's nice of you both to worry, but I think I'm fine. The locksmith started today, and he'll finish tomorrow. I'll bring the spare keys to the vicarage when he's done. And I do look forward to hearing whatever you find out."

"Okay," said Ellie, feeling dismissed. "I'll keep you posted." She stood up to go, but then added, "By the way, I met Lila Ashton this morning. Do you remember much about her?"

"No. I didn't even know she existed until I saw her in court."

"You weren't aware of her relationship with your brother?"

Corinna shook her head. "No," she said sourly, "and it wasn't because of any of the reasons she may have dreamed up. My brother didn't have relationships. He used people and told them whatever they wanted to hear to ensure he got what he wanted. If that girl imagined it was about something more, she was unhappily mistaken."

"I see. Well, I was going to say I don't think her campaign against you is going anywhere. And Graham agrees."

"He told me that too. One way or the other, I really don't have the time or energy to care what she does."

"Okay," Ellie said again. "I'll let you know what I find out tomorrow." And then she left, thinking the triangle had become a three-way conversation, in which Corinna was the only one who heard everything.

As she walked home, she tried to figure out why she felt so crabby and dissatisfied. No, more than that. Angry. Was it because Corinna so casually dismissed the campaign and threats against her? Or was it the way she talked about Pindar, the brother she murdered? Or was it the casual way she referred to Graham and their obvious connection?

. . .

Later in the evening, as Ellie and Graham drove to Chipping Martin for the weekly practice session of The Beecham Morris, Ellie was determined not to reveal her uneasy feelings about Corinna and instead told Graham about her visit to Pen Whittaker and her encounter with Lila.

"The nurse is probably right about Pen," he said. "I don't think you need to worry too much about her. But Mrs. Wiggins thinks Lila is working for a client?"

"That's what she said. That there was a meeting of the minds behind the campaign—and one of them is putting up the necessary dosh. The only person I could think of for that role is Geoff Stephens."

"Which seems highly unlikely," said Graham, as he dodged a badger waddling across the road in the dark. "Stephens does seem bloody anxious to get his hands on that cottage, but I can't fathom him hiring Lila to help speed Corinna out the door. And he's certainly not breaking in or writing threatening letters."

"I agree, but then that means there must be at least two people, if not three, who are working on it. Separately? Together? That seems unlikely too. Unless there's something big at stake. Like revenge. Or a million pounds worth of gold Greek and Roman coins."

Graham glanced over at her and smiled. "You like that idea of the missing treasure?"

"It's the more appealing option. Finding yourself living happily ever after with a pot of gold sounds better than going to prison for settling an old score."

"True. But regardless, they both sound like matters for the police to investigate," he said, giving Ellie a look that she well understood.

"I thought Corinna was dead set against involving the police."

"Yes, she is. And it wouldn't be the first time she made a bad decision, would it? And two bad decisions don't make a good one, do they?"

"I can't imagine what you're suggesting," said Ellie, who decided it was time to change the subject to The Beecham Morris's upcoming performances celebrating the arrival of spring.

Personally, Ellie had no interest in taking up Morris dancing, but she was usually happy to tag along to Graham's rehearsals and performances. The jaunty pipe and tabor music, the intricate steps, the thwack of the wooden sticks the dancers held, and their sweaty banter brought her in touch with an older time in England she had only read about before. That evening, however, one hour of sitting on a metal folding chair in the church hall where they practiced was enough for her, and she decided to take a walk.

Chipping Martin had been a prosperous market town, so a Victorian town hall had been built in the center of its 300-year-old market square, where shops, offices, and a hotel were crowded into the older stone buildings.

For Ellie, the main attraction was a bookstore that had installed a café in one corner. She'd become a regular there, and Tish, who ran the café, would start her latte as soon as she walked in the door. Of course, Lila's petition was there on the counter, but people in Chipping Martin were unconcerned about who lived in the village of Little Beecham, and no one had signed it.

Ellie was scanning the latest barrage of anti-Corinna tweets on her phone, with an eye for any that echoed the language of the threatening letters, when she saw DI Derek Mullane enter the bookshop. He didn't notice her at first, but after he had bought a book and a coffee, he came over to her table.

"Hello there, Mrs. Kent," Mullane said. "I received your message, but there was no time to call back. Are you free to talk now?" From his casual manner, she understood that he was off duty. The transformation from his on-the-job persona—all hard eyes, square jaw, and terse words—to this amiable, attractive, dark-haired man always took her by surprise.

She smiled and said "Sure," so he sat down. "I called because I came across your phone number in a very unexpected place."

"Not, I hope, a telephone box. 'Call Derek, if you're into handcuffs.'"

Ellie laughed. "Hardly. It was in a fifteen-year-old diary belonging to Graham's late wife, Louise Kent."

"Really. Would I have ever met her?"

"I don't know, but I think she must have called you about Pindar Matthews' murder."

"I see. And you came across this information because . . ."

"We're trying to support Corinna, and, I admit I've gotten interested in her history."

"I can imagine. But what does that have to do with Louise Kent?"

"She was a good friend—and was certain that Corinna was not guilty. I suppose you hear that all the time. But, coupled with some of the strange things that have been happening in the present, I've begun to question whether the whole story ever came out back then."

"As I recall, from the evidence, the Matthews case was a clear-cut domestic. And no, not everything came out, because both of the Matthews sisters were remarkably unforthcoming. Do you know why the first Mrs. Kent questioned the confession?"

"She thought there were a lot of things that didn't add up about Corinna's mood, her hopes for the future, the atmosphere at the house. She was actually at Odyssey House a couple of hours before the murder must have taken place—and it didn't seem possible to her that everything could erupt and change so dramatically in that time."

Mullane stirred some sugar into his coffee, before speaking. "You know, most murders do happen very quickly. They're rarely plotted in advance the way they are in books. From what you're saying, she didn't see Ms. Matthews or her brother, so who knows where they were? I could write you a dozen scenarios explaining the scene you've described.

"I remember that day very well. I was quite new on the job and hadn't seen a murder in a setting like that. You know. The big house. The pretty young women.

"The younger girl was shocked by the blood at the scene, but not the elder. She was horrified at first, but I think she quickly understood what had happened and locked herself down tight, long before any of us could draw conclusions about what we saw.

"And she was adamant about that confession, despite the efforts of the police and her solicitor not to let her condemn herself precipitously. You may not believe it, but the police try not to rush to judgment, especially when dealing with a first-time offender. Well educated and from a good family.

"Her solicitor insisted she take a polygraph test, which only confirmed that she had no memory of what occurred. You can't lie about what you can't remember. At any rate, she insisted on her confession without wavering, and there was no evidence to contradict her, so it was eventually accepted. Believe me, the team knew they would be crucified if they weren't careful about that."

"And no one thought she might be attempting to cover for someone else?"

"We considered it, of course. We looked very closely at the alibi of her sister, who was the most obvious alternate suspect, and the person she would have been mostly likely to shield. But we could find no flaws in her story, and the complexity of the physical evidence against Ms. Matthews would have been impossible to fabricate on the spur of the moment."

"There wasn't anyone else? Any other explanation?"

He shrugged and leaned back in his chair. "No, and she offered no explanation or extenuating circumstances. But if you really want to spend your time diving down that particular rabbit hole, I can give you the name of the one person on our team who was the most skeptical about the whole setup. He's retired now, but he may have paid more attention to Louise Kent than the rest of us. That is, if she got any traction at all."

"I'd like to do that, thanks."

He took out his cell phone and texted her a name, Charlie Bynum, and his number.

"I'm sure he'd be happy to talk with you, but I would hate to think you're starting a campaign to prove Ms. Matthews innocent. That would be no more productive than the village campaign against her I've been hearing about."

"That's a bloody nuisance," said Ellie. "I wish you could stop it."

"We can't . . . not unless someone is breaking the law."

Ellie bit her lip, thinking of the intruder, the letters.

"Is someone breaking the law?" he asked.

"Someone has been harassing Corinna in very personal ways. Graham thinks it's a police matter, but she won't hear of it. And he believes she deserves to decide about that herself."

"Well, you know our number. She does too. But a word of advice. Corinna Matthews' problems are not going to be solved by stirring up the past. And don't worry, we are keeping an eye on the situation there.

"If you really want to hear more about the investigation, talk to Charlie. He was a good detective, and he was famous for testing the evidence by looking at the other side. The opposite of what seemed to be true."

"Was he ever right?"

"Once in a while, Mrs. Kent. But only once in a while."

CHAPTER SEVEN

Tuesday, March 13

B efore she set off to see Clio's old friend and executor, Melissa Engelthorpe, in Oxford, Ellie placed a call to Charlie Bynum. There was no answer, so she left a voice mail saying DI Mullane had given her his number and that she hoped to talk with him about the Pindar Matthews case.

The drive down the A44 through the greening countryside and the picturesque town of Woodstock was usually easy enough, but Ellie didn't relax until after she had survived what she thought of as the Russian roulette of the Peartree Roundabout. Once that spit her out onto the Woodstock Road, she was drawn block by block into the infectious energy field of Oxford, which never failed to please her.

The Engelthorpes lived in a large house on a quiet tree-lined street near University Park. The woman who came to the door was about Ellie's age, in her mid-30s, but her heavy makeup and expensively dowdy clothes gave the impression she was older. Her immaculate home, with its evidence of growing children and an accomplished husband—his treatises on global economics were prominently displayed—only made this impression stronger. Ellie found it hard to imagine her as the intimate friend of Clio Matthews, whose passion was making marionettes.

Melissa seemed to feel the same reservations about her. She welcomed her and served tea with practiced grace, but Ellie could tell her role as Corinna's representative made for an awkward beginning. "I appreciate your meeting with me," she said, when they were both settled on the edge of their chairs with delicate cups of China tea.

Melissa gave her a smile without warmth or encouragement. "To be perfectly candid, I was expecting someone else. I had you mixed up with that vicar's wife who took such an interest in the terrible business with Clio's brother and sister."

"That would have been Louise Kent, my husband's late wife," said Ellie. "Graham and I met when he was on sabbatical in California and were married last fall."

"Oh," she said, primly. "Then what is your interest in Clio's affairs? I can't say I was surprised that Corinna would avoid meeting me herself, but to involve a complete stranger seems rather odd even for her."

Ellie gulped. She hadn't expected awkwardness to become hostility quite so quickly. "As you may know, Graham has known the Matthews family for many years, so we've offered to assist Corinna in her current situation any way we can."

Melissa pursed her lips. "I see. Well, I think we should be clear about one thing from the start. There was no need for Corinna to come to Oak Cottage now, any more than she needed to write or call or reach out to Clio in all these years. Clio got along without her in life, and, as I am her executor, I would have made sure she did so now as well, despite the fact that she died in France. And what a lot of bother that is, let me tell you."

Ellie felt herself flush. "I'm sure you're completely equal to that task, but, since Clio did invite her to come, and the cottage is now hers and contains all that's left of her family history, Corinna is trying her best to sort through what's there before she makes a decision about the future."

"Clio invited her to come?" Now it was Melissa's turn to look surprised.

"Yes. I saw the letter myself."

"I must say I'm amazed, but then Clio always was generous to a fault when it came to her family, no matter what they did."

Ellie sipped her tea and said nothing.

"So, what exactly is the purpose of your visit? I'm sure Corinna is aware that the family's assets are still governed by their father's trust—of which she is now the sole beneficiary." The way she said this suggested she thought Corinna had been planning that outcome.

"My role is only to handle Clio's personal estate, which doesn't amount to much. She lived on whatever income she received from the trust. I know she had a few personal things at the cottage, but the rest is in Paris, and, frankly, I'm hoping that Corinna, as heir, might take care of that."

"I have no idea what she'll do," said Ellie. "She's out of prison on license, and I am not sure what that means in terms of travel outside of the country. As for the cottage, she's had some problems with break-ins and wanted you to know that she had to have the locks changed, so if you need access when she's not there, you will find the spare keys at the vicarage."

"Break-ins? Has anything been stolen? I should have been informed about that."

"As far as she can tell, nothing has been stolen. The person who comes in seems to have known the family and leaves little traces around that are intended to unsettle her. She also suspects the person may be searching for something, but what, she has no idea."

"Well, that sounds annoying, but not very consequential. I have no idea who that person might be, if that's what you came to ask."

"I'm sure she'd welcome your suggestions, if any names do occur to you, but she also wondered if you knew why Clio had decided to give up the cottage and live full time in France. If she had shared anything about her plans with you."

"No, she didn't. In fact, I knew nothing about that. I don't think you understand the situation with Clio. She and Janet Shah and I were as close as could be when we were girls, and we certainly tried to help her at the time of the murder, but I know almost nothing about her life since then.

"Once Corinna was in prison, Clio dropped out of uni and shut herself away from everyone, including us, for quite some time. The next thing we knew, she had sold Odyssey House and gone off to some place in France to study puppetry. We thought it was quite symbolic, under the circumstances."

Ellie perked up. "What do you mean it seemed symbolic, if you don't mind my asking?"

"Her brother called her Poppet, and he treated her like one too, but she adored him and he could do no wrong. She would do anything he asked—and, believe me, he pulled the strings, pushed the limits, and thought it was all amusing.

"For example—and it's only one—Janet and I were with them the day she almost drowned in King Lake because Pindar told her to hold her breath and stay under the water while he counted to one hundred. He said he would wave his shirt when she should come up, but he kept stopping the count to tease us, while Clio frantically tried to stayed under. It was terrifying, and we were screaming for her to come up, but her faith in him was never shaken for a moment."

Ellie was appalled. "Did she never get angry? Fight back?"

"No." But then a shadow passed across Melissa's face, and she stirred her tea thoughtfully. "Actually, I stand corrected. There was one time I know of. Pindar was mad at her for some reason or no reason, so he took a doll she loved and tore it apart. He was taunting her with it, and, instead of begging or crying, Clio became completely still, then picked up a pair of scissors and ran straight at him."

Ellie drew in her breath, while Melissa paused, as if stopping a film.

"You know, I'd forgotten about that," she said, sounding a bit stunned. "Afterward Clio made me swear never to tell anyone, and I thought it was because she was so humiliated."

"Humiliated?"

"Pindar stopped her, of course. He was nineteen, and she was only eleven, a featherweight girl. He grabbed her by the wrists and shook her until she dropped the scissors. Then he held her in the air and laughed at her until she apologized."

"And she still thought he could do no wrong after that?"

Melissa nodded with a shudder. "If anything, she became more dependent. Love can be strange in that way, can't it."

"Yes," said Ellie, who was deeply shaken by the image of the girl dangling from the hands of her brother, old enough to be a man.

They were both silent for a moment. Then Ellie said, "Have you ever seen Clio's artwork?"

"No, although I received an exhibit announcement out of the blue a few weeks ago. She'd written on the back that she hoped we might come to the opening."

"Did you go?"

"No, I threw the announcement away. Frankly, I thought it

was absurd that she imagined I would travel to France for some event, when she never made the effort to see me when she was right here. Janet might have felt differently, but I think she may already have been in India visiting her husband's family."

"Do you remember the image on the announcement?" asked Ellie.

Melissa frowned. "It was something odd. Ugly. Not at all what I expected. I thought she made puppets."

"She may have at one time, but lately she'd been making marionettes and kinetic sculptures out of dismembered dolls."

Melissa's eyes widened. "Good Lord. Now that you say that, I do remember something like that. But are you connecting that with the story I told you?"

Ellie shrugged. "Who can say?"

"I can't imagine anyone would buy something like that," Melissa said, retreating to her prim voice.

"I think they do. Or did. Michael-John Parker at The Chestnut Tree in Little Beecham took some of her pieces for his shop. And he'd talked with galleries in London that were interested, but, of course, now that's not going to happen." Ellie paused.

Melissa shook her head and sat up straighter. The grown-up again. "Well, Corinna is the heir, so I hope I don't have to worry about any of that kind of thing. When I agreed to be her executor, it was long ago. Her parents were gone, and she was told she should have a will. I agreed because it was just a formality, and neither of us thought it would ever matter. I was surprised to find out she'd never changed it. Hadn't found someone else long since."

"One last question about the cottage. I assume you've been there since Clio's death?"

"Yes, of course. I went to see what state it was in."

"How did it look?"

"Very much as I remembered it from the Murphys' time. There were a few of her clothes and books about. That's all I saw."

Melissa looked at her suspiciously and set down her tea cup with a rattle. "This is about the break-ins? Corinna thinks Janet or I could be behind them? That's utterly preposterous.

"Clio's solicitor gave me the key I have, and Dr. Stephens has one. He's the neighbor, after all, and Clio was often away. The Murphys must also still have keys. They came to keep the dust down and see to the garden. Of course, I would have no idea what newer friends she might have given them to.

"I hadn't set foot in that cottage since I was little more than a girl," Melissa went on to say, "but I remember going there for tea with fondness. Mrs. Murphy had no daughters of her own, so she loved to feed up us little girls.

"I must say, the idea of Corinna living there is unsettling. It's hard not to feel that she's the one who should have lost her life after all that happened. For it to be Clio seems terribly unfair. I still can't quite take it in that I'll never see her again. But such is life.

"By the way, I've heard some people are saying she committed suicide, and I thought 'Never.' But now, considering what she was doing, I'm not so sure. Do you think that's how she saw herself? Dismembered? Dancing on strings?"

"I don't know," said Ellie. "But you could look at it another way. She was putting broken pieces back together. Giving them a new life. And she was the one who held the strings."

Melissa looked at Ellie as if she were seeing her for the first time. "Well, I must say that's putting a good spin on it. I'll tell you one thing about that accident. Clio was always rubbish as a driver—nervous and distractable. Janet and I never let her drive, if we were going anywhere together, and I can't imagine how she ever managed driving over there on the wrong side of the road."

"I'm afraid I can empathize with the challenge of that," said Ellie.

"Yes, of course, you would," said Melissa, as if it were self-evident that all Americans would be a threat on English roads.

This seemed as good a moment as any for Ellie to wrap up the conversation, so she stood to thank her, and Melissa looked glad to see the back of her. She didn't offer to be in touch with Corinna and said only that she hoped to be finished with any business related to Clio's estate shortly.

On her way from Oxford to Red Hill, the village where the Murphys lived, Ellie stopped for gas and bought a packaged chicken-and-bacon sandwich and some apple juice. As she sat in the car to eat, she couldn't escape the image of Clio rushing at Pindar with a pair of scissors. The young man holding the girl dangling in the air like a puppet. She didn't believe that Melissa could have ever forgotten that. Especially in light of the way Pindar died. But she did believe she'd kept quiet about it and wondered why she had told Ellie now.

Every version of the murder that she'd heard so far had convinced Ellie that Clio could not have been involved in Pindar's death, but, with this new information, the questions came flooding back: if jealousy had been the motive for the killing, it would have been far more likely that Clio—who loved Pindar in some very tangled way—would react badly to the news that he planned to marry. And she had demonstrated her capacity to react violently.

Was the secret, then, that Corinna had collaborated with Clio's friends to provide Clio with an alibi and fabricated the evidence that would point to herself and thereby shield her more vulnerable sister?

Mullane said the police had not neglected the possibility of Clio as a suspect. But between those who might have lied and those who never spoke, how could they have known for certain?

On the other hand, it was hard to imagine Clio keeping Oak Cottage as her bolt-hole if she had been the one who killed Pindar. There was her letter to consider as well. It didn't rule out the possibility of a shared secret, but nothing about its tone or content suggested she feared seeing Corinna. She was looking forward and sounded content.

It was immediately clear that Geordie and Ruby Murphy had no intention of telling Ellie anything if they could avoid it without being downright rude. She was a foreigner and an incomer—an outsider through and through. A sign of what was to come was evident when they did not even offer her the oblig- atory cup of tea.

Geordie had wiry hair, a sturdy frame, and the large, well- used hands of a gardener, while Ruby was the quintessential motherly dumpling with round cheeks that flushed easily. Reluctantly, they invited Ellie into their lounge, where photos of Clio took pride of place, ranging from a grinning baby picture, where she clutched a large teddy bear, and a proud photo in her school uniform at about the age of seven, to one taken in the kitchen at Oak Cottage, where the teen wore an outsize apron and was rolling out biscuits with a younger Ruby.

They both sat on the edge of their chairs, ready to spring up and show Ellie the door at the first opportunity. All Ruby would say was, "I can't imagine why you want to see us. All we have done is keep the cottage and garden nice for Miss Clio, so she'd feel easy and at home whenever she was there."

When Ellie tried to elicit any idea of what Clio's life had been like, Ruby cut her off completely. "It was never our business what she did," she said. "We couldn't say whether she had friends in with whom she shared keys or anything else. She was a grown woman and deserved her privacy."

"I'm sure she was very grateful for your long friendship and support," said Ellie, hoping they would stop seeing her as an antagonist.

"It was never about that," said Ruby, whose black dress underlined her bereaved state. "We loved her as much as if she had been our own. More, in fact, than those who were blessed to have her."

"Will that arrangement for the care of the cottage continue now?" asked Ellie, fishing for what Corinna could possibly have hoped to learn from these stony-faced people.

"No," said Geordie firmly, before Ruby could answer. "We've done our duty by the family, but we're retired now. Miss Clio saw that we would have a good pension from the trust, and that's that. Miss Corinna will have to shift for herself, as she has always been more than happy to do."

"I see. Well, I am glad to know you're taken care of."

Geordie Murphy gave her a what's-it-to-you look.

"It's nice to have met you," said Ellie, getting to her feet. She felt she had failed but didn't know what else she could have said or done. As she was going to the door, she turned and added that it was a shame Clio had died when she was just beginning to be successful with her art and happy with her life in France.

The Murphys glanced at each other and blinked. "Art?" said Ruby.

"Yes, you know. The marionettes and sculptures she made in her studio. That upstairs room in the cottage."

"I never went in there," said Ruby. "She kept that room

locked. I only did for the rest of the house." She paused, then, with a hopeful expression, and asked, "Are you saying Miss Clio was happy? Might she have found a man? Someone she loved?"

"I'm not certain, but she referred to being newly happy in a letter to Corinna," said Ellie, knowing Clio had not been at all specific, but she wanted to see their reaction.

Ruby blushed, and her eyes filled with tears. "It's what I've hoped for all these years . . . that she'd find someone to love her properly. Not like . . . ," but then she turned, gave her husband a pleading look, and hurried out of the room.

Geordie frowned, and Ellie knew, that as welcome as any such news might have been, it was now also unutterably sad. Regardless of what she may or may not have done, for them, Clio's death was a terrible loss. Geordie said goodbye to her tersely, holding back his own emotion, and Ellie left, feeling somehow ashamed.

She drove back to Little Beecham in a drizzly rain that made the landscape, despite the haze of new green growth, as forlorn and gloomy as she felt. She was tired of talk about the Matthews family, but decided to stop at The Chestnut Tree on her way to tea with Miss Worthy anyway. After all she had heard about Clio's past, seeing her work might give her a clearer perspective on the person she became.

Brass bells jingled as she opened the door and entered the elegantly arranged antiques shop, which had once been where the village blacksmith worked. Whistler woofed and came to greet her, but when he saw Hector was not with her, he turned and went back to his bed.

Michael-John looked up from unpacking a delicate lady's desk, and smiled. "Ah, Mrs. Kent. You are just the person I was hoping to see," he said. "I can't persuade Kidder to help me lift this out of the crate. He writes a blog about investing, real estate, or something—I have no idea, actually—I don't read blogs, but he says he can't be interrupted while he does his research. Few would understand that so well as you." He glanced toward the office at the back of the shop, and Ellie saw the blond American ensconced at Michael-John's computer.

She was tempted to ask whether Jeremy Kidder was staying with Michael-John, but it was none of her business. Instead, she said, "In my experience, research is too often an avoidance tactic more than anything else. It's so much easier than writing. Not that I would ever judge anyone else by my own tricks."

Michael-John laughed. "Of course not. You are much too just to do that. But, you see, now that you're here, we can leave him to it without disturbing his concentration."

"Or conscience," she added, with a smile.

She steadied the crate as he carefully lifted out the desk. It was made of burled walnut and had long, curved legs and many small drawers inlaid with ivory and mother-of-pearl. They had set it on the floor and were admiring it when Jeremy emerged from the office after all. "Did I hear you calling me?" he asked.

"No, no. Never mind. I explained to Mrs. Kent that you were busy, and she came to the rescue," said Michael-John, which made Jeremy flush with embarrassment, or maybe, thought Ellie, resentment.

"Of course, she did. I hear that's one of your special talents, Ellie."

From the way he stood, he seemed very at home. He was wearing slippers and a cardigan she was sure she had seen on Michael-John not long ago.

He ran his hand over the desk in a proprietary way. "This is quite nice. It should sell quickly for a good price."

"Naturally," said Michael-John, with a grin. "I wouldn't

have bought it otherwise. But Ellie—I think you've probably come to see some of my other treasures, haven't you? Go back to your work, Kidder. I know you don't like these."

"I hope you're not referring to those grotesque dolls, are you? They're as bad as some sideshow exhibit like the two-headed baby. In fact, one of them *is* a two-headed baby."

"And just as popular."

"If you want to cater to that kind of appetite," said Jeremy, who nodded to Ellie, and went back to the office.

"I did warn you, they are not everyone's cuppa," said Michael-John, as he led Ellie to the back corner of the shop. Under a bench, there were two long boxes. "In fact, I still haven't decided whether to display these for sale or keep them for myself." He brought out the first box and laid it on a table to open it.

When he lifted the lid, Ellie involuntarily stepped back at what she saw. It was a figure more than three feet tall assembled from the body parts of antique dolls: the kind with bisque porcelain faces, glass eyes, real wigs, wooden torsos, and jointed limbs. This one did indeed have two heads—one with eyes and one with holes where the eyes had been, as well as multiple arms and legs. It was painted dark blue and wore a tunic and pants made of gauzy turquoise chiffon elaborately embroidered and decorated with beads and sequins.

"Wow," said Ellie. "That looks like some kind of strange goddess. Beautiful and scary at the same time."

"I know," said Michael-John. "And to think she was forged from sweet baby dolls."

Ellie studied the way the figure was put together. The craftsmanship of the sewing and construction was impeccable. "What's the other one like?"

"Different," he said, opening the second box. While the first was designed with a stand, this one was a marionette, also assembled out of doll parts and dressed in an elaborate, colorful costume that made Ellie think of a court jester. He lifted it out so she could see how sinuously it moved.

"Now that, in its own way, is even more creepy!"

"Isn't it just. I love it," said Michael-John, making the figure dance. "Apparently she used to perform with this—or one like it —at her exhibitions."

"No kidding. I would have liked to see that. They're very powerful. Beautiful. I can't say I'd want to live with them, but I hope you'll keep them, so I can see them again."

"I'm in no rush to do anything," he said, setting them back in their boxes. As their limbs collapsed and their eyes closed, the life that animated them left, and Ellie had a sharp feeling of loss. For them and their maker.

"I'm so sorry I never met Clio. I never even knew a person who could create something like that lived here."

"I wish I'd tried harder to connect with her too," Michael-John agreed. "She was elusive, though. Rather fey, but elegant, in that understated way the French have, which is utterly foreign to the English. At the same time, you would never have guessed what she was up to, if you met her on the high street."

Ellie laughed. "It just goes to show. Never jump to conclusions about your neighbors. Now I have to run."

As she headed toward the door, she noticed that Jeremy had left the computer again to watch them from the doorway of the office. He had a strange expression on his face. Was it jealousy? Or envy? When Michael-John said goodbye to Ellie with quick kisses on each cheek, he turned away sharply and did not see her wave to him.

Priscilla Worthy lived on Chapel Lane, which was lined with old thatched cottages and dead-ended by a former Methodist chapel converted into a fancy weekend home by Londoners. Although Miss Worthy had only recently returned from a long book tour in the US, her Wisteria Cottage, with its winding wisteria trunk and vines, looked as tidy as ever, and yellow primroses bloomed along the flagstone path to the front door.

When Ellie rang the bell, and Charlotte Worthy answered, she almost didn't recognize the girl. She had become her great-aunt's assistant and accompanied her on the tour. Since then, the sullen, blue-haired, chubby teenager had been transformed. Her hair had grown back to its natural blond; she'd lost her baby weight; and her skin was tawny from their time in Florida. Charlotte's son, Dolphin, had grown too and stood on plump, wobbly legs beside his mother, clutching her jeans.

"Hello, Mrs. Kent," said the girl, with her usual laconic inflection, so not everything about her had changed. She was still a teenager. She replied to Ellie's "How are you?" with a monosyllabic "Good," picked up her baby, and led the way to the sitting room, saying, "Auntie will be down in a minute."

Ellie seated herself on the sofa to wait. On a low table in front of it, there was a pile of five different foreign editions of Ramona Blaisdell-Scott's latest book, *Love and Desertion*. They appeared to have just arrived, since the wrappings were still in the trash.

When Miss Worthy came in and saw her looking at the books, she blushed and said, "Oh my, I thought I asked Charlotte to put those away and empty the bin, but perhaps I forgot."

"I'm delighted to see them," said Ellie. "I've been reading *The Buried Heart* aloud to Pen Whittaker, and we're both completely hooked."

"Are you? I think I've improved since then," said the old lady, who, despite the approaching spring, was dressed as usual in woolly layers. She sat down with a sigh of pleasure. "Well, put those over on the shelf out of the way, would you? I'm quite like one of those animals that doesn't enjoy seeing its offspring once they're weaned."

Ellie did as she asked and sat down again, just as Charlotte came in with the tea tray and set it down. Then Miss Worthy busied herself with pouring the tea and passing scones. "Now," she said, after she finished buttering her scone, "tell me the news. How is Corinna managing with all the nonsense going on? Charlotte keeps me up to date on the dreadful social media chatter."

"Fine, it seems," said Ellie. "According to her, she doesn't give a rap about Lila Ashton or her campaign."

Miss Worthy sipped her tea. "I'm not surprised at that. But . . . there is a but . . . isn't there?"

Ellie nodded. "Someone has been getting into the cottage, searching it, playing pranks, and possibly stalking her. Why and who this might be are questions to which she claims to have no answer."

"Claims?"

"I find it hard to believe she doesn't have any idea. There's no forced entry, so it has to be someone with a key. And the pranks involve leaving things around the cottage that suggest other members of her family have been there. I would find this very unnerving, but she says she doesn't.

"So far, the only people known to have keys are not credible possibilities, but it must be someone who knew the family and is able to observe the cottage closely enough to know when she leaves the house—yet remain unseen."

"That sounds like a neighbor," said Miss Worthy. "Or someone local without a demanding job."

"I know, but who? She's having the locks changed and hopes that will be the end of it."

"I have a feeling that won't help," said Miss Worthy, stirring her tea.

"You do?"

She cocked her head from side to side. "Picklocks are readily purchased over the internet."

Ellie frowned. "So, you think this is not just a person who's being a nuisance, but someone who doesn't mind breaking the law?"

"What do you think?"

"I think you might be right, because she's also received hate letters, which she gave to me to read. Most are innocuous, but some are truly threatening. She insists they're nothing to worry about. All of a piece with the kind of things she's received for years.

"Graham wishes she would alert the police, but she won't, and he believes that has to be her prerogative. However, he also insists the murder is history, and I'm not so sure."

"Tell me why," said Miss Worthy. She sat back in her chair and folded her hands, watching Ellie intently.

Ellie tried to put her thoughts in order. "What first caught my attention was learning that Louise didn't believe Corinna's confession. So that was my starting point to consider what happened from a different perspective. All of the evidence pointed to a domestic argument turned violent, with Pindar the victim and Corinna the killer. But, why would Corinna never offer any explanation for this explosive event? Even if, as she said, she could not remember killing Pindar, she must have had reasons for assuming she did.

"Everyone I've talked with knew that she and Pindar hated each other, but hate seems too general, and a quarrel about money too common. Besides which, she told Louise the day before that she thought the money situation with Pindar was finally going to be worked out.

"Another question is about the body. If she killed him right in their own home, what was the point of disposing of the body? What evidence would the body have provided that she was so anxious to conceal that she drove through the night to dump him into the Severn?

"And why did she and Clio never communicate again? What kept them silent for more than fifteen years, only for Clio to write a letter inviting her to Oak Cottage—to take it over if she wished? What changed?"

Miss Worthy smiled at her encouragingly. "And have you come up with a theory that answers these questions?"

Ellie blushed. "Not exactly. But I think something happened between those three that was much more threatening—and much more untenable—than anything that came out at the time."

"And Corinna was the judge of that," said Miss Worthy. "Judge and executioner."

Ellie was taken aback. "Is that how you see it?"

"Well, that's what happened, isn't it? To understand the three of them and their conflicts, you have to remember that Cleve dominated the family and Corinna was his favorite. She was the only one whose temperament and interests were sympathetic—and aligned—with his, and the only one who would go to any lengths to please him. I think everything she did has to be viewed through that lens."

"It's funny you should put it that way. Because, when I spoke with Clio's friend Melissa Engelthorpe today, she described Clio's devotion to Pindar in a similarly intense way."

"Quite," said Miss Worthy. "And there you have it. The cost of overpowering Pindar turned out to be the loss of any relationship with Clio."

"I see," said Ellie, who was surprised that she could have missed this.

"You know, Mrs. Kent, we are never permitted to know the whole story of anyone's life, and the pursuit of such knowledge is not necessarily justified."

"You mean, it doesn't serve any purpose. Especially now, they're all gone. Only Corinna is left to live out her life as best she can."

"Exactly. She gave fifteen years of her life to keep her family's secrets. Do you think she wants them to be revealed now?"

"I guess not. So, you think, it doesn't matter now that it might actually have been Clio who committed the murder in a jealous rage over Pindar's prospective marriage? With Corinna setting the stage to take the blame and a false alibi attested to by Clio's friends?"

"Oh, I don't think that's what happened," said Miss Worthy. "There would be too many people involved in keeping the secret and the police are not that easily gulled."

"But she did once try to stab her brother, and you might view her differently if you'd seen her marionettes made from broken and dismembered dolls."

"Good Lord. I hope you aren't suggesting that's why they disposed of the body. Even for one of my books that would be too noir."

"Well. . . no. Definitely not." Ellie picked up the scone on which she had slathered strawberry jam, but set it down again. Unaccountably, her appetite for it had vanished.

"I'm sure you appreciate that most people's creative work is based only very tangentially on their secret lives and memories," said Miss Worthy, as she topped up their tea. "You are, of course, free to sift through the old story as much as you want. The same elements can be used to create any number of plots. I do it all the time when I'm writing, but I'm more curious about the present and the stalker you mentioned.

"You think that's part of Lila's campaign?" asked Miss

Worthy. "It doesn't really sound like her style. She organized a campaign to clear up a local creek that I volunteered for, and it was vigorous in challenging the mill and other businesses that were polluting the water, but it was strictly legal."

Ellie thought about the pieces of her puzzle. "Okay, but, as you said, the intruder and the person watching Corinna still might be one person, who is probably local and knew the family."

"Yes, and you think that person is searching for something. Has anything been taken?"

"Corinna doesn't know. She's still trying to figure what's there. . . so to know what's not there is impossible."

Miss Worthy nodded. "The writer of the threatening letters could be someone quite different. Less close to the scene, but somehow affected by the murder," she said. "Especially since Corinna told you the letters sound like ones she's received throughout the years."

"True, although she never actually read these particular letters herself, so it's hard to say. If you're right, they might not be as threatening as they seemed to me. More the pastime of a crank."

Miss Worthy nodded. "That's perfectly possible."

"I was wondering if the intruder is searching for Professor Matthews' coin collection."

"Cleve's coins? Oh, my goodness. I had forgotten all about them. What a lot of bother he caused by hiding the collection, instead of using the bank. He could be a silly man at times."

Ellie perked up at her tone. "You knew him?"

"Oh yes, we became quite good friends after Lady Anne died. But that's a story for another day."

Ellie sighed and put down her cup. "Do you think I've gone completely off the rails in championing Louise's idea? I admit I have probably been hoping to show she was right all along."

"And you would clear Corinna's name the way you did your own?"

Ellie blushed.

"It's a noble idea, my dear," said Miss Worthy, "but it has very possibly sent you down the wrong track. Not that there's anything to be discouraged about in that! All great discoveries have involved exploring many dead ends along the way."

"Of course," said Ellie, who, at that moment, felt entirely surrounded by dead ends. But Miss Worthy only smiled, gave her an encouraging hug, and reminded her to let her know how she got on.

While Ellie at Miss Worthy's, dark clouds had gathered and begun to drop an icy rain. As she walked back to the vicarage. her one thought was of the warm kitchen at home until Seamus MacDonald came whizzing around the corner from the B road on his bicycle and hailed her.

"Guv!" he called, and from his eager expression, it was clear he was totally oblivious of the rain. "It's too perfect that I should run into you," he said cheerfully. "We desperately need your advice. That is, Simon and I do."

"About your hunt for the missing coins? My advice is: give up."

"But it's not about that," he said. "It's Simon's story, really, but he doesn't know what to do, so I said I would ask you."

The cold rain had begun to trickle down the back of Ellie's neck, so she pulled up her hood and waited. This was clearly going to be a story that would take some time.

"Simon does a lot of birdwatching in the woods around Odyssey House, but his special interest is badgers, which mainly come out in the early evening. He has the most amazing binoculars that let you see them in the dark."

Ellie's interest quickened. "But, in the process, he's seen something else? Something unexpected?"

Seamus nodded. "He has to wear dark clothes, a hat, and gloves, so he's invisible, really. With badgers, you have to be super careful that they don't see you or even smell you, so he sits in a tree near their sett.

"The woods are posted, of course, but, twice now, he's seen someone there watching Oak Cottage."

"Really?" Ellie tried to sound calm, but she was almost certain this had to be the mysterious intruder. "What kind of someone?" she asked. "Male? Female? Tall? Short?"

"Whoever it is also dresses in black and wears a hoodie, so it's hard to be specific, but I grilled Simon, and he guesses it's a man, tallish and not fat."

"Did he tell you when he saw this person? Which days and times?"

"Definitely Sunday. About four o'clock. The other time he can't remember for sure, because he thought he must have been mistaken. It was so odd, you know. No one is ever in those woods except him. And me. And, I guess sometimes, you know, someone his father has hired."

"Has he asked his father about it?"

"No. Simon doesn't talk much to his father. They don't get along. And he didn't want me even to tell you because, he said, the man wasn't doing anything except watching. He manages to disappear very quickly, though, so, if he hadn't seen him twice, Simon would have just thought he was tricked by the shadows."

"I see," said Ellie, thinking about Sunday. That was the day Corinna said she stayed home until she brought the bags of letters to the vicarage. Ellie wondered whether or not Toby had accompanied her, leaving the cottage unguarded. Regardless, this sounded like the first step toward identifying the intruder.

"The thing is," Seamus went on, "we're worried about Corinna, and we'd like to help. Like her guardian angels. That old hound she has is great, but he's not much use. I'll bet he couldn't smell his dinner at ten paces."

"I'm not sure what you're imagining about being guardian angels, but I cannot state strongly enough that neither you nor Simon should confront this person. Assuming he exists. Do I make myself clear?"

Seamus shrugged, looking disappointed. "We haven't done anything yet, except for tell you. But there must be some way we can help. Simon has a bad crush. He has all those old pictures of Corinna hidden in his room."

"If he keeps them hidden, how do you know?"

"I'm a detective," said Seamus, as if this were obvious. "You need to know what the people you trust are up to."

"That's your idea of trust? Remind me never to let you into my room! Now look, I am very serious. You both know perfectly well there's a campaign going on against Corinna, and the people behind it, their motives, and what they're capable of are not known. Do I have to spell that out more clearly?"

Seamus's eyes were shining. "You mean there may be some connection back to the murder."

"I did not say that. And don't you go there! I'm glad you told me what Simon saw, and I hope you or he will let me know if he sees that person again. But, so far, the man has done nothing except trespass, and it's not up to you boys to enforce that."

"It's Simon's property."

"Seamus, if you want to help Corinna, do nothing to stir up excitement or memories of the past. Do you read me?"

"I do, but you know, Dr. Stephens' attitude is such bollocks. Every old house has a history. Look at the Tower of London. How many tourists pay good money to go there and see where people had their heads chopped off. I've been three times myself."

Ellie put her hands on the handlebars of his bike and looked him in the eyes. "Do nothing," she said.

In an instant, she could see that he'd leapt beyond her thinking, and he looked immensely pleased.

"So, something *is* going on," he said, and Ellie pulled her hands back.

"Do nothing!" she repeated.

He grinned and saluted. "Aye, aye, Guv. Whatever you say. We watch. We do nothing. But I hope you'll tell Corinna that we're on her side."

And before she could say anything else, he sped off down the high street.

"I've had an exhausting, but interesting, day," said Ellie, when she and Graham sat down later to a quiet sherry by the fire. Mrs. Finch had finally gone home, but a lingering odor of cleaning fluid competed with the fragrance of the lamb stew heating on the Aga. Outside the icy rain had turned into sleet, which clattered against the windows.

Graham looked up expectantly, and Ellie launched into her summary of the high points.

"After meeting Melissa Engelthorpe, I decided Clio must have been the one who committed the murder, since she once attacked Pindar with a pair of scissors because he broke a doll she loved—and her suppressed guilt inspired her to go on to a career of making marionettes out of dismembered doll bodies— which incredibly creepy things I saw at Michael-John's shop. The Murphys, who are deeply grieving and undoubtedly believe Clio could do no wrong, were not about to share any information about her life with me or Corinna, but Miss

Worthy was glad to see me. She convinced me that I was probably wrong about Clio and should forget the past.

"Which idea I was swallowing like medicine, when I ran
into Seamus, who told me that Simon Stephens has seen a man
dressed in black watching Oak Cottage from the woods on two
occasions. One being last Sunday late in the afternoon."

Graham looked suitably astonished. "He must be the
intruder!" he said.

"That's what I thought too . . . but who can he be? I don't
see how we'll ever be able to figure that out—unless he's caught
in the act, of course."

"True, but hopefully, we won't need to. The new locks will
deter him, and Corinna will move on, and that will be that. But
explain to me, please, where you ended up with the murder.
Clio is innocent, but was slightly deranged, and Corinna is still
guilty as charged. Is that it?"

"I guess. Melissa ruled out the idea of Clio's committing
suicide—she was always a crappy driver, apparently—and Miss
Worthy thinks whatever family secret Corinna and Clio would
never talk about is surely their business to keep secret now and
forever."

"I'll drink a toast to that," he said, holding up his glass.

Ellie toasted back and said, "I guess we're going with 'Suffi-
cient unto the day is the evil thereof.'"

Graham laughed. "I never thought I'd hear you quoting the
Bible."

Once they had eaten and cleaned up, Graham had some phone
calls to return, so Ellie went up to her study. She saw that
Charlie Bynum had emailed her to say he would be free to
meet her on Thursday morning. She stared at the message and
wondered whether she should tell him she no longer wanted to

meet. But what harm could it do to hear what he said? This was the man who had most questioned the given story about Pindar's murder—and he had possibly spoken with Louise. It was worth an hour or two to be thorough. To hear all sides. So, she thanked him for his message and said 10 a.m. on Thursday would be perfect.

She was about to close up shop for the night when she remembered what Michael-John said about a video of Clio on YouTube, and a quick search found a performance from two years before in Paris.

A black screen opened up, then lightened to show Clio, dressed in a black bodysuit like a mime, with blue hair and makeup matching the painted face of a two-headed figure, also in black. Electronic music began to play, and the two figures began to dance. Their parallel movements were haunting and beautiful, going on and on, until the music faded back, and the two were once again motionless.

Ellie watched it three times, then ran downstairs to see it again with Graham.

"I would never in a million years have guessed she could do that," he said. "When she lived here, she had a way of being invisible."

"Even within her family, she seems to have been invisible," said Ellie. "Which could be how she got away with murder."

"You're not going back to that idea again?"

"No. I was only joking. Miss Worthy thinks Corinna's personality is the key to what happened. How she was her father's favorite and devoted her life to doing what he wanted.

A sad look crossed Graham's face then, but he gave her a hug, and said, "I don't really think Cleve is to blame. Corinna is an alcoholic, and when she's drunk, she is perfectly capable of doing terrible things all on her own."

CHAPTER EIGHT

Wednesday, March 14

E llie woke up thinking that Graham and Miss Worthy were right. She was burrowing down rabbit holes, not conducting an investigation. And to what end anyway? Whom would it help? Certainly not herself . . . and probably not Corinna either. But when she went up to her study after breakfast, she dove right back in. Outside her door was a cardboard box marked "CM."

Before she even carried the box inside, she was certain what it was and wondered whether Mrs. Finch had always known about it. After all, she had been cleaning the attic every year, though it may have only been recent events that brought to mind what the label signified.

Ellie slit the tape sealing the box and found it contained neatly labeled file folders. Louise's research on the murder. She lifted out the first folder, feeling grateful. Without saying a word, Mrs. Finch had taken a stand.

She wasn't surprised that Louise had been thorough, but

the range of her inquiries was certainly much greater than the few penciled notes in her datebooks would have predicted. These files included information on bloodstains, alcoholism, and blackout drinking; finding bodies with ground-penetrating radar; tide charts and stories about bodies recovered at sea; as well as maps and timelines for the crime.

Louise had figured out the driving times from Little Beecham to different points along the Severn and studied the terrain and access to the water. Her notes made it clear that it was possible for a woman on her own to reach a spot with no CCTV cameras where she might dispose of a man's body in the time available and in a way that made its recovery unlikely.

This material was covered with Louise's penciled notes and questions, but there was no summary showing what conclusions she had drawn—nor was there a single fact that undermined Corinna's assertion of her guilt. Nonetheless, this careful work showed that Louise's concerns about the accepted version of events were much deeper than either Graham or Morag had understood.

There were also loose items that Louise had saved:

- A sheet of information for visitors to the women's prison, which had been crumpled up, then flattened, and saved.
- An obituary for Cleve Matthews, clipped from *The Times*. It attributed his death in Athens to a sudden heart attack and listed his survivors as his son, Pindar Anthony Matthews of Little Beecham, Corinna Anne Matthews of Cambridge, and Clio Jane Matthews of Edinburgh.

If only they had stayed put! Ellie thought, as she laid this aside and continued on to see:

- A photo of Corinna and a young Isabelle in the garden of the vicarage with shining faces and their arms around each other.
- A program for the performance of *King Lear* in Stratford, which Louise and Corinna had attended the day before the murder.

Ellie thought this latter item was only a poignant memento from "life before," but when she flipped through the pages, she discovered that someone had written "Now, gods, stand up for bastards!" in black ink above the bio of the actor who played the treacherous, illegitimate Edmund. The handwriting was not Louise's . . . so did that mean it must be Corinna's? And was this significant? Did she know that actor and think he was a bastard? Or was she merely highlighting the famous declaration from the act 1 soliloquy in which Edmund declares he will seize his legitimate brother's lands.

Louise's own program had not been saved, so was this one kept because it was a clue? A key to Corinna's state of mind? How could Ellie ever guess?

At the very bottom of the box, there was one last item: a white cardboard jewelry box about two inches square. Ellie picked it up and opened it. Inside, wrapped in worn tissue paper, was an exquisite gold Greek coin carved with the image of an owl. Set in a gold bezel with a chain to make it into a necklace, the tiny 2,000-year-old coin was battered, but its beauty was undiminished.

Of all Ellie had seen that morning, this was the most moving—and telling. She was certain the necklace must be Corinna's, and that she had entrusted it to Louise for safe-keeping when she went to prison. Holding the coin, which was connected to so much of the Matthews family story, Ellie thought it was not too great a leap to imagine that it was also somehow connected to the reason Louise felt so certain the truth about what happened the night Pindar died remained unknown.

But a glance at the clock showed it was time to get ready for The Soup Car, so Ellie carefully put everything away and tucked it under her desk. Down in the kitchen, as they packed the lunches, Ellie thanked Mrs. Finch for the material she'd left her.

Mrs. Finch looked up from wrapping sandwiches in foil and gave Ellie only the barest glance, but it showed she'd guessed what the contents were. "It was Mrs. Kent's, but I thought you'd be the best to decide whether it was time to throw it out" was all she said, and Ellie said she was right.

There was no time to dwell on the Matthews family for the next couple of hours, as she navigated from village to village, home to home, with her hot lunches. But when she reached Upper Shortfield and pulled into the drive at Hermione Tuttle's large stucco house, it all came back. Another visitor was already there. Someone who drove a British-racing-green BMW.

As she hurried across the winter-worn lawn, Ellie could see Mrs. Tuttle talking with Lila Ashton at the front door. The thin, wiry woman was speaking, her normally bitter expression more animated than Ellie had ever seen it.

Lila was half-turned toward Ellie, holding a large bundle, and grinned when she saw her. "Hello again! We keep crossing paths!" she said, as if this were a happy coincidence. She shifted the bundle, so Ellie could see it contained a variety of bright-colored hats. This reminded her of the way Lila had made sure she saw the signed petitions against Corinna. She couldn't imagine what colorful hats had to do with anything, though, so perhaps she and Mrs. Tuttle were working together on behalf of some other cause.

Before Ellie could do more than fake a polite smile, Lila had hitched up the bundle on her hip, waved, and saying, "Thanks again," departed.

Mrs. Tuttle welcomed Ellie with a flustered greeting, as she hurried her into the kitchen. Although her large, gloomy house had a dining room, the kitchen was far warmer, and she ate all her meals there.

The Tuttle family had once been wealthy, but, from what Ellie had heard, Hermione had run so amok on the Stock Exchange that her husband divorced her and moved to Canada. Even her two daughters had cut off contact with their mother.

Now, on Soup Car days, she ate so heartily that Ellie wondered what she ate between free lunches. Once the last drops of soup were gone, and the dishes were cleared, she asked the older woman whether she was working with Lila Ashton on some project.

Her face settled into its habitual aggrieved expression, as she said, "It's more of a common cause than a project."

"What about?" asked Ellie, thinking of Miss Worthy and the polluted stream.

Mrs. Tuttle poured herself some tea, then stirred in three lumps of sugar. "Justice," she said. "Purely and simply, justice for a wonderful young man whose life was viciously cut short."

"Ah. Would that happen to be Pindar Matthews?"

She nodded sharply, as if there could be no other, so Ellie asked, "Did you know him?"

"Know him? I was more of a mother to him than his own foolish mother from the time he was a young chap."

"How did that come about?" Ellie found it hard to imagine how Mrs. Tuttle and the young Pindar would have ever met.

"He came by here the summer he was fourteen, looking for work mowing lawns. He'd ridden his bicycle all the way to Upper Shortfield so his family wouldn't find out what he was up to. His father would never approve—he was that proud of marrying Lady Anne and thought it made them all above such menial work. I suspected the lad didn't know the first thing about mowing a lawn, but he had a cheeky grin, so I hired him.

"I was right about the mowing, but he was delightful and an excellent whist player. He turned out to be too clever by half with cards, but he made me laugh, the way he could imitate people. I was sure he was a goer with a brilliant future—and so was he. He even gave me his autograph and told me it would be worth a fortune someday, when he became a film star. Would you like to see it?"

"I would," said Ellie, who waited while Mrs. Tuttle went to her sideboard and took out an old-fashioned leather autograph book.

"Here it is," she said, as she pointed to a yellowed page where Pindar had written:

> *Mrs. T,*
> *Learn what you are and be such!*
> *Your devoted friend,*
> *Pindar Anthony Matthews*

The handwriting was bold and a little clumsy in the way he attempted to give his signature a flourish. Mrs. Tuttle ran her finger over the writing and said, "That saying was written by the Greek poet his father named him after, and he had made it his motto. His goal in life."

"That's very sweet. Did you continue to see him when he was older?"

"Certainly. He always came to tell me about what he was

doing. His dreams and plans. And I gave him the help and encouragement he never got from his family."

She looked proud, but Ellie wondered whether she was referring to financial support and thought it was likely she was. Perhaps not all of her unwise investments had been in stocks.

"I will never recover from the shock of learning he'd been murdered by that awful sister, just as his career was about to begin. He was a marvelous actor, you know, and he'd made the contacts he needed to take off. 'Per aspera ad astra,' he used to say, and we'd laugh and laugh."

Ellie felt a shock herself when she heard those words again, and Mrs. Tuttle must have seen the change, because she abruptly switched from reminiscence to condemnation:

"I thought this country believed the punishment should fit the crime," she said, "and no one will ever convince me that justice has been served by making someone sit in a prison cell for a few years, when he will always and forever be dead." Then she rose abruptly and went to the sideboard to put the autograph book away.

Ellie was still trying to think what she should say, when the older woman sat down and said, "I heard about the vicar's sermon on love thy neighbor . . . and I suppose next he'll be telling us to 'forgive them for they know not what they do' . . . but they *do* know, and that's the point.

"You don't imagine that girl didn't know what she was doing when she killed him and then pushed his body into the sea. Do you? Really? Because I don't, and I'm not satisfied."

Ellie took a deep breath, and then said, "I can hear that. But, if you stop for a minute to think about it, you don't actually know what happened or why. All you know is how you feel about it."

"That's bollocks!" said Mrs. Tuttle, who stood up and stormed out of the kitchen, leaving Ellie alone to pack up and leave. Obviously, she had failed to say what the woman wanted to hear, and that was that.

As she drove away, Ellie remembered the news story about some local who had declared the most suitable punishment for Corinna would have been to be hanged on the village green— and wondered whether she might have just been talking with that person. If she ever went back to the Tuttle home, it might be interesting to see what Hermione's handwriting looked like. It wasn't hard to imagine that bitter woman treating Corinna to a steady stream of nasty letters over the years. It was also not surprising that she had found in Lila someone who shared a common cause regarding Corinna's release from prison.

Ellie had intended to go straight home, but she knew Mrs. Finch was still cleaning, and Graham would not yet be back from his various morning meetings. She was debating what to do next, when she saw a fingerpost pointing the way to King-brook and decided it was a sign that she should stop to see how Pen Whittaker was doing.

But when she arrived at the pretty brick row house, Ellie rang the bell, and no one answered. This was a bit worrying— Pen had a buzzer and intercom next to her bed that enabled her to find out who was at the door, and open it, if she wished. Of course, no answer could simply mean she was asleep or, better still, had recovered enough to go out.

However, just as she was about to give up and go back to her car, a stout gray-haired woman in a long, flowered apron emerged from the house across the street and called out, "Aren't you the lady who sometimes brings Mrs. Whittaker a lunch?"

Ellie nodded, and the woman came across the street. She introduced herself as Mrs. Jennie Sanders, and said, "I guess you haven't heard the news. Someone broke in, and Mrs. Whittaker has had a stroke. No one knows exactly when it happened, but the visiting nurse found her when she came a couple of hours ago."

"Omigod! And here I was hoping she wasn't at home because she was feeling better," said Ellie.

"I know, and she did seem to be getting better. But I checked on her last evening, and, to be honest, I was concerned. I couldn't make sense of what she was saying, and I meant to drop by this morning, but I got busy, and you know how it goes. When the ambulance came to take her to hospital, you could have knocked me over with a feather."

"I feel the same way. Do you have any idea how she's doing now?"

"I don't. But I saw them taking her out, and she looked very poorly."

Ellie thanked her and went back to the car, but she couldn't drive away. The memory of how worried Pen had been about that strange man breaking in would not leave her; and she struggled with the feeling that there must have been something more she should have done.

After a few minutes, she texted Graham: *Did you know there was a break-in at Pen's and she has had a stroke?*

His reply came immediately. *Yes. I just heard. I'm tied up now, but I can meet you at home in an hour. We can go to see her together.*

Ellie thought about the time that would be lost waiting for him and wrote back: *I'd rather meet there. I am going now.*

She started the car, but then changed her mind, turned off the engine, and went across to ring Mrs. Sanders' doorbell instead. "I'm sorry to bother you, but you said Mrs. Whittaker didn't make sense when you saw her yesterday, and I wondered if you understood anything she said."

Mrs. Sanders shook her head. "I'm not sure she even recognized me. She was frightened when she saw me come into her room, even though I've had a key to her house for ten years. Usually, we have a cup of tea and a chat, and I do some little task for her. But this time she kept insisting there was a man in the garden trying to break in. So much so that I went down and looked, but there was no one there. It was quite unnerving how certain she was . . . and she must have been right!"

"I know. I feel terrible because she was confused and worried when I saw her on Monday too," said Ellie. "I did call the nurse about it, and she told me it was probably a reaction to the antibiotics she was taking."

"Is that so. Well, she may have been right, but Pen was too. I just wished I'd known."

"You couldn't have done anything more," said Ellie, and Mrs. Sanders looked grateful to be reassured, but it was much harder to do the same for herself.

When she arrived at the hospital, Ellie explained to the matron that she was the wife of Mrs. Whittaker's vicar, and he was on his way, but she would like to sit with her until he arrived. The matron was reluctant, but Ellie insisted that she herself was also a friend.

Finally, she was escorted to a private room, where Pen lay unconscious, attached to heart and lung monitors, as well as various IVs. Ellie sat down next to her and held her unresponsive hand, as she listened to the stertorous breathing and the hum of machinery. Hoping she might bring her some comfort, she whispered all the prayers and poems she could think of.

After what seemed like an age, the hand under hers suddenly twitched, and she clasped it gently. Then to her surprise, Pen's eyes opened, wide with fear. In a hoarse whisper, she said, "There was nothing I could do. I couldn't give him what he wanted. He had it all wrong, but he wouldn't listen!" Then she gave a little gasp and was gone.

Ellie tried not to gasp herself. She had never seen anyone

die before, but in the moment of that final exhaled breath, it was almost as if you could see the spirit leave. The body lying there was no longer Pen Whittaker. It had been abandoned as completely as her empty house, her unmade bed, and the garden she would now never finish planting.

Just then, the door opened and Graham came in, looking flustered and upset at the sight of the dead woman. "I'm so sorry I couldn't get here sooner," he said, pulling Ellie into a hug. "I'll explain why later."

Then he went to Pen's side and began to quietly recite the prayers for the dead. Ellie bowed her head, but her thoughts were busy trying to parse Pen's last words. What had this intruder wanted—and what had he been wrong about?

When Graham was finished, he put his prayer book back into his pocket and came to stand by Ellie with his arm around her shoulders.

"Are you all right?" he asked.

Ellie leaned into him and sighed. "I don't know yet. She looks so peaceful now, but I'm afraid it wasn't a peaceful death."

"I heard," he said. "Matron told me when I arrived."

"What do you mean?" Ellie asked. "How could she know? She wasn't here."

"The EMTs who picked Pen up saw the mess in her house and called the police. One of them came to the hospital, hoping to have a word, but she was no longer conscious."

"But she was," said Ellie. "She spoke just before she died."

Graham looked surprised. "She did? But that could be terribly important. What did she say?"

Ellie thought and then recited: "There was nothing I could do. I couldn't give him what he wanted. He had it all wrong, but he wouldn't listen!"

"Who wouldn't listen?" Graham asked.

Ellie shook her head. "I don't know."

"Well, we'll need to go by the Chipping Martin station and tell them about this right away." But as they headed to the parking lot, Ellie suddenly remembered Barney, who was always at Pen's side. She was sure she could almost hear Pen saying, "Forget the police! Find the cat!"

"You know, there's something I have to do first," she told Graham. "And that's check on Barney. Pen's cat. He was everything to her, and I want to know that he's safe."

"All right, but how about if you go to the police, and I'll see to the cat."

"No, he doesn't know you, and I'm sure he'll be terribly upset. Let's both get him and then call the police from home."

Graham looked as if he wanted to argue about these priorities, but, wisely, he didn't.

Ellie had to force herself to think only about driving as they headed back to Pen's house.

When they arrived, in tandem, they had to squeeze in among the police panda cars to park. Mrs. Sanders was standing in front of her house, looking anxious, and called to them.

"Oh, Mrs. Kent, I'm so glad you've come back. The police have taken over the house and won't tell me anything other than that Mrs. Whittaker has died."

"Yes, that's true. We came back because I suddenly remembered Barney. He was so important to Pen," said Ellie, equally anxious.

Mrs. Sanders nodded. "Luckily, I went in just before the police came and found him. He was under the bed and that upset, but I was able to get hold of him."

"I'm so glad. Will you be able to keep him?"

"Keep him?" She sneezed at the thought. "I can't have a cat. I'm allergic. I've hardly been able to breathe ever since I brought him into the house."

"I see," said Ellie. She glanced at Graham, who could read her expression and nodded. "If you think it will be all right, we can take him. Does he have a carrier or anything?"

Mrs. Sanders said yes, and disappeared back into her house, reappearing a few minutes later, laden with a cat carrier and another large bag containing food, litter, and a cat box. The big gray tiger cat was howling, his face pressed against the screened opening in the carrier.

"Hello, Barney. Do you remember me?" asked Ellie, looking in at him.

"I'm not sure he does," said Graham, as Barney continued to howl.

"You like cats, don't you?" she asked him.

"Not so much when they're howling, but yes. I like cats, and so does Isabelle."

DI Mullane's sergeant, Alan Jones, came out of the house as they were securing the cat in the back seat of Ellie's car. She had always disliked him from the days when he was assigned to follow her as a murder suspect, so she was not surprised by the look of suspicion that crossed his face when he recognized her.

"Mrs. Kent? Father Kent? What brings you here? I was just going to get in touch to say that DI Mullane would like to come around and speak with you about the deceased. We understand you were one of the last people to visit her."

"I was," said Ellie, who endeavored to be civil. "I was also the person with her when she died. What happened here, do you know yet?"

"The DI will fill you in as soon as possible" was all he would say and made a note in his ever-present notebook.

Ellie half expected he was writing: "Ellie Kent found at the scene of the crime, Wednesday, 4 p.m."

But their immediate job was to take care of Barney. She leaned in to put a finger through the mesh of the carrier window and stroke his striped forehead. He looked at her with big sad, yellow eyes and did not say a word. It made Ellie tear up to think of how he and Pen used to lie side by side on her bed in such comfortable companionship.

"I think he knows she died," Ellie said to Graham as she slipped into the driver's seat. "And he's the only one who knows what happened."

"Not the only one," he said. "Someone human knows too."

Ellie half expected to find DI Mullane already on the doorstep when they arrived back at the vicarage, but instead a different surprise awaited them: Isabelle Kent was sprawled on the sofa, with her arms wrapped around Hector. Both were sound asleep and looked utterly content.

The dog woke up the instant Ellie entered the room with Barney in his carrier, and his barking woke Isabelle, who shook out long, untidy blond braids and stretched. "Dad! Ellie! Where have you been? I got here hours ago," she said.

"We didn't know you were coming today," said Graham, giving his daughter a hug and a kiss. At 19, Isabelle had a remarkable resemblance to the photos Ellie had seen of her pretty blond mother, but with her father's height, lanky build, and sparkling, intelligent blue eyes.

"I sent you a text," she said. "Didn't you get it? I was offered a ride door-to-door, so I decided not to wait until Friday to come home. Besides I'm working on an essay that I dearly hope you can help me with. But who is this?" she asked. Hector had leapt down and was trying to sniff the cat, who backed himself into a corner of the carrier and hissed.

"This is Barney," said Graham. "A good fellow who rather suddenly needs a new home. Do you think you'll be okay with that?" he asked, squatting down to pet Hector, who looked only slightly mollified by the attention.

"Where did he come from?"

"A member of the parish who died unexpectedly."

"And you guys said we would take him?"

"Only if you and Hector approve."

"Of course, we approve, don't we, Heckie?" she said, picking up the dog. "We love cats. But I would say, for now, we'd better keep them apart. I'll take Barney up to my room and get him settled."

A few minutes later, the doorbell did ring, and there was DI Mullane. He was in a hurry, he said, but they persuaded him to sit down in the kitchen and have a mug of tea. He had the look of a person who'd been on the job for hours without pausing to breathe, much less eat.

"As you've heard, the emergency medics who attended Penelope Whittaker were concerned about the circumstances of the stroke that led to her death. The home was in a state of considerable disarray," he told them. "We're interviewing everyone who saw her in the last few days of her life to try to get a picture of what might have led to this event. Your name, Mrs. Kent, was mentioned by several different people."

"That's because she'd had pneumonia, and I've been helping out a bit."

"How did she seem the last time you saw her?"

"The last time I saw her was today. But the last time I took her lunch was on Monday. I thought she was recovering, but she'd suddenly taken a turn for the worse."

"In what way?"

"She decided to go out to the newsagent's shop on the corner, when she really should have stayed in bed. She had several gardening magazines that she bought each month, and, for some reason, she did not want to wait for me to pick them up. Which I surely could have done. It's horrible to think that none of this might have happened if she had only let me run that errand for her."

"You mean she caught cold? Had a fall?"

"No, nothing like that. There was someone in the shop who frightened her. She told me she thought he recognized her, and she was afraid he had followed her home. She kept asking me whether there was anyone else in the house."

Mullane nodded, making hurried notes. "He seemed to recognize her—and there was something threatening about that? Did she not, in turn, recognize him?"

Ellie thought back to that morning, which already seemed long ago. "She didn't tell me who he was or why he frightened her, but she must have known who he was, because she was definitely convinced that he was going to come after her."

"But she gave no reason?"

Ellie shook her head. "The only thing she said that seemed related had to do with a quarrel she'd had with her husband, where she gave in to him and she told me 'Now look what's happened.'"

"That sounds like a consequence, doesn't it?" said Mullane.

"Yes, except her husband has been dead for several years," pointed out Graham.

"I wish I could tell you more," said Ellie. "But that's all I know. When I was with her in the hospital, before she died, she regained consciousness briefly and said, "There was nothing I could do. I couldn't give him what he wanted. He had it all wrong, but he wouldn't listen!"

"That sounds like she was telling you what happened. Not about something from the past. Do you know whether she told anyone else about this man she saw?"

"Mrs. Sanders, her neighbor, heard about him, when she visited yesterday. Pen told her she thought he was in the garden trying to break in. I don't know about anyone else."

"How did you leave things with her on Monday?"

"I assured her that there was no one in the house, and I checked the locks on all the windows and doors. I also called the visiting nurse, but she basically laughed it all off as a hallucination caused by antibiotics."

"If that were the case, it was a very persistent hallucination," said Graham. "It sounds like you think she didn't die from the stroke."

"It's early days," said Mullane, as he finished off his tea, closed his notebook, and stood up. "Aside from the fact that the house looks as if someone searched it, Mrs. Sanders noticed something when she came looking for the cat. There was a window in the kitchen that had been broken and neatly covered with cardboard. She says the house was tidy and there was no broken window when she was there the evening before. It's not the sort of thing you'd expect a robber to do, but it was clever. I gather a few people took care of Mrs. Whittaker, so everyone would assume the repair had been done by someone else. You don't know anything about that, do you?"

"No, everything about the house was fine on Monday."

Mullane pursed his lips. "We'll follow up on that, of course. Her valuables, such as they were—a wallet, a bit of jewelry—were not disturbed, but it seems likely the break-in precipitated her death."

"Rather an odd thief to go to all that trouble with the window and leave the house obviously searched," said Graham.

"Indeed," said Mullane. "But the doors have locks that can't be opened with picklocks, so the thief had to resort to another way to get in—and he may have thought to conceal or delay discovery of the fact."

"You mean he might have done that before things went wrong and he ended up killing her," said Graham.

"Quite." As he stood up to go, Mullane looked directly at Ellie and said, "I assume you are aware of the connection between Penelope Whittaker and the Matthews family."

"No, I'm not," said Ellie, surprised.

"Her husband, Jock Whittaker, was the estate manager for Odyssey House—and Mrs. Whittaker's brother, Geordie Murphy, was the gardener there."

"As in the Murphys who lived in Oak Cottage?" asked Ellie. "Graham, you must have known that."

"Yes, but Whittaker retired a dozen or more years ago and died quite awhile back. How can that matter?"

"I believe he retired shortly after the murder that has generated so much local interest lately."

Ellie blushed, and Graham looked angry. "I hope you're not suggesting there is any link between Corinna's release from prison and the death of Mrs. Whittaker!"

"We're not jumping to conclusions, and neither should you. I hope you'll respect the importance of keeping this conversation confidential."

"Of course, and I will come to the station to sign my statement," said Ellie.

"Much appreciated." Then Mullane smiled his un-smile— the one he used on the job that had not one iota of warmth to it.

. . .

"What are you thinking?" Ellie asked, when Mullane had left. Graham was drinking his cold tea.

"To be honest, I was thinking that I hope some good-hearted person fixed that window and will come forward quickly to say so and that it will turn out Pen herself messed up her house looking for something. Which is another way of saying that I hope she died from natural causes, and there will be no possible connection between this event and Corinna."

"I can't see any connection to Corinna herself, but what about the man who has been stalking her? Breaking in there?"

"Why would they have been connected?"

"Maybe he thought Pen had whatever he's been searching for in the cottage. The coin collection, for example."

"Why on earth would she? Pen didn't work for the Matthews family, did not live on the estate, and Jock was one of the most rigidly self-righteous men I've ever met. If he had found those coins, he would have turned them over immediately. As in more than fifteen years ago."

"Okay. But you have to admit, there's something unsettling about break-ins at both places within such a short period of time. Don't you think Mullane might look for a connection?"

"Why would he? Corinna has never reported the break-ins at the cottage."

Ellie blushed. "True. However, I did mention someone was harassing her when we ran into each other at the bookstore in Chipping Martin on Monday. We were discussing the past, and the present sort of crept in."

Graham frowned. "I see. Well, as far as I'm concerned, Pen's death is a matter for the pathologist, coroner, and the police. I trust you agree."

"Of course," said Ellie, and, from his expression, she could tell it was not a good time to tell him about what she'd discovered about Louise's extensive research into Pindar's murder.

CHAPTER NINE

Thursday, March 15

I t turned out that Isabelle's essay topic was "The Resurrection: What Really Happened." Ellie knew from her years of teaching that there was no point in telling students they had selected an unwritable essay topic. It was something you had to learn for yourself. She had once tried to prove why Chaucer was ahead of his time in five pages, and the long nights of increasingly desperate efforts to boil her mountain of research down to a concise argument had provided her with an unforgettable lesson. Not the one assigned by the professor . . . but useful all the same.

When they had finished breakfast, she hugged both Graham and Isabelle goodbye and left them deep in a discussion of the different factions viewing Christ's resurrection as a real, mythical, or symbolic event. She was setting off for the village of Maltby to talk with Charlie Bynum as part of her own amorphous wrestling match with life, death, and the meaning of the past in the present.

. . .

Charlie Bynum had been a detective chief inspector at the time of Pindar Matthews' murder, but now he lived with his wife on the outskirts of Maltby in a tidy stone cottage with window boxes full of winter-worn geraniums along the front. When he greeted Ellie at the door, she thought he was playing the role of pensioner to the hilt with his misbuttoned cardigan and worn slippers, but she soon discovered he had lost none of his memory or intelligence.

"I remember Louise Kent," he told her as his wife poured coffee for them before disappearing from the unused-looking lounge, where a crackling fire helped take the chill off the stale air. "She was a beautiful woman, but perhaps too sure of her own understanding of people."

He looked at Ellie intently. "After what happened to her, I would have thought your husband would choose someone who was more interested in flower arranging than murder. But apparently not. I've heard about you: no waiting around for the misguided to confess their sins."

Ellie didn't know what to say—whether he was praising her or calling her a complete nincompoop—so she smiled noncommittally and waited, sipping her coffee.

"What exactly are you trying to find out about this case? The sinner confessed. As you surely know."

"Yes, but, as you may recall, Louise didn't believe it."

He shook his head. "My point about her exactly. And what good did that do anyone involved? I'm sure you're aware that even when you have a dozen eyewitnesses to an event, they will all have seen something different."

"Of course. And I've heard that you were the one person who was willing to say that more than one perspective should be considered."

He looked pleased. "That's true. When you turn the facts upside down and shake them, you often discover something that was there, but hidden."

"Did that happen in this case?"

He shrugged. "Yes and no. The official conclusion was that the murder was an open-and-shut domestic. I had to agree to some extent, since the circumstantial evidence certainly supported that. But if you questioned the story, you had to wonder why that young woman was so quick to condemn herself and practically ran all the way to prison."

Ellie felt her interest quicken.

"I always believe evidence. You can't ignore that," he admonished. "It's the interpretation of it that I like to explore."

"And, in that case, what did you find?"

"Two things struck me right away. I saw a lass in a kind of terror I recognized. I know what it's like when the drink gets the better of you. She was certain it had taken her over the cliff and she had killed her brother, even though she had no memory of what happened. From that standpoint, confessing was a relief, but I thought she also used it is a way to shut off questions about something even more important to her that she wanted to keep secret.

"I would have had no trouble believing either one of those lasses wanted to kill their brother—he sounded like a right sociopath for all his good looks and so-called charm. But I would have expected them to do it impulsively—and the drink fitted in with that, but the disposal of the body did not. Impulsive killers leave the body at the scene or dispose of it in a hasty, haphazard manner."

"That's one of the points I've been curious about too," said Ellie. "If it were a spur-of-the-moment thing that happened during a fight that got out of control, how did Corinna come up with the plan to get rid of the body so quickly? Louise was disturbed that someone could be happily looking forward to a party the next day and then, within a few hours, do what she purportedly did. Especially since Corinna had told Louise she hoped the problems with money for Pindar had been resolved."

The old detective gave her a dismissive smile. "I remember Mrs. Kent's story about the sweater Corinna wanted to wear to a party. Red with silver buttons, as I recall. But, you know, her story didn't really have any bearing on the investigation. And the fact that Corinna thought the financial problems had been worked out could well have been what triggered her violent response if she found out they weren't. The brother wanted to get married, according to that young lass from the pub. For that, he would surely need money.

"No matter what, they'd all been under a lot of stress over the way their father left the estate. He basically tied them to the trust—and, to some extent, each other—so anything Pindar said or did that showed there was once again no agreement could have been unbearable."

"Yes, I can see that," said Ellie. "That's actually very helpful."

"What Mrs. Kent saw at ten o'clock was obviously a very different situation from what occurred later. Pindar had reportedly had a lot to drink, and although he may have been in an excellent mood at the pub—as the girlfriend claimed—he could easily have felt aggrieved and aggressive by the time he returned home."

"The girlfriend being Lila Ashton?"

He nodded. "Yes. And, as I am sure you know, she was another one who was utterly shocked by that night's outcome. Fancied she'd be walking down the aisle with that bloke, not out searching for his body.

"She wanted to think their plans had something to do with the murder, but I never believed that. Those two—Corinna and

Pindar—had been struggling their whole lives for whatever it was they wanted from that family—attention, praise, love, money—and any number of things might have lit the fuse for the explosion that went off that night.

"Anyway, the girlfriend's opinion was not evidence. What the evidence showed was first, that the murderer made no attempt to clean up the crime scene, and second, that the victim was removed—and so successfully disposed of that he was never recovered."

"How did you resolve that contradiction?" asked Ellie.

"Some people on the team argued that she would have cleaned up the scene if she hadn't been exhausted by getting rid of the body or that she would have but she simply ran out of time to do both. Others thought she wanted her sister to see the scene and know he was dead. If he had seemed to disappear, she might have spent years hoping for his return."

"What did you think?"

"Well, for one thing, I am always a bit suspicious of murders where there's no body. You have to look carefully at the situation from every perspective of who gains and who loses. Sometimes the one who gains is the missing victim."

"Are you talking about faked deaths?" asked Ellie, suddenly visualizing all those folders of research in Louise's box.

He nodded. "You have to consider that possibility."

"Did you find any evidence of that? Because, you know, it occurs to me that Louise may have wondered about that. I've discovered she did a lot research in the months after the murder . . . and it shows her concerns went way beyond the issue of Corinna's mood."

"Did she now? I'm not surprised. She was always polite, but I had the feeling she didn't trust us to do the job right." His expression showed he thought Ellie was the same type.

"Believe me, we considered every angle, but disappearing

would not have helped that bloke get what he wanted. To live like a lord. He wanted to break that trust, which tied up the money with his sister and some friend of their father's holding the purse strings.

"All the evidence pointed to the fact that he badgered Corinna until she snapped. She may have been drunk, in a blackout, and acting on impulse, but I believe she must have fantasized about killing her brother often enough that, when the moment came, she knew exactly what she wanted to do, and she did it.

"Most people when they kill are shocked at what they've done, and I am sure she was, but her anger, her fantasies, managed to carry her through all the time it took not only to kill him, but also to dispose of his body. That took a lot of nerve, but she also had luck—if her goal was that he never be found. There was no way she could control that. Bodies don't disappear in the sea all that quickly or easily."

"There is something particularly horrible about that," said Ellie. "Although from her point of view the job was over and done with a lot faster than if she had tried to bury him, my impression is that the reason she did it was not about him. Not about revenge or anything like that. For some reason it was important to achieve finality for herself—and her sister."

Charlie raised an eyebrow and smiled. "You've thought about that, have you?"

"Yes. From what I've been told, Pindar's relationships with both of his sisters were very toxic, but Corinna was defended by her hatred, and Clio was vulnerable because she loved him."

He nodded. "That's a good description. It points to the 'Why now?' question one always has to ask when considering motivation. What happened that night that was so different from countless other nights? What caused Corinna to snap?"

"The team thought it was all about the money. And the

girlfriend thought it was because Corinna was jealous. I didn't agree with either. I think the answer was in the committed silence of both sisters, which was very telling. But not revealing!"

"Did you think there was a conspiracy between them?"

"Not the way you probably mean. The younger girl's alibi was solid, and her shock could not have been faked. I suspected they may have been silent for different reasons, which were possibly linked, but, no matter what, we couldn't get at them."

Ellie suppressed a smile of satisfaction: this, at least, seemed to support her own idea.

"Well," she said, "that brings us to the present day. In your opinion, was there any other person involved—someone on the periphery who might be still alive?"

As Ellie described the watcher, the break-ins, and the threatening letters, Charlie Bynum's eyebrows danced with excitement. She was sure this meant it confirmed something he'd guessed at. But when she finished, all he said was, "I actually have no idea. I suppose there's still money there somewhere. Someone who hopes to inherit. But I'm sure Derek is on top of that. He's a good man."

"Did you never consider that the root of the problem was not money?"

"You mean why the girls didn't talk."

"They weren't girls anymore."

"True." He set his coffee cup back on the tray. "It could have been something else. But, in a way, that wasn't relevant. You think the question you need answered is why, but for the police the essential questions are who and how."

"I get that. 'Who' closed the case. But 'why' is the reason the story still isn't finished."

"I'm afraid the only person who can ever tell you why is

Corinna herself. And she's kept her secret a long time. Why should she explain herself to you?"

Ellie blushed, hearing Miss Worthy's words echoed in what he said. "No reason at all," she said curtly. "I did have one other question, though. Were the Odyssey House staff interviewed about that night? That would have been the estate manager, Jock Whittaker; the gardener, Geordie Murphy; and his wife, Ruby, who was the cook and housekeeper."

Charlie scratched his chin and said, "I'm sure they were, but I don't recall those names."

"The Murphys lived in Oak Cottage on the estate."

"Oh, yes. I remember the housekeeper. She said they heard nothing, but their cottage is set quite a distance from the main house and drive, so that's not surprising. The estate manager didn't live on site, so he wasn't there."

"Right," said Ellie.

"Why do you ask?" he said, standing up.

"Pen Whittaker, Jock's widow, died suddenly this week, apparently or possibly as the result of someone breaking in to search her house."

"Oh," he said, and that was all. Ellie could tell from the look in his eyes that he grasped the implications, but he wasn't going to explore them. That was the job for someone else now.

So, what had she learned from him? In the end, all it added up to was the past was past, Corinna's secrets were hers to keep, and the present was not his problem. Ellie felt low as she drove toward home, stopping at the Chipping Martin Police Station to sign her statement about Pen's death. The sight of those last words she witnessed typed onto a form made her feel even lower.

What was it the intruder had wanted her to give him—information? Money? Some object? And why was he so angry that he was beyond listening? Pen's brother Geordie might know—or suspect—the answer, but he would never tell Ellie. No, the only person who might do that was Ruby, and she would have to figure out a way to get her to talk.

When she arrived home, Ellie learned that Mullane had called and told Graham there would be a coroner's inquest into Pen's death, and she would need to testify.

"Oh, damn," she said, "I guess, like you said before, I was hoping they'd decide . . . I don't know what."

"I think that *is* what they decided," said Graham. "That they don't know for sure what happened, and they want the coroner to rule on the cause of death."

Ellie fell silent, but then she couldn't resist asking, "Have you seen Corinna again? Does she know about all this—and the possibility people will say there's a link to her return?"

"No, I haven't," he said, "and I think that information would be better coming from you."

"Why do you say that?"

"Because you are you—an excellent ally. Besides, in this situation, I'm not the best person to help."

Ellie considered her reply, probably not long enough because she was already feeling bad before she said: "You mean it's not because Lila has been putting it about that you're supporting Corinna because she was your lover?"

For the first time ever, in her experience, Graham turned white, instead of blushing. "She's doing what?"

"I might be wrong about the source, but Mrs. Bigelow hinted to me with her most lascivious grin that you had a motive for wanting Corinna to stay—and I had one for wanting her to go. I might be wrong, but I assumed Lila must have picked up that bit of history from Pindar and added it to her tool kit for her current campaign."

Graham shook his head in disbelief and said, "You know what that makes me want to say? Women are impossible!"

"But of course, you won't. To be fair, I haven't heard anything that suggests this tidbit has caused much excitement. But, while we're on the subject of Corinna, I think you should see something Mrs. Finch brought down from the attic yesterday." And with that she ran up to her study and came back down with the box of Louise's research.

"You thought Louise's objection to Corinna's confession was only an emotional reaction . . . but I think this makes it clear it wasn't. She conducted a very thorough investigation."

Graham looked taken aback and sat down hard as she laid out the neat folders labeled with his late wife's handwriting on the farmhouse table.

For a few minutes he was silent, as he leafed through the files. Then he sighed and said, "I did know she was very upset. She thought the police didn't question either Corinna or the circumstantial evidence as closely as they should have. But Corinna wanted her to stay out of it. She even went so far as to call me and ask me to tell her she was not helping—and later, when she was in prison, she told Louise to stop visiting. I thought that was the end of it."

"It wasn't. From the dates on some of these articles, she clearly kept thinking about it and looking for answers for years.

"And here's another thing." Ellie reached down to the bottom and brought out the little jewelry box. "Corinna must have entrusted this to Louise . . . so she may have been annoyed about her persistence, but she still knew Louise was a friend."

Graham opened the box. "Oh God," he said. "She was wearing that the first time I ever saw her. Cleve gave each of the children necklaces like this when they were born. As they grew up, replacing the chain was a ritual he enjoyed."

He stood up then and pulled Ellie into a hug. "And what

did my first sleuth wife find out from all this?" he said, speaking into her hair.

"I'm still working on that. She put down all the dots, but she didn't connect them."

"And you, I suppose, will."

Ellie smiled. "If I can," she said, giving him a kiss. "You know, if I can, I will."

When Graham retreated to his study—nominally to write, but more likely to work on the medieval Latin translation project that he turned to when he was upset—Ellie picked up Hector and headed over to Oak Cottage. Corinna might prefer solitude and popping in on Graham, but she wanted to fill her in on what had been happening.

Toby bayed loudly at her knock, and she heard the scrabble of paws racing down the stairs as she waited on the stoop, but this time Corinna followed quickly and opened the door after checking the new peephole to see who was there.

She had not lost her prison pallor, but today she looked stunningly different. Geordie Murphy's gardening clothes had been replaced with a pair of close-fitting jeans, a fine black wool sweater over a white T-shirt, and fur-lined leather slippers. She saw that Ellie noticed the change, blushed slightly, and grinned.

"Michael-John didn't approve of my wardrobe," she explained. "The other day he left some bloke in charge of the shop and drove me into Oxford, so I could go to an AA meeting. While I was there, he used the time to buy me new clothes. Rather high handed of him, but he did quite well, don't you think?"

"I do," said Ellie, with a laugh, and followed Corinna into the kitchen, where they set to work together on preparing some tea. Ellie noticed the biscuits had also been upgraded to ginger-lemon. Probably another improvement instigated by Michael-John.

"I see your security system now includes a peephole. Have the new locks put a stop to the intruder?"

"Unfortunately, no," said Corinna, turning on her new electric kettle. "He uses picklocks, so I guess that settles the question of whether he was a friend of Clio's with a key. I'm debating whether to take further measures or ignore it. I don't like feeling pulled into an escalating war. And I rather hoped I was done living behind barred windows and locked doors."

"I am sorry that it seems necessary. Do you remember a woman named Penelope Whittaker? She was the wife of your family's estate manager, Jock."

Corinna nodded. "I do. Vividly. She taught me how to deadhead roses when I was eleven. I don't remember exactly how we came together—or what she was doing at Odyssey House that day—but I've always remembered how carefully she clipped off each dead rose. With reverence. I loved doing that, but the gardener, Geordie, got mad because we children weren't supposed to touch the garden. Only look and sniff from a distance. What makes you bring her up?"

"An intruder broke into her home in Kingbrook this week."

Corinna looked at her sharply. "Are you hinting there's a link?"

"So far, no one knows, but the experience frightened her so badly, she had a stroke and died."

"How very odd. And sad," said Corinna, who turned away to the window and sighed. "Sometimes I feel as if everyone associated with my family is fated to die a sudden death. But if you're worrying that my intruder could frighten me, don't. I am not defenseless."

Ellie glanced at Toby, who'd fallen asleep in a sunny spot

on the kitchen floor, and wondered what she meant, but decided it was better not to ask.

"Are the Murphys all right?"

"I saw them, and they're fine. Grieving over your sister, but otherwise okay."

"Well, that's a relief anyway," she said, returning to the business of making tea. "You know, most people from here I have hardly thought of over the years, but Mrs. Whittaker has always been with me. There was one scraggly rose bush outside the chapel at the prison, and I used to take off the dead blooms —with my fingers, not secateurs, of course—and I would think of her as I did it. That's my idea of immortality."

"I like that," said Ellie. "Mine is pretty much the same."

"I know I will always and forever be defined by the murder of my brother—but I hope over time I might be able to add some new bits to that."

"You know, Isabelle doesn't remember you that way at all. She still thinks of you as Aunty Corinna, and she's looking forward to seeing you now that she's home for the Easter break."

Corinna's face brightened, as if another piece of her old self had suddenly been infused with new life. "Thank you for telling me that. She was such a shining little girl. I'd love to see her again."

"She still is a shining girl, but tall like Graham. You know, another person who never thought of you as a murderer was Louise, and I believe you asked her to keep this for you," said Ellie, taking out the little jewelry box and pushing it toward her.

Corinna looked at it and grew still, but she didn't touch it. "Where did you find that?"

"In a box where Louise kept the research she did. She

really did try to understand what happened. How it happened."

Corinna shook her head. "You'd think a vicar's wife would be better at knowing there is often no answer to how or why."

Ellie took a chance and laughed . . . which did bring a shadow of a smile to Corinna's face.

"I am grateful to her, you know. When I could allow myself to think about it, I appreciated that she was out there in the world believing I was a better person than I am. I have to say she was heavily outnumbered, though."

At that, she got up and went to the dresser, where she opened a narrow drawer designed for cutlery.

"I found this stuck on the refrigerator with magnets today," she said, pulling out an 8x10-inch black-and-white photo, which she handed to Ellie.

It was an original of the photo taken at the Parthenon that she'd seen online—and all of the family's faces had been crossed out except for Corinna's. "You won. For now," had been written along the bottom.

"My God, that's horrible! The intruder left this?" said Ellie.

"He did." Her expression remained stoic. "And I can't guess why he thought I needed to be reminded that I'm the only one left, but clearly I should be glad my own face isn't crossed out. Yet." She took the photo and put it back into the drawer.

"The weird part is that I have now been through all the boxes of papers Clio kept, and I didn't find any photographs at all. So, I don't know where he found this, but I hadn't seen it here—and it's notable as the only photo I can remember of our whole family together."

"But you still don't have any idea who this intruder is? I mean, he has to be someone connected to you. A cousin?

Someone who might inherit if all the members of your immediate family are gone?"

"I have thought about it, of course. But the answer is still
no. My parents had a mixed marriage when it came to class and
culture—my great-grandfather on my father's side was an
Italian stonemason, and, on my mother's, the younger son of a
duke. So, from the get-go, we were out of step with both sides
and never had much to do with them. Besides, all the money in
the trust goes to Oxford, if there are no direct heirs."

In that case, money was not the motive for these latest
events. *Unless it was the coins*, thought Ellie. *Those bloody,
wild card, coins.*

Ellie was about to ask Corinna to explain the significance of
the necklace and the coin collection, when Toby woke up and
went to the window with an anxious expression. Hector got up
too and danced around the bigger dog, trying to see what he
couldn't possibly see.

That's when Ellie first noticed the distant sounds. Drum-
beats and then, gradually, more. Banging, clanging, cymbals,
whistles, and chanting.

"What the hell is that?" she said as they joined the dogs at
the window.

Dusk was just turning to darkness, but through the trees,
they could see flickering torches and a parade of people coming
down the winding drive. The cacophony increased as they
approached. Two women at the front were carrying effigies of a
man with a knife stuck through his heart and a woman with a
rope around her neck. As they approached the yard, others
dressed in black ran ahead with their phones held out, making
videos and taking photos.

The parade that followed was made up of people in
colorful pointed hoods with eye, nose, and mouth holes that
took Ellie only a moment to recognize. She'd seen them before,

when Lila Ashton picked them up from the home of Hermione Tuttle. Then she had thought they were hats. Now that she understood what they were, she couldn't escape the ominous reminder of hooded marchers back home, who were always up to no good.

As they pooled in front of the cottage, the women shook the effigies up and down, and the racket became deafening. Spoons banged on cooking pots, cans full of rattling stones, horns, cymbals, drums, whistles, and garbage-can lids created a din that lessened only when they joined together to shout:

"Killer!"

"Killer!"

"We don't want you!"

Then they threw eggs that splattered across the front of the cottage and cracked the glass in the windows. Toby's baying and Hector's high-pitched barking became frantic, and Ellie grabbed their collars, saying, "You and the dogs had better go upstairs and keep away from the windows. I'm calling the police right now."

Corinna had watched, paralyzed, her white face a blank mask. But she did what Ellie said, as if she were reverting to a time when following orders was automatic; and it took only a moment for Ellie to get them all up the stairs and to shut them in the bedroom.

Then she put in a 999 call and went back down. She was more angry than afraid, when she grabbed the old tweed coat hanging by the door and went out onto the front stoop. These were her neighbors, after all, and she thought their behavior was appalling.

She had no idea what she planned to say, but before she could even open her mouth, a barrage of eggs flew through the air, all but one missing her. The bull's-eye smacked against her chest painfully and splattered.

Then the hooded crowd surged toward her, and the people taking videos recorded them shouting and banging their noise-makers, as they repeated their chant:

"Killer!"

"Killer!"

"We don't want you!"

"Oh, put a sock in it!" Ellie shouted back. "Stop this noise right now!" She tried to spot the tall blond Lila and her side-kick, Mrs. Tuttle, who had surely planned this event and wouldn't dream of missing it. But she couldn't recognize anyone—and it didn't occur to her immediately that the crowd didn't recognize her either. They saw a slim woman with dark hair standing outside Oak Cottage and assumed she was Corinna.

"What good do you think this is doing? It's outrageous!" she said, trying to raise her voice above the din. The delighted crowd answered her with frantic banging of their noisemakers, as cell phone cameras flashed on all sides.

Ellie ducked the next egg to fly by her head as the hooded protesters began to dance gleefully in the torchlight like figures in some Hieronymus Bosch painting.

"You've made your point. Now get out of here! The police will be arriving any minute—and it's you they'll be arresting!"

But they didn't care what Ellie said. This was undoubtedly Lila's grand finale, meant to flood social media with images and even, perhaps, attract other news media.

Some people continued throwing eggs, but one woman, who apparently realized that Ellie was not Corinna, shouted back, "You don't belong here either! So don't think you can tell us what to do!"

Ellie was taken aback, but before she could respond, several things happened almost simultaneously. Seamus MacDonald burst out of the woods at a run, shouting something she couldn't make out. But she did see the angry crowd surge toward the boy, so she rushed to protect him, and they collided just as a loud bang like a firework went off.

Both fell to the ground at the feet of the marchers, who seemed momentarily stunned, and, in the sudden silence, they could all hear the singsong whine of approaching police cars.

Immediately the torches went out, and the crowd melted into the woods as two panda cars tore down the drive, followed by Graham in the red Mini. Three constables jumped out and took up the chase, while a fourth ran over to see whether Ellie and Seamus were injured.

"Corinna!" shouted Graham as he jumped out of the Mini and then stopped dead when he saw Ellie's face in the circle of light from the constable's flashlight. "Ellie! What are you doing here? Are you hurt?" he asked, emotions moving quickly across his face.

The constable had already helped them both to their feet, and Ellie began to shiver, as Graham pulled her into his arms.

"I'm all right really, I'm totally fine," she tried to assure him, although she sounded to herself as if she were babbling, and her ears were still ringing with the noise. "Is Seamus all right?" she asked, turning to see the constable helping the boy to sit down on the front stoop.

"There was a man with a gun!" he kept saying, and the constable just patted him, as if he were overexcited.

When Ellie sat down on the stoop beside him, she asked, "A man with a gun? Is that why you ran out of the woods?" She couldn't believe it, but Seamus nodded.

"I thought he was going to shoot you, Guv—and, if you hadn't knocked us both over, he might have," he added, with a wobbly grin.

The constable looked surprised. "You mean someone in that crowd really did have a gun?"

Seamus shook his head. "Not in the crowd. In the woods."

"You'd better warn the others," said Graham. "I can stay here with them," and the constable took off after his colleagues.

"Are you sure you're not hurt, Seamus?" he asked. "Because if you're both okay, I think you and Ellie should get into my car and lock the doors until we know better what's going on.

"Ellie, what happened to Corinna? Where is she?" he asked, as if the crowd might have dragged her away. Not an unlikely thought since the two effigies lay sprawled in the drive like victims of a massacre.

"I made her stay inside," said Ellie, wiping at the smears of egg on her face and clothes. "We were talking in the kitchen, and then we heard the noise. I still can't quite take in what happened. I never imagined . . . I mean, I thought if they knew I was here, as a witness, they would go away. But they didn't."

"They thought you were her, Guv," said Seamus. "You were wearing her coat. Even Simon and I thought you were her until you spoke."

"You mean Simon Stephens? He's the one who called me, but where is he? Is he all right?" asked Graham.

"I expect so. He was up in a tree. We were in the woods checking on the badgers, you see. Then we heard the noise and started to watch the riot. Simon had his night binoculars, so that's how he caught sight of the man with the gun. It was same man," he said to Ellie. "The one I told you about. Only this time he had one of those masks that covers your whole face."

"What man is that?" asked Graham.

"The one who's been watching the cottage."

"Do you think he saw you?"

"Not at first. We were all watching the crazy scene here, but when Simon saw him pull the gun, I knew I had to do something to get you to move fast. So, I told him to stay put and jumped down to try to warn you."

"That was very brave, Seamus," said Graham. "Also very foolhardy, but at times they do go together."

Just then the police began to filter back into the yard, so he added, "Please take my keys, get into the car, lock the doors, and stay warm, while I try to find out what's happening."

They did as he said, but watched him talking with the police, who had not been able to catch anyone. When Graham gestured toward his car, they could tell he was explaining that the person attacked by the mob was not Corinna Matthews, but his wife, Ellie Kent. Then they watched as Graham and one of the policemen went inside.

One of the others busied himself taking photos of the scene, while the third came over to the car to take their statements.

After they left, the silence seemed to Ellie as deafening as the noise had been. If it weren't for the abandoned hoods, noisemakers, and effigies littering the drive, she wouldn't have believed her memory of what had happened there.

"Are you sure that loud bang was a shot?" she asked Seamus. It was completely dark now, and, as the adrenaline ebbed away, she felt cold, sore, and sticky. She could tell that before long she would have a bruise where that egg had pounded into her chest.

"Simon could see him clearly. For me, he was more like a shadow. But when Simon thought he saw a gun, I ran. There wasn't time to be sure."

Ellie hugged him. "I'm just glad that you didn't get shot, you crazy boy, but thank you. You may have saved my life."

He didn't say anything, but he leaned heavily into her arms, and they stayed that way.

A long time seemed to pass, and Ellie couldn't figure why Graham hadn't returned, so she climbed out of the car and walked gingerly across the yard. Through the shattered kitchen window, she could plainly see him with Corinna sitting at the kitchen table in deep conversation. She looked shattered, and he was holding her hand.

Bloody hell, she thought, and went back to the car, remembering how he had torn into the driveway bent on saving—not her—but his onetime love. As far as she was concerned, he could walk home.

She was still fumbling with shaky hands to start the car, so she could take Seamus home, when Graham and a police officer emerged from the cottage with Hector.

"I'm sorry we kept you waiting," he said, climbing into the car, as Seamus moved to the back. "It took a long time for the officer to persuade Corinna to tell him the whole story. About the intruder, the break-ins. Everything. I was afraid if I left, she'd shut down, and that can't happen now. Pranks are one thing. Attempted murder is something else again."

"Attempted murder?" said Ellie, her voice breaking on the words. Seamus, on the other hand, leaned forward from the back seat with an expression on his face she could only describe as thrilled. After all, from his point of view, the danger was over. All that was left was a good story.

"What else would you call it?" said Graham. "The police found a bullet in the lintel over the door. Where you were standing."

"I'd call it a bad shot, then," said Ellie testily.

"Please don't try to laugh this off, Ellie. It was near enough," he said as he turned the car to head back down the drive. They were all silent as he drove Seamus home.

It was no surprise that, when they pulled up in front of Blackthorn Cottage, Morag rushed out demanding to know what had happened. "The phone has been ringing off the hook with people telling me they saw you on the internet at some riot!" she said. "I've been too afraid to look myself."

"It was nothing, Mum. I'm fine," said Seamus, climbing out of the car. "I was helping Simon with the badger watch, when some trouble took place next door."

Morag looked from him to Ellie in her egg-stained, bedraggled state.

"What do you mean trouble? I heard it was a riot," she said, and Graham got out to talk with her.

"It was Lila Ashton. You know she wanted there to be a fuss about Corinna, so she organized some rough music."

"Rough music?" howled Morag. "What is this? The nineteenth century? Someone has to shake that woman until she admits the past is over and done with."

"Yes, well . . . I don't think she's quite there yet."

"So how did you get involved?" she asked Seamus.

"Simon and I saw a man with a gun in the woods, but no one got hurt."

Morag looked down at her son's dusty, rumpled clothes and shook her head. "A gun? Oh, my God. Why can't you get interested in something safe like stamp collecting!"

Ellie gave Seamus a look, and he did not repeat his line about detection being his destiny.

"Would you like us to come inside and talk further?" Graham asked, noticing that a few neighbors were now watching.

"No," said Morag, glancing around. "Thank you. I just want my son to come inside and have his tea, do his homework, and go to bed. In one piece."

Ellie and Graham hugged them both before they went inside, but Morag was still stiff with outrage. She undoubtedly guessed that this was not the end of the incident, since the police would be around to question Seamus and who knew what else would happen to disrupt their lives after that.

As Graham drove home and pulled into the drive, Ellie felt the events just passed became more and more unreal. She was glad Isabelle had gone out with friends for the evening, and she could strip off her sticky clothes without having to give any explanation. Graham saw her settled into a hot bath and left her to have a good soak in peace. She had dozed off when he came back and sat down on the edge of the tub.

"You're getting wrinkly," he said and passed her a glass of brandy.

Ellie smiled. "I'm trying to wash off the whole day."

"I don't blame you. Are you sure you're not hurt?"

She rubbed the spot where the egg hit her breastbone. "I have a bruise on its way here, but that tweed coat and Seamus took the brunt of my fall in the driveway."

"I'm very grateful," he said, bending down to kiss her.

"You thought I was Corinna," she said, trying not to sound sulky.

"Of course, I did. I wasn't expecting to find my wife lying in the driveway of Oak Cottage surrounded by a mob!"

"I suppose not."

"Ellie, I have learned in six months to expect the unexpected, but you still manage to take me by surprise."

Ellie sipped her brandy and gave him a wry smile. "Well, that's good, isn't it? We're not bored yet?"

"It's good," he said, kissing her again. "I just get terrified sometimes about losing you."

"I know," she said. "I do too. About losing you," then she stood up to hug him, regardless of the water streaming down her body.

When she was warm and dry, dressed in her flannel nightgown and warm robe, they huddled together on the sofa in the sitting room and let the fire do the talking for a while.

Then Ellie remembered something she'd meant to ask. "What did you mean by what you said to Morag about rough music?"

"Rough music is what you witnessed tonight. One of those wonderful English folk traditions you love so much. Long before petitions, hate mail, and social media, it was how the community expressed its displeasure."

CHAPTER TEN

Friday, March 16

E llie was exhausted, but too overwrought for restful sleep. Hooded figures danced through her dreams, and she was awakened with a pounding heart when a man in black stalked through the village with a gun to prevent her from revealing that Corinna was innocent. It had been the photo from Greece that proved it, but, from 4 a.m. on, she lay awake trying to think why.

Nothing came to her, but finally she gave up on sleep and crept quietly out of bed to go up to her study and see what was happening online.

The demonstrators had been quick to post lurid videos, and their footage managed to make the march look not only much bigger than it was, but also more exciting. Some of the tweets wrongly identified Ellie as the convicted murderer, Corinna Matthews. This was corrected by early morning, but the tone of the self-righteous chatter didn't change until the news broke that someone had shot at the Little Beecham vicar's wife. Then opinions began to ricochet from celebrating the marchers' efforts to rid the village of a murderer to calling Ellie a heroine. This was a stretch. The more she looked at the scenes, the more she felt like a fool for trying to confront a mob singlehandedly.

A tweet from the Thames Valley police saying they would be questioning everyone who participated as suspects in an attempted murder did more than Ellie ever could have hoped to put a spoke in the social media campaign. By 6 a.m., the majority of posts were condemning the march and calling for people to live and let live. *Graham ought to be happy about that,* she thought, and went down to the dark kitchen to make herself some tea.

Ellie had not been aware of any reporters turning up for Lila's big show, but as the social media chatter shifted, the news momentum spread to the mainstream media. The shooting attracted attention, but that was just one of the news angles available. Some opted for the quaint Cotswold village reenacting an old custom, while others went for a rehash of the Pindar Matthews murder, the threat of increasing gun violence in the UK, and the need to revamp the justice system. Ellie thought Lila must be dancing on the rooftops as she watched this unfold.

By the time Graham and Isabelle came down for breakfast, there was a TV news truck parked in front of the church, and they could see a crew walking around the churchyard shooting B roll as background for some planned version of the news.

After the fourth time he'd gone to the door to turn away reporters with "No comment," Graham said, "I hope the gates to Odyssey House are locked." Ellie handed him a mug of tea and reminded him that he'd said the night before the police would be posting a guard at the cottage. That ought to keep the media at bay.

She could think of only one reason why journalists would

be interested in St. Michael's, and that was her reputation for solving local mysteries. It was not the sort of publicity welcomed by the locals—especially the Bells, who were always worried that notoriety would put Little Beecham on the itinerary of tourist buses and other undesirables.

Ellie felt again the folly of her behavior. Any sensible vicar's wife—correction, any sensible person—would have called the police and then stayed inside with Corinna and let the mob have its say without responding.

Regrettably, she was not that person.

"What do you think," she said to Graham, "are those reporters going for the body-in-the-churchyard or the live-baby-in-the-manger angle?"

"I don't know," he said, with a thin smile. "You have to admit you're a better story than most vicar's wives. And a shooting is always good copy. There aren't nearly as many here as you have back in the States."

"Attempted shooting," Ellie corrected and went back to the table, where her porridge was getting cold. She checked her phone and found it was flooded with texts, including ones from her parents in California, as well as Morag, Seamus, and Michael-John. All wanted to know what was happening.

Mrs. Finch arrived, dismayed by this new round of violence involving her vicarage, and she was mollified only when Isabelle offered to help her with the day's cooking and to take over Ellie's Soup Car visits so the housekeeper could finish spring-cleaning the downstairs.

Ellie tried to make light of her experience, pointing out that photos of her on the internet being hit in the chest with an egg were erroneously captioned: "Vicar's wife takes it on the chin for murderer."

"I did not get hit on the chin. That egg hit me right here," she said, rubbing her bruised breastbone gingerly. "It only splattered on my chin."

Isabelle, who could usually be counted on to be a good sport, laughed, but Mrs. Finch bustled around the kitchen with her face screwed up in a knot. No one had thrown eggs at the vicar's wife in all her years of service, much less shot at her. She was furious at the demonstrators, but Ellie could tell she blamed her too.

Graham was none too happy either, but he did a better job of hiding it. He had been very solicitous and loving the night before when they were alone. With reporters on the prowl now that it was morning, all he could say was "At least you weren't injured. Thank God for that."

Ellie was hurt by his tone and said, "You mean no thanks to me," and then regretted it, when she saw Mrs. Finch's back stiffen. They tried never to have disagreements "in public," and that included their own kitchen when the housekeeper was present.

"I thought you were very brave," said Isabelle staunchly. She was disappointed to have missed all the excitement because she'd gone out dancing with her friends in Oxford. "Those people needed to know that someone was willing to stand up to them. I'll bet they were very surprised."

"So surprised they reacted violently," said Graham. "They might have left, if there had been no response. Going out to face them was a big risk."

"What would you have done?" Isabelle asked.

"I would have called the police and stayed inside."

"I don't believe you," said his daughter. "Those people were from Little Beecham. Some of them were probably in church last Sunday. Wouldn't you have wanted to go out there and talk to them further about loving their neighbor? I think Ellie did the right thing. It was just an unfortunate coincidence that she and Corinna look so much alike."

Graham blinked, then shook his head as if to rid himself of that image, and said, "All right. I'll admit I might have gone out to confront them."

"I hope you aren't thinking 'because I'm a man' as the end of that sentence," Isabelle said.

He smiled wryly. "Maybe I was. But, to be honest, I don't know what I would have done. Staying inside would have felt like letting them win. Letting them intimidate me. That's a universal feeling."

"Thank you," said Ellie. "Although I admit I can't claim to have had any idea what might happen. I think I imagined they'd be ashamed when they realized there was a witness to their attempted intimidation. I wanted them to know they couldn't harass Corinna in secret, hiding behind those hoods."

"Except people wearing masks and hoods are not ashamed. They feel impervious and powerful, and when they become a mob, they've surrendered to a collective identity that protects them even more. They're beyond shame. Beyond conversation and beyond reason. That's why they continued to attack you, even after some of them must have realized you were the wrong person."

"Oh, I don't know about that. One woman seemed to take pleasure in the opportunity to tell me to go back where I belonged. She knew exactly who I was." The memory made her angry, as if that unidentified woman had spoken for the whole village.

Graham sighed and said he wished they could all stay in and not answer the phone or door, but that wasn't possible. He'd already received a dozen calls from worried parishioners. Besides, Ellie had to go to Oxford to testify at the inquest into

Pen Whittaker's death, and Isabelle would be doing The Soup Car rounds.

"Also, don't forget Mullane is coming, and, after the inquest, I'm visiting Clio's friend, Janet Shah."

When the doorbell rang, Ellie assumed it would be Mullane. But when Isabelle went to the door, Ellie and Graham could hear a loud voice even before Geoff Stephens barged into the kitchen. He was a tall, good-looking man, wearing an expensive, well-cut suit, but at the moment, just another red-faced bully.

He looked from Graham to Ellie and back, saying, "This village is completely out of control. I've had the police at my house this morning, questioning my son about a riot, a shooting, and even an attempted murder—within yards of my home. I hope you understand now why we wanted you to support the effort to remove that woman."

"I'm sure that was very upsetting, but it's ridiculous to blame Corinna for it," said Ellie. "People are wound up because Lila Ashton and a few others have been working very hard to make them that way. Corinna hasn't done a thing."

"Except commit murder," said Geoff, looking at her with disdain. "I have no idea who this Lila Ashton is, and I certainly hope you aren't implying that I have any responsibility for that fiasco, just because I don't care to have a murderer living on the doorstep of my family home."

Ellie didn't reply, but Graham stepped in to say, "Ellie is right, you know. None of that was Corinna's doing. Her behavior since she returned has been irreproachable. Which is more than I can say for some others. I'm not presuming to tell you how to feel about her presence, but I'd be careful what you say about it, and where you place the blame for the events last night—especially if you're speaking with the police or journalists. They have their own ways of interpreting what they hear and the sources they hear it from."

For a moment, Ellie thought Dr. Stephens looked taken aback, but it didn't last long. "I was in London!" he declared. "And I will not have *my* reputation sullied because of a woman who baldly admits to stabbing her brother to death."

"Perhaps, then, you might want to go back to London until the dust settles on this episode," suggested Ellie. "You might also want to leave now, because we're expecting the police here for an interview at any moment."

Which was true. And, it was obvious their visitor did not want to have any further interaction with the police, because he did leave, still huffing and puffing, and had barely reached his car when, on cue, DI Mullane arrived with Sergeant Jones in tow.

Ellie showed them into Graham's study rather the sitting room, since Mrs. Finch was cleaning there. They sat on the sofa with their backs straight, as if they were at an interview table in the police station, while Graham and Ellie took their usual places.

"How are you this morning, Mrs. Kent?" Mullane asked, as Jones took out his notebook and pen. Mullane was dressed in his official gray suit, and it was hard to believe that only four days ago, they had been drinking coffee together almost like friends.

"I'm fine," she said, absently rubbing her bruised chest. "How is Corinna?"

"Holed up. Anxious for the police to finish collecting evidence so she can clean up the mess. You were extremely lucky, you know. That shooter might very well have hit you."

Ellie shook her head in disbelief. "You know, if you hadn't found the bullet, I'm not sure I could believe that the shooting really happened. Why would someone want to shoot a gun in the midst of that bacchanalian scene?"

Mullane frowned. "It does look like that on the internet. But those videos have an unhelpful way of distorting reality. As far as we can tell, there were fewer than twenty people involved. It was the noise, those hoods and torches, that made it seem like a bigger group."

"But the danger was real enough, and everyone's aware of it. People are usually closemouthed about who takes part in such activities, but shooting is out of bounds. We're not talking about some villagers reviving a traditional way of expressing dissatisfaction with a neighbor. We are talking about assault with a deadly weapon or even attempted murder. As a result, we've had a stream of people contacting us, quick to exonerate themselves. Even to cast themselves as victims."

"You mean they think they were tricked into participating?"

"Something like that. They were there willingly, and they were certainly whipped up to feel it was warranted."

"By Lila Ashton?"

"Mainly."

"But surely, she didn't have anything to do with the shooting, did she?"

"Everyone we've interviewed denies being armed, and we're pretty certain they're telling the truth. The angle of the shot makes it clear that the gunman was in the woods, as Simon Stephens and Seamus MacDonald reported. The video footage we've seen does not show any of the demonstrators near there. They came down the drive and stayed in the clearing until the police arrived, which was after the shot had been fired. Unfortunately, the way they dispersed so quickly into the woods gave cover to the shooter."

"And no one else has reported seeing anyone who wasn't part of the rough music?"

"Other than the two lads, no, and their description is not helpful. Simon claims to have seen a man, also dressed in black and of similar build, in the woods before. And Ms. Matthews has admitted that someone has broken into the cottage on several occasions. She and her hound tried to track him, but only determined that he left via the woods. Nothing substantial ties these reports together yet."

He paused before going on. "We're working on the theory that you were mistaken for Ms. Matthews. Very few of the people involved ever knew her, and those who did have caught little more than a glimpse of her since she returned, so, in the excitement of the moment and the uncertain light, this would not have been a difficult mistake to make. The marchers—and presumably the shooter—all saw the person they expected to see. Do you have any reason for doubting that?"

"I should hope not! But why would anyone want to kill Corinna either? Avenging her brother and going to prison yourself seems like a very poor plan."

Mullane shrugged. "There's no accounting for what some people call justice," he said, in a way that made Ellie think of Hermione Tuttle. Public hanging aside, what might she think was acceptable to do?

"It's early days, and we've just begun collecting information. Ms. Ashton is cooperating with our investigation and has admitted to organizing the campaign against Ms. Matthews. She says her goal has been to pressure the Parole Board into reconsidering her release—or at least her freedom to return to Little Beecham. Another poorly conceived idea, in my opinion.

"So far, she has declined to name anyone else who might have been involved, but we'll find out, and they will be called to account, especially if violence was planned."

Ellie opened her mouth to tell him that she knew who made those colorful hoods and then stopped. She wanted to talk with Mrs. Tuttle herself first, and, fortunately, Mullane didn't notice her hesitation.

"Ms. Matthews claims she has no idea who has been breaking into Oak Cottage, much less who could want to kill her. In fact, she's more than anxious to put the whole incident behind her, since you and the MacDonald boy were not injured. However, we hope you will press charges."

Ellie glanced at Graham and sipped her tea to buy some time. "I don't know what to say, to be honest. It seems odd to call it an accident, but, in a way, it was, and there was no harm done."

Mullane frowned. "Discharging a firearm into a crowd of people is not the kind of behavior we can ignore, Mrs. Kent. It may have been an accident in that you were the wrong target—and the shooter missed—but the person who fired that gun acted deliberately and should face the consequences."

"How can you possibly identify him—or her?"

"We're the police. That's how."

"Well, I can't be of any help. I was watching the mob. They looked like demons."

"Yes, and it was dangerous for you to confront them, but keeping Ms. Matthews out of sight was wise. I'm very glad no one was hurt, and the damage was limited.

"If it's any comfort, the people we've interviewed are chastened by the way things turned out and regret that you were involved. They've all been warned that there will be no tolerance of any more such incidents or harassment."

"Do you think Corinna might still be in danger?"

"I certainly wouldn't assume she's not, as she wants to do. But rest assured, we are paying attention to all of these events. We're not totally lacking in imagination, you know."

"Are you trying to apologize for telling me the case was wrapped up fifteen years ago?"

"No," he said.

Graham frowned. "Ellie has to testify today at the inquest into Pen Whittaker's death. After last night, do you still believe there's no connection?"

Mullane frowned. "I don't think it would be wise to get ahead of ourselves on that" was all he would say, and then he and Jones left.

Ellie half expected the next event to be an angry call from Morag blaming her for Seamus's entanglement in last night's fracas, and she was cowardly enough to be glad it didn't come. She had decided to leave early so she could stop by Hermione Tuttle's house on her way to Oxford. It was obvious Mrs. Tuttle had been involved in the rough music plan, but Ellie didn't want to jump to conclusions about how involved.

When she pulled into the drive, she saw that all the drapes were still drawn, and no lights were on inside the house, but she went to the porch and rang the bell until, at last, Mrs. Tuttle unlocked the door and opened it a crack.

Her face was ashen, and she looked 10 years older. When she saw it was Ellie, hope flashed in her eyes, but when she realized there was no lunch box in her hand, she said, "What do you want?"

"I want to talk to you," Ellie said and stuck her foot in the door before the other woman could close it. "The police will probably be here before long, and I wanted you to know that. For reasons I can't explain or justify, I did not tell them about your involvement in that near disaster last night. Despite the fact that both an innocent boy and I nearly got shot."

Mrs. Tuttle shrank back at her words. "I had nothing to do

that!" she said, turning even more pale. "You're the one who ruined the whole thing! All our plans. What were you doing there? You stuck up for that killer and stole the limelight! Now everyone's talking about you, instead of justice for my boy."

"I ruined the whole thing? I nearly got killed, and you're blaming me? Are you mad? Were you really hoping Corinna would be shot? That's your eye-for-an-eye notion of avenging your boy, as you call him?"

Mrs. Tuttle crossed her arms and stuck her chin in the air.

"She, at least, would deserve her fate, and by her own admission."

"Is this what Lila thinks too? Do the two of you sit around drinking tea and saying things like this?"

"No one else has ever known or understood how deep our loss has been. So why shouldn't we? I've never seen any reason why that woman should live when he didn't."

The hairs on Ellie's arms stood up as she recognized the phrase from one of the threatening letters.

"You sent those threatening letters too, didn't you?"

A proud little smile crossed her face. "I've been a faithful correspondent over the years, yes. And why not?"

Ellie took a deep breath, looked around at the cold, musty house where the Tuttle family had once lived and now Hermione lived alone, and realized that she was out of her depth. It was time to bow out and let Mullane take this bit over.

"Well, I can see there's nothing I can say to help or hinder you, but I suppose I do hope, for your sake, that the police have a broader view of justice than you do."

With that, she left, and she would have thought the day couldn't get much worse, but it did. The Oxford Crown Court was held in the County Hall, and Ellie sat transfixed as a series of witnesses presented the pieces of the puzzle that added up to a picture of Pen Whittaker's last two days, and the circumstances of her death. By the time it was all laid out, she was more or less prepared, but still shocked, to hear the coroner's conclusion: unlawful killing.

She was crying by the time she reached Graham on the phone and stood on the street with tears running down her face as she told him that the evidence showed Pen had been nearly strangled in her bedroom, and that's what precipitated her stroke and subsequent death. The killer had entered through the kitchen window and covered it with cardboard to disguise what he'd done and then left through the back door to the garden, which relocked automatically as he pulled it shut.

Nothing had been discovered that would explain the state of the house, since the few valuables were undisturbed. The search had been more frantic than methodical, and it had probably taken place after the failed confrontation Pen described to Ellie. No fingerprints or other DNA evidence was left behind, and the police reported they had no leads on the perpetrator.

Graham did his best to comfort her without resorting to any platitudes such as "She's at peace now," and Ellie was grateful for that. After she got off the phone, she walked around Oxford in a daze, and finally went into The Turl to have coffee in one of its dim corners. She could imagine a mad person wanting to kill Corinna as revenge for Pindar. But Pen Whittaker, lover of roses and cats? The attack on her was inexplicable. Yet someone had done it.

Ellie considered canceling her meeting with Janet Shah, but finally decided the drive through the countryside to Townsend's Mill might restore her spirits better than being surrounded by the throbbing, youthful life of the university. The day had turned warm with puffy clouds, a blue sky, and early daffodils that bobbed along the verges of the greening fields. This was the English spring as she had always imagined it, and she found herself wishing she could simply focus on that, rather than pawing around in the darkness of human behavior.

Townsend's Mill was a hamlet, surrounding an old stone mill, where the brook that once kept its wheels turning still bubbled along, but the mill itself was now a craft gallery and café.

The Shahs lived on the outskirts in what was called the Manor Farm House, a sprawling complex of stone house and barns with a courtyard full of bicycles. If there were a manor associated with it, Ellie didn't see it.

The sound of exuberant children's voices came from within before the door was even open. As Janet greeted her, Ellie caught a glimpse of several children running up the main staircase, followed by a young teenager with a long black braid, wearing a colorful salwar kameez. Janet was dressed in this traditional silk tunic and loose pants too, though her sandy hair was cut very short. She welcomed Ellie, apologizing for the ruckus with a smile, and led her into a spacious kitchen with a conservatory at the back overlooking a walled garden.

"You'd think jet lag would slow them down, but it seems to have the opposite effect. Thankfully, my niece came back from India with us for a visit. She has much more sway over them than I do at the moment," she said as she loaded one large tray with fruit juice, thick sandwiches of date-nut bread and cream cheese, samosas stuffed with spiced chick peas, and sliced apples and baby carrots for the children, and then set up another smaller version of the same with a pot of tea for them.

She picked up the big tray and said, "I'll be back in two ticks. Why don't you settle down for now out in the conservatory, but if it gets chilly, we can move back inside."

She disappeared with the tray, and Ellie sat down in a comfortable wicker chair overlooking a lush green lawn bordered with freshly turned flower beds. It was shaded by an old apple tree, and the peacefulness of the scene was a balm to her fractured spirit.

Janet returned and poured out the tea with a smile, urging Ellie to take whatever she would like for food. To her own surprise, she found she was very hungry and helped herself to some of everything. Janet did likewise, and, for a few minutes, they both concentrated on eating.

Then Janet sat back and sighed happily. "I'm always amazed at how peaceful the house suddenly becomes when the children are feeding. Do you have children yourself? I got a late start so I had four in six years, and I'm still dealing with little ones."

"I've just recently acquired a nineteen-year-old stepdaughter," said Ellie, "so getting to know her is my priority. She's at university, and before I know it, she'll probably be off living somewhere far away."

"Some days I look forward to that," Janet said, with a laugh. "Mostly I'm grateful, though."

She closed the conservatory door when the noise began to pick up again. "They eat as fast as dogs, but I tell them to interrupt me only if there is blood or someone stops breathing. Otherwise, I never get a thing done."

"Does that work?"

Janet laughed again. "Of course not," she said as she sipped her tea, then helped herself to another sandwich. As she took a bite and chewed, she regarded Ellie.

At last, she said, "So, Corinna is finally interested in Clio." Then she shook her head. "Sorry. I didn't mean to say that out loud, but I suppose you're aware that growing up with Clio didn't give her friends a very positive view of the Matthews family. Of course, I know families look different from the perspective of each person, so I really shouldn't comment on what Corinna felt then or now. But I'm happy to talk with you for Cli's sake."

"Thank you," said Ellie. "It's terribly sad that they were not able to reconnect. I saw the letter Clio sent, inviting Corinna to use Oak Cottage. The tone was generous and open to a new start."

A shadow crossed Janet's face, and her eyes filled with tears. "I guess I'm glad to know that. There's no resolution for Corinna, but it was a good thing for Cli to have written that." She cleared her throat and poured them both more tea. At the sound of small feet tearing back down the stairs, accompanied by gales of laughter, Janet looked toward the sound and sighed again.

"You hear that? There's never a time when it doesn't remind me of Clio, Mel, and myself. We were like that as kids, and we had such fun together. It's heartbreaking to think about everything that happened afterward. All that Cli missed out on then—and will miss out on now."

Ellie nodded encouragingly and took a samosa. She knew there were questions she should ask, but at the moment she preferred to bask in this woman's friendly presence and hear whatever part of the story she wanted to tell.

"Our favorite game was playing dress-up in the Odyssey House attic," she went on. "Lady Anne—Cli's mother—had a trunk of clothes that had belonged to her mother, Lady Eloise, and some from her grandmother, Lady Claire too. They were the most amazing dresses . . . beautiful fabrics, heavily beaded and embroidered, with lace and flounces and fringes, you name it. Lady Anne's family had a duke somewhere in the family tree, which was all we needed to become little Lady Mucks in our games. That attic was our own world. Trunks became carriages and ships and caves and hollow tree trunks. It was magical.

"I remember it was always kind of a shock to come back downstairs. The light would be so bright, and the tension, so thick and oppressive. Her parents never got along, and it was my first experience with that kind of unpleasantness. Professor Matthews was terribly brilliant and admired in his work, but he was disappointed in his wife, and all the children were expected to somehow erase that by living up to the strict standards he set for them.

"Life downstairs was not easy, but for those hours in the attic, Cli was free and a happy, amazing child."

"When she got older, she took apart those clothes and made the most beautiful things for us. Vests and skirts, jackets and shoulder bags. She could make anything. We used to dress up— the three of us—and go into London on the train to parade around. People stared too. We loved that. After the invisibility of school uniforms, you know."

"Of course, we all thought our lives would be fine once we left home. But then, I guess you do think that when you're young, even if you have perfectly nice parents, which I did."

"Did you know Corinna and Pindar too?"

"Not really. They were six and eight years older. That's a big difference when you're young. Pindar was an adult in our eyes. He was tall and very handsome, so we were all a little in love with him. We didn't know enough to see the signs of trouble."

"Were there signs back then?" asked Ellie.

"Oh, yes, I think so now. He was always playing mean tricks on Corinna, who would become very angry, but he was also a great one for goading Clio to take risks, and he would push the limits to see what she would be willing to do to keep his approval. Neither Mel nor I had brothers, so we thought this was the way they were. And it can be hard to know whether a naughty, rambunctious lad is going to turn into a sociopath, but looking back, I would say Pindar was headed that way from an early age."

"Where carefree becomes without conscience."

Janet bit into a slice of apple with a thoughtful expression. "Yes, exactly. It's a bit frightening to think of, isn't it?

"I heard from Melissa about some incidents that sounded very scary to me," said Ellie.

Janet nodded. "Nonetheless, we could never have imagined how terrible the true outcome would be.

"I can't say I knew Corinna—she was always quite remote and busy with her studies, but she also seemed to be very close to their father, who, from a child's perspective, was definitely a person to avoid. In a way, she was sort of forced to play the role of the professor's wife, which is strange to think of, since she was only a girl herself. But, you know, despite what happened, I have always thought of her as an honorable person. If that makes sense. She was brought down by someone who was ruthlessly dishonorable, but she owned up and paid the price."

"Did you ever wonder why it happened? I mean, I know Corinna has no memory of the events of that night, but from what I've heard and read, neither she nor Clio would ever talk about what led to that last confrontation."

"Of course, I did. And it's always bothered me. You think you know what's going on in your friends' lives, and it's startling when you realize you don't. Didn't. We spent that night together in Oxford where Melissa had a flat, and I remember Clio was very nervy from the moment she arrived. Things had been difficult for them ever since their father's death, but I thought she was even more on edge that night. Looking back at that time, I would describe her as devastated by the murder, but also weirdly unsurprised, and I've always wondered about that."

"That's very interesting," said Ellie. "Did you ever think that might be because she was involved in some way?"

Janet raised her eyebrows. "No," she said. "I mean, she was definitely with us when it happened. And there was no question she was terribly shocked by Pindar's death. It may have been that she suspected something was about to blow between Pindar and Corinna—in a way we could all see that coming for years—but I never dreamed it would play out the way it did.

"Once it happened, I wasn't surprised that Cli kept silent about whatever triggered the explosion. They were all trained from an early age to keep the family secrets—mainly about their mother's drinking during the time I knew them best—so it was natural, I guess, that she and Corinna reacted the same way around the murder."

"And did you have the same experience as Melissa? That she cut all ties with you soon after Pindar's death?"

"Yes, but I didn't resent it the way Melissa does. I always believed she'd come back to us when she was ready, and she did. She sent a postcard announcing an exhibit in Paris that included her work, and I was amazed. Those figures she makes —I mean, made—I think they're fabulous. And the costumes made me laugh, because they reminded me of what she made for us back in the day. To me that said she was still the same Clio that I had known and loved.

"Vijay and I were looking forward to going to the opening— it coincided with a business trip he had to take to Paris—but we were also getting ready to go to India, and two of the kids came down with strep, so there was no way I could take the time."

"Did he go anyway?"

"He did, and he said Clio was there with a man—an art collector or something, French, I believe—and I was delighted because I really thought she'd never get together with anyone. You know, even up to the time he died, Pindar was her one and only in a disturbing sort of way. But Vijay said she seemed happy. And her work was well received.

"He took some photos for me so I could see how well she looked and her work on display. If you want, I can email them to you. Corinna might like to see them."

"I'm sure she would."

"I haven't even asked how she's doing. Clio's accident must have been a terrible blow for her."

"Yes. And it hasn't been easy to come back to where Clio lived and deal with the cottage and all that's left of her family. To say nothing of putting up with the very unwelcoming attitude of the village."

"Oh, my God, Vijay told me he saw something online this morning, but I've been so busy unpacking and catching up on laundry, I forgot all about it. There was some riot or shooting in Little Beecham? And that was at Corinna's? Were you the vicar's wife someone shot at by mistake?!"

Ellie nodded.

"That's incredible! Do the police know who's responsible?"

"For the rough music, yes, I think so, but not the shooting. And Corinna says she has no idea who could want to harm her. But there's definitely someone behind a whole series of threatening events."

"How bizarre. You wouldn't think there could be anyone left around here. I mean, Clio was hardly ever in England . . . and Corinna has been away all these years . . ."

"Exactly. It's very strange, and she would appreciate knowing if you have any ideas at all who might be behind it."

"I'll give it a think, but no one comes immediately to mind."

"Thank you. Meanwhile, she's determined to start picking

up the pieces of her life, and I can tell you the first thing she did was to get a dog."

Janet's face brightened. "A dog? Really? You know their father would never let them have a dog, and Clio used to make up stories about the family's invisible dogs. They were very funny. Always doing a poo under the professor's desk and peeing on his books."

They both laughed, and then were interrupted by the thunder of five sets of feet running down the hall and voices shouting, *"Jaldi! Jaldi! Jaldi!"* Hurry! Hurry! Hurry!

Janet looked toward the kitchen door and laughed. "Whenever we go to India, the kids come home speaking Hindi . . . or their version of it." Then they tumbled in, demanding attention: two boys and two girls with shiny black hair and dark eyes, but their mother's affecting smile, and the teenager who tried to hold them back from assaulting what was left on the tea tray.

Janet stood up and addressed them. "One moment, please. Settle down. This is Mrs. Kent, and I'd like you to say hello. Nicely."

They stared at Ellie, then said, "Hello," burst into giggles, and ran out into the garden to chase each other around.

Janet laughed again as she watched them. "So ends the quiet grown-up time."

"I should be getting on anyway," said Ellie, "but I would love to see the photos from Clio's exhibit—and if you happen to think of anyone from the past who might still be around and have an interest in making trouble, it could be helpful."

"Of course, and please do tell Corinna I'd be happy to see her again. And you too. I knew Louise, you know. Vijay and I didn't move here until the third baby came along, and our house in Little Beecham began to burst at the seams. We used to go to Saint Michael's from time to time, and I thought both

Louise and Graham made it a very welcoming place. Not, you know, all stuffy C. of E.

"Anyway, I didn't want to say that right off, because I'm sure you're tired of hearing it and feeling compared. Being a vicar's wife—it can't be easy."

Ellie grinned. "The vicar's worth it—and I'm getting used to it. I'm just sorry I never met Louise myself. If you know what I mean."

"I think she'd be pleased that you're supporting Corinna. She stuck by her when no one else would."

"I've heard that, and I've also heard that she thought Corinna might have been innocent."

"I'm sure she wished she was. It was a hard truth for all of us to swallow. An object lesson in how life can go completely pear-shaped in an instant," said Janet, as she watched her children trying to scramble up the trunk of the old apple tree. "Then we deal with the consequences however we can."

As Ellie headed back out to her car, she was struck by how different Clio, Janet, and Melissa had become as adults. But the story of their childhood friendship rang true, and Clio's evolution into an artist who had managed to move past her history did too. Tempting as it was as an alternative solution to the mystery of the murder, Ellie realized it was time to lay to rest, once and for all, any notion that it was Clio, not Corinna, who had been the killer.

Ellie hoped the journalists would be gone when she got back to Little Beecham. After all, nearly a whole day had passed, and surely the events of yesterday were old news now. But one game young woman jumped out of her car as soon as Ellie parked and rushed over to intercept her before she could reach the back door of the vicarage.

"Ellie," she called boldly, "what do you think about the verdict in the Penelope Whittaker inquest? Is her death linked to the shooting last night? Do you think someone hoped to silence you before you could testify? And what about the link with the Matthews murder?"

Ellie looked at her hungry expression and pulled back from the insistent hand waving a microphone in her face. "No comment," she said and pushed past her.

Undeterred, the woman smiled, and turned the camera on herself. "And there you have it, folks! Ellie Kent says, 'No comment!' The words everyone understands to mean yes!"

"Everyone" again! thought Ellie, so even though she was already halfway through the door, she turned back and said, "No, those words do not mean yes. Believe me, I am an English teacher, and the words 'no comment' mean exactly that." Then she went in, closed the door, and locked it. Okay, maybe the door slipped and sounded as if she slammed it. This wasn't a movie, and she couldn't redo the scene even if she would have liked to. She sighed and tried to imagine how this latest encounter would look on YouTube. Or Twitter. Or wherever.

But once she was inside, the reporter's questions replayed in her mind. What made her think that the death of Pen Whittaker was linked to the shooting? Or Pindar's murder? And why would anyone want to silence her?

She pulled out her phone and sent a text to Mullane. *A reporter just raised the question of whether the intended target of the shooting was me. Have you considered that?*

The answer came back immediately. *Yes. More later.*

Good grief was all Ellie could think as she wearily made her way up the stairs. She wanted to be alone, but when she heard a voice coming from Isabelle's room softly saying, "Come on, sweetie. Come on . . . ," she stopped.

Peeking in the half-open door, she saw Isabelle sitting

on the floor with a can of tuna and a spoon, presumably trying to coax Barney to eat something, despite his being holed up in her closet. The fact that Hector was eagerly peering around her legs to see what was going on did not help.

"May I come in?" asked Ellie.

"Sure. You might be more successful with this. After all, Barney knows you."

"I'm not sure he does in this context." Ellie pulled up a chair and looked into the dark corners of the closet. All she could see was a pair of yellow eyes.

"You look knackered," said Isabelle, glancing up at her. "Hard day?"

"Mind scrambling," said Ellie. "Just as a start, the coroner ruled that Pen's death was an unlawful killing."

"Does that mean murder?"

"Yes. To put it bluntly. And I have to say it's beyond my comprehension how she could have come to such an untimely and uncalled-for end."

"Well, I hope you aren't looking for me to say it's all in God's plan," said Isabelle, and, when their eyes met, blue and brown, they both smiled.

"I'm not, but thanks. That's exactly what I needed to hear." She slid down and joined Isabelle on the floor. "So, what do you think . . . is this going to work out? The dog and the cat?" she asked.

Isabelle handed her the tuna and backed away from the closet on her hands and knees. "It will happen," she said, confidently, brushing her hair out of her eyes. "Barney just has to get used to us."

"And vice versa," said Ellie, who handed Hector over to keep him out of the closet. Then she crawled in and set the tuna down in front of Barney, who stared at her until she moved back out again. After a long moment of consideration, he crouched down and began to gobble.

"Your gracious offering has been accepted," said Ellie, when she'd fully emerged.

Isabelle laughed. "I can see I'll need to provide special services for a while, but that's okay. It gives me an excuse to avoid work on my essay."

"About the Resurrection?"

"Yes. And the trouble is, when it's a question of belief, it doesn't matter what really happened to Jesus."

"Probably not. Even figuring out what really happened to Pindar Matthews fifteen years ago seems impossible."

"My task might be easier. Who can say I'm wrong?"

"Very true. And, in my case, the answer is 'everyone.' My new favorite word."

"You know, I remember how shocked Mum was about what happened to Aunty Corinna."

"You do? I thought you were way too young."

"Oh, I was. But Mum used to remind me of her now and then. I think she liked to talk about her, the way she was when they were friends. Kind of like the way you reminisce about someone who's died, you know? I had a doll she gave me, and Mum would get this wistful look on her face and say, 'Aunty Corinna gave you that. Don't forget it.'

"At the time, I didn't know why she left or where she'd gone, but later, when I did, I could still recall the way Mum said that. Like it was really important to her that I remember Corinna had been our friend and kind to me."

"Did you ever have the impression that your mother didn't believe Corinna committed the murder?"

"No, and that didn't seem to be the point. She wanted to me to understand that good people can do irrevocably bad things, but you can still love them."

"Did your dad feel the same way?"

Isabelle wrinkled her nose. "In principle, yes, of course. About Corinna . . . I don't know. She was Mum's friend. They did things together, and she stayed with me quite often when Mum and Dad went out, but Dad was rather standoffish. It was a bit odd, really, because Mum and Dad usually liked the same people.

"They were very comfortable together, you know. Like you and Dad now, but different, because they were different people then."

Ellie blushed, but she was pleased. "You think your dad is different now?"

"Oh, definitely. Mum's death changed him, for one thing. It was like he'd gone into a small, dark space, although he did his best for me and the parish. But when he came back from California with you, I could see how he'd changed. The world had opened up again and was bigger than ever before."

"Thank you for telling me that, Isabelle. Meeting him has done that for me too."

"It's made the world bigger for me too, you know. Having you in the family. I don't have to be afraid of leaving him anymore, and I can work on being me instead of the vicar's daughter." She smiled then and, when she stood up, she held out her hand to pull Ellie to her feet.

CHAPTER ELEVEN

Saturday, March 17

As it turned out, Ellie was alone in the kitchen reading the dregs of the news coverage about the rough music in Little Beecham, when DI Mullane finally returned her call. At the sight of his name on her phone, she was glad Graham was already holed up working on the string of sermons he had to give in the lead-up to Easter; and she'd just seen Isabelle off to Oxford with her face painted green for the St. Patrick's Day parade.

"Mrs. Kent?" said Mullane, when she answered the phone. "Can you talk?"

"Yes," she said, with a sudden feeling of dread. "What have you found out?"

"Nothing specific yet, but tell me this. How many people did you tell what Pen Whittaker said to you before she died?"

Ellie was taken aback. Whom had she told? "Graham . . . and you. I don't think there was anyone else."

"Not Corinna Matthews?"

"No, definitely not."

"Did you mention to anyone else that Mrs. Whittaker spoke to you?"

"No."

There was a pause, as if he were thinking. "You're sure that's it?"

"I might have said something to Pen's neighbor right after it happened, but I don't remember. Why?"

"If even a couple of people heard that she spoke to you, it's possible that others came to hear about it too. Including the person who was responsible for her death."

Ellie felt herself turn hot and cold all at once. "I never thought—"

"Of course not. But we believe we're dealing with someone local, and that means someone who knows your reputation, shall we say? So, there is a risk that you might divine the meaning behind whatever Mrs. Whittaker said and that could lead you—and the police—back to him."

"But how could he know I would be at Corinna's on Thursday night? That I would step outside?"

"He couldn't. Let's just say, as regards that, he lucked out and took the chance. But we suspect there is one person—aside from Lila Ashton—behind all the events that have happened since Corinna's release."

"How?"

"When we figure that out, you'll know. And, if you figure it out first, you'd better tell me. Immediately. I hope I've made myself clear."

"Brilliantly," said Ellie, but he had already hung up.

"We need to talk," Ellie said to Graham, opening his study door. He looked up from his typewriter with that dreamy look writers get when they are far, far away from the world around them.

"Okay," he said, blinking, and turned his chair toward her. He regarded her with the calm, neutral expression he would present to a parishioner in urgent need of help. Which indeed she was.

Rather than taking her usual spot beside him, Ellie sat down on the sofa facing him, her arms crossed and one hand over her mouth, as he waited patiently for her to begin.

"I heard something yesterday I haven't told you yet," she said.

A stillness came over him that she recognized as his way of preparing for bad news.

"You know about that reporter who stopped me in the drive, and I cut her off with no comment?"

"Yes . . . it was all over the internet briefly until someone was busted for drugs over in Red Hill."

She nodded. "I know, but that's not the point. The point is, afterward I started thinking about the questions she asked me . . . especially the one about whether someone shot at me to prevent me from testifying at the inquest. At the time, I thought that was completely daft, but later I began to wonder. What if I had been the target? Not because of my testimony. That was already in my witness statement. But what if there's something else I know—or heard—that could lead the police to identify the person who attacked Pen? And what if that person has been following me . . . and did take the opportunity of the rough music to try to prevent me from remembering whatever it is?"

Years of practice had taught Graham to listen sympathetically to every kind of confession, but she could tell from his eyes that this one was difficult for him to hear. "Have you had the feeling that someone is following you?" he finally asked.

"No, not at all."

"But you have thought more about what Pen said and what it might have meant?"

"Yes, but, Graham, I still have no idea. I asked Mullane what they thought, and all he said was it's their theory the person must be local. And they think the break-ins, the attack on Pen, and the shooting are all somehow connected with Corinna's release from prison."

"But they're not looking at Corinna as a suspect, I hope." The sudden urgency of this remark did not escape Ellie.

"No. At least, if they are, he didn't tell me."

"Then I don't see what the connection can be. And you being a threat seems like a completely separate issue."

"I agree. Pen's link to the Matthews family is indirect at best and ancient history to boot."

"Was there anything else she said that day she saw the man who frightened her?"

Ellie started to shake her head, saying, "It was all very confusing."

"But still . . . she did say something?" he prompted.

"Yes. What I mentioned before, when we were talking with Mullane. About Jock never believing her."

Then she added, "Now I remember she was referring to something she saw that she thought was important, and he insisted it wasn't."

"The theory being that all these years later that resulted in her death?"

"It does seem like going a long way to connect dots. On the other hand, accepting the idea of random violence against an old lady living alone in Kingbrook takes a stretch of the imagination too."

Graham gave her a long look. "You know, Ellie, when you get that restless expression, it worries me. I appreciate you're not satisfied with having 'no idea,' but that's the way someone out there wants it to stay—and all the more reason why you should let the police have the ideas, ask the questions, and find the answers."

In the afternoon, Ellie was happy to change focus and go over to the church to meet with the organist, Mr. Dunn, about the music for Easter. She would never have much to say about flower arrangements, silver polishing, or the state of the needlepoint kneelers, but she did love music and had found Mr. Dunn enjoyed having someone with whom to discuss his ideas.

For the Easter service, he proposed to play the difficult, but triumphant, "Toccata" by Charles-Marie Widor as his postlude. Although it was by a French composer, this piece had been played during the recessional at the marriage of Prince William and Kate Middleton, so it was familiar and likely to please and impress the congregation.

Ellie wasn't sure whether either Mr. Dunn or the small Victorian organ at St. Michael's was up to the task, but she had encouraged him and offered to turn pages. So far, the run-throughs had been rocky on both sides, but he was improving, and so was she. Most people wouldn't notice if he missed a few notes among so many, but if she turned two pages at once or was so nervous that she knocked the music over . . . well, that would be a disaster.

Today she could hear him playing before she even reached the church. "A Mighty Fortress Is Our God" almost shook the old stones and rattled the windows in their arched frames. She entered quietly and sat down in a back pew to listen.

The church wasn't heated on weekdays, and Mr. Dunn was wearing a wool hat pulled over his flyaway gray hair, a thick Irish sweater, and fingerless gloves as he played. When he reached the final chord, which seemed to hang almost visibly in the air, he turned and greeted her with a pale, drawn face.

"Sorry," he said. "I've only just heard what the coroner had to say about Pen Whittaker's death."

"Don't apologize to me," said Ellie, walking up to join him. "I love to hear an organ let off the leash. Was she a friend?"

"Yes," he said. "She sang in the choir here for many years."

"I didn't know that."

"It was before your time, but she was the mainstay in keeping the sopranos in tune. And she was one of the people I always had in mind when I planned the music. Would she be pleased or not? Even after she was no longer able to come regularly."

"I wish I had known her better. I always enjoyed taking her lunch. She was so enthusiastic about her garden. It was infectious! And she loved to be read to, which was fun for me too."

"It's horrible to realize that her life came to an end like that."

"I know, but if it's any comfort, she was safe in the hospital, and I was with her when she passed."

"I'm glad," he said, fingering his music, with a sad, abstracted expression.

"Did you know her husband too?"

"No," he said. "Jock wasn't a churchgoer or a music lover, and I don't think he much approved of Pen's involvement. But, you know, it was hardly something he could object to openly." He gave Ellie a fleeting smile.

"He sounds quite authoritarian, from what I've heard."

"I believe he was. An absolute ruler, and the Odyssey House estate was his kingdom."

Ellie started to laugh, then stopped. "I suppose that was difficult at times."

"I believe it could be. Pen never said a word against him. At least not in my hearing. Do you think it would be all right if we dedicated the Easter music to her memory?"

"Of course. I'll mention it to Graham, but I am sure he will agree that it's a lovely idea."

"Thank you," he said and turned back to his keyboard. "Shall we start, then?" he asked and Ellie nodded, sitting down on the organ bench beside him. After a ripple of warm-ups, he plunged into the Widor, filling the church with a glorious sound, and the task of watching for the moment to turn the page wiped every other thought from her head. By the time they successfully reached the last sequence of resounding chords, they were both smiling and ended their rehearsal with a long hug.

Ellie's heart felt lighter than it had for two days when she left the church and set off for Oak Cottage. Since Thursday night, she had spoken only briefly with Corinna—a perfunctory "How are you?" conversation. In other situations, a dramatic experience such as the one they'd been through might bring people together, but she still found communicating with Corinna difficult. Uncertain.

She was surprised to find the cottage already back to normal with the cracked windows replaced and every sign of the mess created by the mob expunged. The daffodils in the bed along the front had survived and had begun unfurling their blossoms.

Corinna came readily to the door to let Ellie in, but said she was busy in Clio's workroom and did not want to stop yet. That was fine with Ellie, who followed her upstairs, curious to see where Clio had made her marionettes and sculpture. Neither of them referred to the last time they were together.

The workroom was the biggest of the three bedrooms on

the upper floor and had been fitted out with a large worktable over which hung full-spectrum lighting. Shelves lined all four walls and were stacked with plastic boxes holding tools and materials.

A jumbled pile of doll body parts, tools, fabric, beads, buttons, braid, and more was spread across the worktable, and Corinna had obviously been sorting them into boxes.

"Has there been another break-in?" Ellie guessed, looking at the chaos.

"Not since the other day—I just didn't realize he'd been in here until this morning because the door was locked, and I hadn't found the key. Fortunately, it seems the focus was search and not destroy." She indicated a dozen finished marionettes, which were hanging from hooks and sitting along the uphol-stered window seat. Like the ones Ellie had seen at The Chestnut Tree, these were assemblages made from dolls as much as a century old with expressions ranging from a frozen sweetness to a macabre, eyeless stare. All of them wore costumes that looked as if they had been made from the vintage dresses that Janet had told her about.

"She was a very talented artist, wasn't she," said Ellie.

"Yes," said Corinna, who nodded, but didn't look up or pause in what she was doing. "I'll take a break in a minute," she added and gestured for Ellie to sit on a wooden chair. Working quickly, she finished sorting the pile into separate boxes and set them back on the shelves. Then she sat down on a stack of art books, wiped her face with her sleeve, and lit a cigarette.

"The main thing I've learned from being here is that I had no idea who my sister was. Nominally, I lived with her for her first eleven years. After that, I went off to uni, and we saw each other only occasionally. It's surprising and hard to discover what I missed. What, I would wager to say, everyone in the family missed. Better too late than never, I suppose."

"Six years is a big age difference," said Ellie, and Corinna shrugged.

"It wasn't only that. From the get-go, she found in Pindar the one family member who paid attention to her, and he made a point of keeping her in his thrall." She frowned at the memory as she stubbed out her cigarette.

"She was his poppet," said Ellie.

"What?!" She looked up suddenly.

"According to Melissa Engelthorpe, Pindar called her Poppet."

"Ugh," she said, shaking her head. "I'm glad I never heard that. Do you know what it means?"

"I thought it was a term of endearment."

"It can be. But it also refers to a small figure used in witch-craft. The actions you perform on your poppet are transferred to your victim by sympathetic magic."

Now Ellie was taken aback. "Wow. But, if she was the poppet, who was the victim?"

"I don't know. Once I might have thought it was Clio herself. But seeing all this," she said, gesturing to the dazzling color and creativity in the room, "there was obviously a lot to Clio that was beyond Pindar's reach. Not that he would have noticed. He never could see anything beyond himself and what was useful to him."

Something in her tone made Ellie go on alert, but Corinna ended the conversation, saying, "I've done enough here for now. Let's go downstairs." Toby, who had appeared to be dozing, leapt to his feet at her words, and Ellie followed them down to the kitchen.

It was clear that Corinna had been at work there too. An old cardboard box full of cassette tapes and a cassette player that must have been more than 20 years old sat on the kitchen table.

As Corinna turned on the kettle and took out the tea, milk, and sugar, Ellie offered to get the mugs from the cupboard where she was surprised to see, behind the simple everyday china, an exquisite porcelain tea set, gilded and decorated with delicate flowers. "That porcelain tea set is lovely," she said as she set two mugs on the table.

"It was my great-grandmother's. Meissen," said Corinna, in a distracted way. She measured some tea into the Brown Betty teapot.

"My mother treasured it, and she would sometimes use it to give us tea up in her room as a special treat. Unfortunately, one day Clio dropped her cup and it broke, so that was the end of that little ceremony.

"I found what was left in the box room yesterday, so I guess Clio couldn't bear either to get rid of it or to look at it . . . but I brought it down to show Michael-John. I thought he might be interested.

"That," she said, indicating the cassette player and box of tapes, "is something I discovered today. It was in Clio's workroom, and most of the cassettes are music compilations that Pindar made when he was a teenager. Radiohead. Queen. U2 . . . It looks as if Clio might have liked to listen to them while she worked.

"There are some tapes of my father's in there too. He used to talk the first drafts of his papers and books onto cassettes, and we kids would record over the tapes after his assistant had finished transcribing them. I found one today that still has Cleve's voice on it, and a couple of others that I used when I was working on my thesis.

"This one was a bit of a shock," she said, picking up a cassette that Ellie could see had originally been labeled "Epictetus: Chapter 6." That had been crossed out and replaced with "Women in Rome #1," written in red ink.

Corinna popped it into the machine and went back to making the tea.

Suddenly Ellie was listening to what was apparently the voice of a long-ago Corinna talking about women's rights—or rather, the lack of them—in ancient Rome. There was a slur in her voice that might have been caused by the age of the tape or the fact that she had been drinking while she worked.

When her voice cut off abruptly, there was a pause before the recorder picked up an angry man saying, "I'm sure you'll be pleased to know Winstead's latest letter came today. The one that deigns to give me an increased allowance. But I hope neither of you imagines politely worded or-else clauses will stop me from finding a way out of that trust—and when I do, things won't go so well for you."

"Don't be such a prat, Pindar. You think threatening me is going to get you anywhere? Sooner or later, you'll have to accept the fact that the trust is not a gravy train. If you want more money, you have to earn it. And the same is true for Clio and me. You are not singled out in any way."

"The trust. Talk about the misuse of a word. You know perfectly well that as soon as Mother was dead, Cleve saw his chance to cheat me by tying up her money, and he jumped at it."

"That is not what happened. Mother left everything to him to avoid the death duties, as was perfectly correct. And he left everything to us. We just can't dive in and spend it all."

"That's how you see it? Well, I don't. But I haven't spent my whole life with blinders on hoping to please the unpleasant Cleve. You have, and all that you've achieved is to turn into Mother! A hopeless lush."

His mocking laughter was lacerating, and it was followed by the sounds of a struggle and a crash, as if a heavy piece of furniture had overturned sending numerous other objects tumbling to the floor.

Corinna pressed the stop button. Her face had paled, and her hand shook as she poured out the tea.

"That was some argument. Do you remember it?" Ellie asked hesitantly. "I mean, it's not a recording of the fight that led to Pindar's death, is it?"

Corinna shook her head. "We had virtually that same argument many times in the months after my father's death."

"What about the letter he mentioned? Would that fix it in time?"

"No. My fellow trustee sent Pindar numerous letters. He had a touching faith in the written word. The impact of a registered letter."

"I see. It must be upsetting to hear no matter when it was."

Corinna lit a cigarette and looked away out the window. Ellie wondered how to keep the conversation going.

To her surprise, Corinna gave her the answer: wait and listen.

"It's not," she said. "I mean, not upsetting in the way you might think. It confirms the reality of scenes that have played in my mind a million times, and that's a relief.

"But I'm certain it wasn't the last argument, because that would not have been about money." She turned back to Ellie then and said, "I may not remember the circumstances of the murder, but I do know why it happened. I have always known why."

Ellie was stunned. "Did Clio know too?"

"Yes."

They both paused for breath. "No one else knew? Not even Louise?"

"No one."

"Was that why you came looking for her when you were

released?" Ellie asked, as if a puzzle piece had suddenly fallen into place.

"Yes. Sort of. I wanted to her know the reason I couldn't see her when I was in prison had nothing to do with her. With anything she'd done. It was a shock to realize both she and Clio —the two people I had most hoped to make amends to—were gone."

Ellie sipped her tea and waited. She thought it was notable that whatever place Graham held in her heart, he was not near the top of that list.

Toby came over and laid his head on Corinna's knee, and she stroked him thoughtfully. Then she took the tape out of the cassette player, and said, "Pindar was right about one thing. I'll give him that. I was on the road to becoming a hopeless drunk. Still functional in my way, at times, but increasingly unpredictable. You might think killing Pindar was my biggest regret from that time of my life, but it was actually the least surprising thing I did in a blackout back then.

"He was always hard on me—he tried to smother me when I was a baby, you know—but his parting gift was sobriety. I have never had drink since that day, and I am grateful to him for that.

"When you're in prison, it's very clear the easiest path is to keep going down. To do otherwise is almost like resisting gravity. But there were some people from Alcoholics Anonymous who came there to hold meetings, and I started to attend. It was a chance to see people from outside who didn't judge, and I certainly needed that. They also offered simple directions for how to live—many of which I soon realized I had heard over and over from my father, who loved to quote the Stoics. Not that any of it sank in when I was growing up."

"You mean like 'I have lost nothing that belongs to me. It was not something of mine that was torn from me?'"

Corinna could not hide her surprise.

"My father was a philosophy professor at Berkeley," said Ellie, "so I heard more about the Stoics than Mother Goose too."

"Well, I never," she said and smiled, for what seemed to Ellie like the first time.

After that, the talk between them flowed more easily.

When the light through the windows began to darken, Ellie said she should get home. As she was putting on her coat in the front hall, she noticed that Corinna had also been at work in the sitting room. This was a fairly large room with an exposed beam ceiling that ran the length of the house and was furnished with the comfortable old pine furniture that Michael-John mentioned. There was a large stone fireplace over which hung the country landscape he thought was by Walter Sickert, but what attracted Ellie the most were the boxes of books.

Corinna had obviously been pruning the overcrowded shelves that lined the walls. On top of one box, Ellie spotted a familiar name: Ramona Blaisdell-Scott. Surely the last author she would have expected to find in the library of the Matthews family.

"Do you know that book? Who that author is?" she asked Corinna, pointing to the hardcover edition of Miss Worthy's first book, *Love at War*.

Corinna shook her head. "I don't have a clue. I found that in the bedroom, so I guess Clio might have read it—or planned to, but I never will."

Ellie took the book out of the box. From its pristine cover and pages, she guessed Corinna was right that it hadn't been read, but, when she opened the flyleaf, she saw an inscription and recognized the handwriting. "For

Cleve, Thank you for the wonderful book—and for your gifts of time and friendship. Yours always, PW." Priscilla Worthy.

"This is inscribed to your father, did you know?"

"No, I didn't look, but I'm sure he never read it either."

Ellie laughed. "Ramona Blaisdell-Scott's a very popular author, who lives in the village. But until a couple of months ago no one knew that. The identity of the person behind the pen name was kept secret for years. From the inscription, it appears she and your father were friends."

"I doubt it. Aside from us, my father's world was made up of colleagues, competitors, and students. Although I vaguely remember he had one friend from childhood he used to visit from time to time. They both collected coins, and I think they smoked cigars together. I always liked the way he smelled when he came home."

"Well, if you're planning to get rid of these books, I'd like to have this one."

"Sure. Take a bag full. Take two bags."

"Thanks! This one will do me," she said and slipped the book into her purse.

Ellie hoped she would find Graham at home when she got there, so she could tell him Corinna had revealed what they suspected: that she had known all along why she killed Pindar. It was never about the money and, whatever the secret reason was, Clio had known it too.

Her thoughts were so wrapped up in speculation about what this reason might have been that she didn't notice Lila Ashton getting out of her car and approaching the vicarage.

As usual, Lila was dressed in her professional armor and looked, from her determined expression, ready to attack. The very idea made Ellie instantly forget that a vicar's wife should always be polite.

"What are you doing here?" she asked, when they met at the front door.

"I came by to be certain you're all right and to be absolutely clear that neither my firm nor I bear responsibility for what unauthorized individuals might have done on Thursday night."

"Is that so," said Ellie. "I assume you're referring to the shooter who nearly killed me. As it happens, I am fine, and I'm glad to hear that wasn't an *authorized* part of your event. It certainly made a splash for you in the news."

"You can't imagine that was planned."

"Having spoken with Hermione Tuttle about your partnership, I wouldn't expect any limits to have been discussed."

"Hermione is not my 'partner.' We do share the same deep distress about the way the death of someone we loved has been dismissed as no longer significant by the legal system and the community. That said, I never dreamt anything like that shooting could happen here."

"But media attention is what you wanted. An airing of your grievances—a fresh public hanging of Corinna in the court of social media and public opinion."

"I have never countenanced violence of any kind. How could I possibly, given my own experience?"

Ellie shrugged. "I don't know. The police are investigating your activities, and that will include not only you and Hermione, but also whoever else you have on your team. Perhaps the creep stalking Corinna, who has been supplied with so much inside knowledge about her family. Rather a nice touch to have the campaign brought right into her home, since she couldn't care less about social media."

Lila's face tightened in anger. "I don't know anything about anyone stalking Corinna or going into her home. And I'd like to point out that Corinna is not the victim here. It's our community. And the goal has always been to ensure that someone who committed a heinous murder does not come back here as if nothing ever happened."

"Look, I am truly sorry about the loss you suffered," said Ellie, "and I am not minimizing it, but I don't think your campaign has ever been about our community. Corinna has never expressed any intention to stay here, but you jumped on this opportunity to stir people up to write hate mail before she even arrived, and the media coverage has practically guaranteed that it will be impossible for her to go anywhere and start over."

"I won't disagree, and, to be honest, I have no problem with any of that. My only purpose in coming here was to be clear about the shooting. I have no need to listen to a lecture about what I or our community needs from a complete outsider as oblivious and arrogant as you are." And, with that, she stalked back to her car.

Ellie found her hands were shaking when she tried to open the door. The whole day had suddenly shifted from positive to negative, and she felt as if she'd become embroiled in a road-rage attack in which she had herself played an unpleasant, aggressive role.

Had she been oblivious and arrogant? Did Lila and Hermione have a valid argument that Corinna's release relegated Pindar's death to an issue of the past? Resolved, no matter how unresolved. On top of that, in seeking a new interpretation of the facts, had she also been seeking a way to blame him, rather than Corinna, for his death—and, to justify that, had she willfully disregarded the feelings of those who still loved him?

. . .

After dinner, she and Graham went for a walk in the woods where the trees were still bare, but the quince and blackthorn were blooming and catkins had formed on the hazel. The breeze was cool and soft, the kind that caresses your skin.

Ellie had so far said little about the day, and he asked her why she was so subdued.

"Comeuppance," she said. "And humility. Lila Ashton made me feel I've been heartless."

"That sounds like a pretty harsh self-judgment. It's always difficult to navigate situations that invite us to take sides. Make things black and white. Nothing is ever that simple."

Ellie nodded. "I know. But it's also easy to forget. I've taken Corinna's side because Louise believed in her, but, I admit, I keep wanting there to be some very good reason for her to have killed Pindar. Something that would make it seem more justifiable."

"You will likely never get the satisfaction of knowing the answer to that. Even back when I was at Oxford, people specu-lated about the skeletons in the Odyssey House closets. Not only Lady Anne's alcoholism, but how the marriage between two such different people ever came about in the first place, to say nothing of what might become of their offspring. No one questioned that Cleve was a brilliant scholar and teacher, but his attempt to control the narrative about his family so tightly was bound to fascinate the students under his thumb."

"Interesting," said Ellie. "I keep hearing different versions of how Corinna devoted her life to pleasing her father, but I hardly think murdering Pindar was the way to achieve that goal."

"No. I expect not."

"Did you ever consider that, if their father hadn't died, Corinna and Clio would have stayed at their respective univer-sities . . . and none of this would have happened?"

"Yes, but I don't think the what if . . . then it would never . . . scenario is ever very helpful."

"Point taken. But you know I do find it a little surprising that Corinna could express her regret about not having a chance to mend her relationships with Clio and Louise—and say she was grateful to Pindar because the murder shocked her into sobriety. But she has never once said she was sorry about killing him."

"What are you suggesting?"

"Well, I guess what I'm suggesting is what I said I'm hoping for. That, for whatever secret reason, she believed the murder was justifiable. He deserved it."

"No one deserves to be murdered."

"No. Of course not. Delete that," said Ellie emphatically.

"Speaking of murder . . . Did you hear anything more from Mullane today about their search for the person who shot at you?"

Ellie shook her head. "Nothing. And, to be honest, I've been trying not to think about that."

Graham put his arm around her shoulders. "That's understandable . . . as long as you're careful, even while you're not thinking about it."

She grinned up at him. "You know I will be."

"Yes, I do," he said. "On another front, there was a message in my email today saying Pen's body has been released. I've scheduled the funeral for Tuesday."

CHAPTER TWELVE

Sunday, March 18

The bells in the church tower began to ring early on Sunday morning, creating a cheerful clamor, but Ellie had to push herself to get out of bed. Suit up for the role of vicar's wife. She had put aside her guilt feelings about Lila and Hermione—they seemed fully capable of making their case without her help—and had lain awake much of the night thinking about what could have happened that would push Corinna to the point of murder. Was it Pindar's endless, insufferable treatment of her? Or something to do with Clio, who was his poppet and victim and loved him all the same?

The other thing that kept coming back to her was the cocksure sound of Pindar's voice as he swore to break the trust and promised things would not go well for Corinna as a result. Were these only empty threats? Siblings bullying each other—as if they had powers they didn't have? It was possible that Corinna had heard her brother make such grandiose statements all her life, so she didn't even hear them anymore, but to Ellie they were disturbing.

She drowned these thoughts with a cold shower, then shivering, threw on her ready-set-go business attire of a tailored gray wool suit with a burgundy silk shirt. A quick fluff of her hair, a swipe of lipstick, and she was downstairs to catch up with Graham and Isabelle as the second round of bells rang.

When she and Isabelle entered the church, person after person greeted the girl, who looked especially beautiful and grown-up with her hair twisted into a knot at the back of her neck and a long-sleeved navy wool dress with white lace at the collar and cuffs. Admiring how well she looked, Ellie realized she felt positively old next to her stepdaughter.

While the congregation took a proprietary pleasure in seeing their vicar's daughter back in the fold, many eyes skittered away from Ellie after a hasty "Good morning." Watching the parishioners scatter to take their places, she guessed more than a few had been part of the rough-music crowd that marched to Oak Cottage on Thursday night.

The ritual of the service offered a chance for all of them to quiet themselves, lulled by music and the sunshine pouring through the stained glass windows. But when Graham asked them in his quiet way to pray for those who thought to bring peace through chaos and for the soul of Penelope Whittaker, a member of the parish who had died tragically that week, a wave of uneasiness swept through the church.

Everyone seemed glued to their pews until the last strains of the postlude died away, but many left without staying for tea. As the remainder moved toward the refreshments, Ellie caught scraps of whispered talk about being questioned by the police, anxiety about the shooting, anger at the disruption of their lives, and the upcoming funeral for Pen. Under the circumstances, she was glad it was her turn to be situated behind the table, where she was too busy doling out tea, coffee, and cake to talk.

Miss Worthy came to join her when it was time to stack the dirty cups and plates in boxes to go back to the vicarage for washing. When no one was nearby, she said in a low voice, "Are you quite all right, Mrs. Kent? I've been feeling terrible that my urging you to support Corinna put you in danger."

"I'm fine, so please don't worry," said Ellie. "What happened was almost entirely my own fault, and certainly not yours."

"Then would you come by to see me? Later today?" she asked. "There is something I would very much like to talk with you about."

"I'd be glad to. And I have something to show you," Ellie replied, so they agreed on 3 p.m.

Graham, Ellie, and Isabelle had planned to eat Sunday lunch at a restaurant overlooking the Thames and then take a walk on the path along the river, but a bank of dark clouds closed in as they were carrying home the tea dishes. By the time they were ready to leave for the restaurant, the wind had picked up, the temperature dropped, and a sleety rain poured down.

So instead, they feasted on leftovers and played a game of Scrabble by the fire. Although Hector occupied the prime location directly in front of the blaze, Barney emerged from somewhere to creep into the sitting room and hopped up onto a bookcase to observe the scene. When Ellie went over to pet him, he pushed his head into her palm, and she felt the tiniest purr. That made her very happy.

The rain stopped as abruptly as it had started, and the afternoon became lit by streams of golden light. Isabelle decided to take Hector for a walk, while Graham dozed off over the crossword puzzle with his tortoiseshell glasses halfway down his nose. Ellie kissed him anyway and set off to see Miss Worthy.

The streets were quiet, and the village was as pretty as a stage set. Yet, there were people who walked these streets who had signed those petitions and flooded social media and Corinna's mailbox with hateful messages, to say nothing of marching down her drive wearing hoods, carrying effigies, making noise, shouting, and throwing eggs. Ellie thought the police must be right: someone local was also behind the more violent acts. The thought of that man with a gun made her angry, but it also induced her to scan the gaps between buildings and walk as quickly as she could without actually running.

Miss Worthy met Ellie at the door herself, saying Charlotte had taken Dolphin on a visit to her parents, and led the way back to the kitchen, where she was baking shortbread.

"I'm so glad to see you in one piece. We've never had a shooting like that here before, where so many people were at risk of being hurt. Have the police found the person who did it?"

"I was just thinking about that. But the answer is I don't know. They aren't telling me much."

"It had to be one of those people Lila riled up. That's the trouble with these social media campaigns. It's impossible to know whose fuse is being lit!"

"The police are operating under the assumption it was someone local," said Ellie, who decided not to mention the idea that she herself might have been the target. "Corinna still says she has no idea who could want to shoot her, and Lila is doing her best to distance herself from the whole issue. She even made a point of coming over to tell me that she and her company were in no way involved."

"Hmph," Miss Worthy said with a sniff. "Afraid of getting sued, I suppose. Or worse."

"Yes. But my understanding is that all her fuses are wet at this point. The police are watching her."

"I'm sure she doesn't like that. And Pen Whittaker's death? Have they found the connection? Surely there aren't two such dangerous people on the loose."

"I have no idea about that either. Did you know Pen?"

"Yes, of course. Not well, but she had a lovely singing voice when she was younger, and she was always generous with her advice about roses. I never much cared for Jock. He was one of those perfectionists that you begin to suspect is a bully at heart. Of course, that meant he ran the Odyssey House estate very efficiently.

"Not that his personality has any bearing on her death. I'm afraid I took that as further evidence that safety is no longer something one can take for granted even in our little towns and villages."

Ellie sighed. "I know. I sure had the wrong idea about that when I moved here from San Francisco! But we must all press on. Despite the break-ins at Oak Cottage, Corinna has made quite good progress on sorting through what's there, which means that I have this for you." She opened her purse and handed Miss Worthy the copy of *Love at War*.

Miss Worthy's expression showed both surprise and recognition. "Oh my," she said, taking it carefully and looking at it, front to back. "It's almost like seeing a ghost, but I remember when I gave this to Cleve as if it were yesterday."

"Is this the story you promised to tell me the last time I was here?"

"No, not exactly. But it's related."

For a moment, she set aside the book to concentrate on cutting her shortbread dough into triangles. Ellie waited patiently until Miss Worthy had put the full tray in the oven, wiped her hands on her William Morris apron, and sat down. "Now," she said. "Is this really a story? It feels more like a saga, but I'll see what I can tell you in fifteen minutes." She set the timer on the table.

"I think you already know that Cleve Matthews and I were friends. It began about twenty years ago, because toward the end of her life, Lady Anne was very ill and virtually house-bound. The consequence of her alcoholism. It's a terrible kind of decline and took an enormous toll on the whole family.

"I had no idea how bad the situation was—they were close-mouthed about her condition—so I was not aware that it was probably the worst possible time to ask for Cleve's help. I had written a simply awful romance set in ancient Greece, and I knew this was one of his areas of expertise, but that's about all. We had seldom crossed paths, despite living in the same village.

"Nonetheless, as new writers often do, I wrote and inquired whether we could meet so I could ask him some questions. It was really very cheeky, because I hadn't published anything yet, but I did it anyway.

"Much to my surprise, he said yes. He came to tea—this was when I was still living in a grace-and-favor cottage secluded in the woods behind Hughes House—and he kindly let me pepper him with questions. He had the reputation in the village of being cold and distant, but to me he was very generous with his time and offered to lend me some books and even to read my manuscript to check my details.

"I had the impression that he didn't know many people outside of academia. I was about his age, and I like to think he did truly find my company refreshing.

"I never published that book. In fact, I never even finished it. I quickly realized I didn't care that much for the classical world, and I would be better off writing about World War Two . . . something I knew about! From that time forward, well, the stories have just rolled out. But that's beside the point.

"After Lady Anne's death, Cleve became quite a frequent visitor, and I realized that, as successful as his career had been, he was a lonely man in a difficult situation."

"And did you come to have a soft spot for him, Miss Worthy?"

She sighed. "I did, and I suppose I was not the first woman in late middle age who thought to change her circumstances with the magic wand of a new relationship. I didn't love him—you know I only ever loved one man in my life—but I liked him very much, and I was guilty of hoping he loved me."

"But then he died."

"Yes. There's no good way to die, but that family has had quite a run of sudden deaths. In Cleve's case, there was nothing mysterious about it, though. He had long-standing heart problems that finally caught up with him. But it was our last meeting that the book you brought pertains to.

"It was the night before he was to leave for a conference in Athens, and he called to ask if he could come by. He sounded agitated. Excited. I confess I thought something special was going to happen." She blushed. "I even imagined he might be planning to propose. A very mad idea, but I was younger then."

At 35, Ellie had a little trouble thinking of 60+ as younger, but then to 80+, it certainly was.

"He did look excited when he arrived, and he was carrying a present, but it was obviously a book. A heavy one, and definitely not romantic!" She laughed. "He was so distracted he didn't notice I was disappointed. Nor that I quickly countered it by signing a copy of my first book, which had just been released, for him."

"*Love at War,*" said Ellie, realizing she had seen the date the book was inscribed without linking it to the professor's death.

Miss Worthy nodded. "I persuaded him to stay long enough for a drink and realized what I had thought was excitement was distress over a row with his son. He wouldn't go into the details, but a good sum of money was apparently involved, and it was clear that he was very worried—not for the first time —about the sort of man Pindar had become, despite his best efforts to direct and even control him.

"After going on about that for an hour or more, he suddenly got up and announced he had to leave. He had started for the door before I realized I hadn't thanked him very graciously for the book. So, I did, and all he said was, "Of course. And I thank you. We'll talk more about it when I get back.""

"Only he didn't come back."

"No. That was the last time I saw him."

"What was the book?"

"A big encyclopedia of the classical world. To be honest, I never even looked at it. I felt embarrassed, because it seemed to me that he must not have been listening to anything I'd said for years. I wasn't writing about that anymore, and I wasn't even interested. As it turned out, my gift was equally inappropriate. I doubt he ever looked at that either."

"What did you do with his book?"

"Oh, I kept it. I thought about getting rid of it, when I moved here, but I couldn't. Didn't. It's one of those objects that reminds you you're a fool. Remarkable how things can do that, isn't it? I stuck it on the top shelf of the sitting room bookcase to forget about it, even though I suppose I've always been aware of its presence."

"You still have it, then?"

"I expect so. I can't say I've looked for it, but I can't think of any reason why it wouldn't still be there."

"May I look for it?" asked Ellie.

"If it will amuse you, of course," said Miss Worthy, who heard her timer ding and got up to take the shortbread out of the oven.

Without another word, Ellie left the kitchen and went to the sitting room. The new foreign-language editions of *Love and Desertion* had been carefully shelved alongside Miss Worthy's other titles on the lower shelf. The shelves above were a mishmash of reference books, nonfiction, classics, and recent novels, but, at the far end of the top shelf, she spotted a thick encyclopedia.

Ellie had to climb up on the sofa arm to reach it, but she managed to get her fingers around it and slide it out. It was about four inches thick and remarkably heavy. She nearly stumbled, stepping down off the sofa with it in her arms.

It did look like a dreary academic tome, but Ellie took it out to the kitchen, where Miss Worthy was sliding the shortbread onto a rack to cool.

"I see what you mean about unromantic," she said, setting it down with a thump. "It seems a very odd choice as a gift for a person with only a casual interest in getting facts right for fiction."

Miss Worthy glanced at it with distaste, as if the very sight brought back her misguided fantasies.

"There must have been some thought behind giving it to you, though," said Ellie, opening it. "He did say he wanted to talk to you about it when he got back."

There was no inscription, and the pages, dense with type and small detailed drawings and illustrations, did not invite browsing.

"Maybe you should give it to—" she began to say, when her fingers noticed an irregularity in the middle of a page. A dent.

She looked up sharply at Miss Worthy, who had washed her hands at the kitchen sink and was drying them with a towel.

Ellie pressed the dent. It was circular, and she began flipping pages to see what was causing it. About a quarter of the way in, she came to the place where a hole had been drilled in the center of the page, just wide enough to insert something wrapped in paper.

"Miss Worthy, you need to see this," she said.

Miss Worthy came and sat down to watch as Ellie held the book open with two hands, flipped it over, and shook hard. A paper cylinder inched out.

"Can you pull that?" she asked, and Miss Worthy grasped it and pulled.

"What is it?" she asked.

"A lot of money, I think. Open it and see."

As Miss Worthy removed the paper wrapping, about two dozen small gold coins spilled across the table. Each was meticulously hand carved, exquisitely beautiful, and more than 2000 years old. Astonished, she sat down, and, for several minutes they examined them without uttering a word. The gold glowed softly in the lamplight, but it was the aura the coins gave off that Ellie found most mesmerizing. Worn and misshapen from centuries of being handed down, person to person to person, the carvings of animals, mythical creatures, heroes, and leaders remained recognizable and as expressive as the artist who made them intended.

When Miss Worthy sat back, her eyes glittered with tears. "I can't believe Cleve entrusted me with this treasure all those years ago, and I never knew it. I thought his gift repudiated what we shared, and it was completely the opposite.

"If only I had paid more attention. Understood what he

told me and what was too painful for him to say aloud. He was so upset about Pindar. He must have felt he couldn't leave the collection anywhere in Odyssey House while he was away.

"It's horrible to think that if I had not been such a prideful fool, I might have prevented the tragedy that ruined his children's lives."

Ellie looked at Miss Worthy's anguished face and said, "If only. Could have. Might have. You know you can't take that all on yourself. Cleve shares the responsibility, for one. He could have told you what he was entrusting to your care."

"I suppose he had no idea I would react the way I did. Never look inside."

"I'm not sure, though," said Ellie, who suddenly thought of Pen Whittaker, whose initials were also PW. "He may have understood that you wouldn't—counted on it, in fact—because, not knowing what you had, you would not be at any risk.

"Miss Worthy, I have a very bad feeling about this, and I think you need to put those coins into police custody immediately."

"Why? I can return them to Corinna in the morning."

"No, that's exactly what you should not do. That would be putting her in danger. Don't you see, in her last letter, Clio told Corinna that she had a new idea about where the coins might be. She didn't elaborate, but this book was in her bedroom." Ellie tapped the cover of *Love at War*, with its warm inscription to Cleve from PW.

"Ever since Clio's death, someone has been searching Oak Cottage. And someone broke in and frightened Pen Whittaker to death. Not you. But another PW associated with the Matthews family.

"An easy enough mistake to make, since—I'm guessing—no one in the family knew of your friendship with Cleve, and no one knew back then or even until very recently that Ramona

Blaisdell-Scott was you—a person far more likely to be of interest to Cleve than Pen Whittaker."

"You're saying Clio shared her idea with someone, even though she didn't tell Corinna."

Ellie nodded, and Miss Worthy picked up the phone.

Within less than an hour, DI Mullane had given Miss Worthy a witnessed receipt, and Cleve Matthews' coin collection was in police custody.

Ellie followed him out to the front steps as he was leaving and asked whether a public announcement could be made about the recovery of the coins to end all the speculation about where they were.

"You think that will stop Ms. Matthews' intruder?"

"I think Clio knew the coins were not in the cottage, but she had an idea about where might be, and I think the intruder was looking for any indication of what her idea had been."

"And he didn't find it," said Mullane.

"I think he did find it, but he didn't understand what it meant. Miss Worthy inscribed a book to Cleve Matthews right before his death, signing her name as PW. The intruder could have spotted the significance of that date, without knowing who PW was. He found someone associated with the Matthews family, who had those initials, but it was the wrong one."

"Are you referring to Pen Whittaker?"

Ellie nodded.

"That's why he ransacked her house. But not the cottage."

Ellie nodded again.

"This is all very clever, Mrs. Kent. But extremely far-fetched. This person has now gone to the extent of causing a death in an effort to find coins that no one has seen for fifteen years and could, in fact, be anywhere."

"The odds are long, I know. But think how many people religiously buy lottery tickets week after week. In comparison, the chance to find a million pounds and walk away . . . how could you not pursue it?"

"Up to a point, but I think he's past that point now."

"You're probably right, but I hope an announcement that the game is over will ensure that he doesn't decide to keep looking and find Miss Worthy."

"All right. We won't say anything about where the coins were found, but that they have been turned over to the police. At least it shows some progress," he said and headed back to his car with a million pounds no bigger than a lipstick tube in his pocket.

On her way back to the vicarage, Ellie went by The Chestnut Tree to see whether Michael-John was free. The closed sign hung on the door, but lights were still on in the shop. She would have liked to tell him this latest news, but he was deep in conversation with Jeremy Kidder. Their discussion—which appeared be about a two-foot-tall jade Buddha—looked rather heated, but her passing caught their attention, and they broke off to look in her direction. Michael-John waved, but Jeremy's expression became clouded with resentment, as usual. She smiled anyway and hoped he was not going to be a long-term fixture in her friend's life.

She had been meaning for days to go on Google to find out more about Jeremy, since it felt awkward to ask, and, when she got home and found no one else was there, she went up to her study and did just that.

Jeremy Kidder was indeed from Los Angeles, and he had accounts on Facebook, Twitter, and Instagram. But beyond posting glamorous selfies and vacation shots, he wasn't very active and didn't have many friends or followers. She didn't know why, but she felt disappointed, and maybe even a little suspicious. These days, such totally unrevealing social media accounts struck her as fake. At the same time, she also thought there were plenty of reasons for avoiding social media altogether, as she was reminded when a quick search told her that her latest adventures had been immortalized in the e-universe.

Before she shut down, she remembered that she hadn't yet sent a thank-you email to Janet Shah and used that opportunity to ask her to please send the photos Vijay took of Clio, as she was looking forward to seeing them and sharing them with Corinna.

When Graham and Isabelle arrived back at home, it turned out they had gone to the chippie in Kingbrook to get fish and chips for dinner. The fragrance of freshly fried haddock and potatoes made Ellie realize she was starving, and nothing mattered more than getting the food on the table with plenty of napkins and bottles of beer.

It wasn't until they had eaten and settled back to finish their beers that Ellie broke the news about the discovery of the long-lost coins. Both Graham and Isabelle congratulated her roundly on solving one of Little Beecham's most puzzling mysteries.

Ellie was pleased, but pointed out that she had not really done a thing. "It only came about because Miss Worthy's whole story about Cleve giving her such a strange present made me want to see it."

"Was she really hoping Professor Matthews would propose?" asked Isabelle, wiping her hands and mouth. "I've always pictured him as a scary gnome."

"I don't know, gnomes can be sweet," said Ellie.

"I am certain no one has ever described Cleve Matthews as sweet," said Graham. "But, if he and Priscilla Worthy became friends, I have probably misjudged him at least a little.

"There is one thing that sounds odd to me, though. You said the book held about twenty-five coins."

"About that, yes."

"Then what happened to the rest?"

"The rest?"

"When Cleve showed me his collection years ago, I would have said there were more than fifty coins."

"Half are still not found?" Ellie was shocked. "I hope no one else knows that. I thought when the police announced the collection had been found, that would put an end to the matter."

"Well, if details are released about what has been recovered, anyone who ever saw—or possibly even heard about—the original collection would know," said Graham.

"Then I've got to tell Mullane right away," said Ellie, who pulled out her phone and texted him: *What you have is only half the original collection! Be sure not to announce any details!*

CHAPTER THIRTEEN

Monday, March 19

E llie expected the news about the discovery of the coin collection to be released first thing, but the morning passed without a word. She didn't hear back from Janet Shah either. The surprise came when Graham climbed up to her study to tell her that Geordie and Ruby Murphy's home had been burgled during the night.

"Are they okay?" she asked.

"They're fine," he said. "They were away visiting their son and his family when it happened."

"What was taken?"

"Nothing, as far as I've heard. But the place was ransacked. I must admit, this puts paid to any hope there isn't some connection between the Matthews family and these incidents. All of them have happened since Corinna was released from prison. There must be a reason for that."

"I think you're looking at it from the wrong perspective. It has all happened since Clio wrote that letter. Or rather since she had her new idea about where the coins might have ended up."

Graham stared at her. "Explain, please?"

"It's just my theory," she said, but went on to outline the links among Clio's letter, the dated inscription from PW in the copy of *Love at War*, and the coincidence of Pen, who was connected to the Matthews family, having the same initials as Miss Worthy, whose connection to them was unknown.

"I see. How do the Murphys fit in with your theory?"

"Um . . . they don't. Except they are the only other people in that close circle who were around the family at the time they lived in Odyssey House."

"But they would have returned the collection immediately if Cleve had entrusted it to them. And so would Jock."

"Not if they didn't know they had it any more than Miss Worthy did. But there is another possibility. When he took the book with its buried treasure to Miss Worthy, Cleve Matthews was desperately upset. He'd had a huge row with Pindar about money and didn't know what to do about it."

"That was nothing new."

"Maybe not. But what if Cleve had discovered that Pindar had pinched some of the coins—perhaps as many as half of them—and he did not want to accuse his own son of the theft. At the same time, he also needed to act quickly to protect the rest of the collection while he was away. He wasn't giving it away. He was buying time. And Miss Worthy remembers that he did say they would talk about the book he'd brought her when he returned."

"But instead, he died."

"Exactly. As a result, no one has known until yesterday what he did—or that his death made it possible for the theft of half a million pounds to go undiscovered for all these years."

"Are you suggesting those facts are linked? No one has ever intimated that Cleve's death was suspicious."

"If the situation was as I have described, it was a pretty convenient fatal heart attack."

"But he was in Greece when it happened. And Pindar—if he's the one you imagine stole the coins—never had two bobs to rub together. He was skint all the time. Playing darts for rounds at the pub. Hassling Corinna about his allowance. And, from what I recall, he certainly had no assets at the time of his death."

"You mean none that anyone knew about," said Ellie. "I haven't had a chance to tell you about my latest encounter with Hermione Tuttle. She more or less admitted that she gave Pindar a substantial amount of money right before his death. So where did that go?"

"I don't know, but Winstead's firm should know. They've handled all the family's financial affairs for decades."

"Interesting. Of course, the coins represent a much larger sum than anything Hermione could have given him, but they might have been tricky to turn into cash."

"Maybe, but I expect there are collectors who buy coins for cash on the quiet, just as they do other antiquities and art objects." Graham ran his fingers through his hair as if to rid himself of this whole problem.

"The more you delve into this story, the more complicated it gets! But I can't spend all day thinking about that . . . I've promised to let Isabelle catechize me on whether I do or do not believe Jesus really appeared to the Apostles in the flesh after his death, among other questions."

"That sounds like a great father-daughter activity," said Ellie. "I will be eager to hear all about it later, but I can't talk more now either. I have miles to go and lunches to deliver."

. . .

Before she left her study, though, Ellie checked her email again for any word from Mullane or Janet—and found none—so she went downstairs to help Mrs. Finch pack up the food for The Soup Car. There, she was surprised to find Isabelle, dressed in particularly ratty clothes.

"I thought you and Graham were dissecting the Resurrection today," she said.

"We are," said Isabelle, "but when I gave him my questions, he said he needed some time to prepare. I won't settle for canned answers, you know."

Ellie laughed. "You should probably record this session for posterity."

"I will. But meanwhile, I've offered to help Corinna with her garden. I guess the Murphys used to look after everything for Clio, but they're not coming anymore. So, we're going to do whatever winter clean-up needs to be done. Which I hope she knows, because I don't."

At noon, Ellie was on her way to make her lunch deliveries, when she heard a news report on the radio about the discovery of the long-missing Greek and Roman coins collected by the late Professor Cleve Matthews. The collection was described as valuable, but there was no mention of how valuable or where they had been found.

She had nearly reached her first stop when her phone rang. It was DI Mullane, so she pulled over and hoped no cars would be coming either way on the narrow lane.

"Mrs. Kent," he said in his usual laconic way. "You left me a message about more missing coins, but no details."

"I wanted to be sure that you didn't mention the number of coins or the value, since I learned from Graham that what I found was only half the collection."

"We knew that, actually. Ms. Matthews gave us a list of the coins her father had with the last valuation, made before his death. And Father Kent is right, half are still unaccounted for, including some of the most valuable. Did you know that a single one of those little gold coins can be worth one hundred fifty thousand pounds? Not that the professor had one of those. Still, the ones not found are worth a very tidy sum."

"Oof! Was Corinna upset that so many are still missing?"

"Hard to say. That one keeps her emotions to herself. From long practice, I assume. But when she looked at them . . . her face was very still, but her eyes were angry. I think she knows—or suspects—what happened to the rest."

"I do too," said Ellie. "In fact, I think Pindar Matthews stole them before his father's death, and that's why the professor hid the rest of them in that book and put them in Miss Worthy's care without telling her."

"If that were the case, what happened to them? Or the money?"

"I have no idea. Graham's understanding is that Pindar had no money at the time of his death."

"The rest might be still hidden in some other book."

"True. But hopefully the intruder thinks they've all been found and the jig is up. There's no reason to ransack any more houses."

"That would be nice. Meanwhile, we'll be posting officers to watch the homes of all the people who have been involved so far. Just in case he doesn't get that message."

"You still think this is someone local?"

"Yes, but you might be interested to know that we've been in touch with the French authorities about Clio Matthews' accident. Inquests had to be held both in the UK and France, you know, but the most important witness testified only in France."

"There was a witness?"

"The driver of the car coming from the opposite direction. He reported that the car behind Clio seemed to draw closer just before she went over the cliff."

Ellie was stunned. "And that driver never stopped?"

"No, and the car disappeared into the fog. The witness was too horrified by what happened to even notice the make or color of the car, to say nothing of the number plate."

"Wow."

"Now don't get too excited. I'm telling you this only so you know that we are not neglecting any angles. Do you understand me?"

"Yes, and thank you for the update," she said, but she felt deeply shaken by the possibility that Clio might have been "helped" to her death.

Ellie hoped to be distracted by her visit to Leora Carpenter's neat stone house in Lower Shortfield. But the Matthews family drama followed her there: she found Mrs. Carpenter riveted to her television, watching the follow-up to the news conference about the discovery of the coins.

"Isn't this remarkable!" she said. "Dudley would have been so pleased to know those coins have finally been recovered. Losing them was almost worse than losing Cleve."

"Losing Cleve?" Ellie asked, as she set a tray of lunch on the TV table in the sitting room where Mrs. Carpenter liked to eat.

"Cleve Matthews and my husband, Dudley, grew up together in Birmingham. They began collecting coins when they were young. Old English money at first, but their passion was always the Greek and Roman coins, and that bond held despite their changing circumstances."

"You mean because Cleve Matthews became so renowned?"

"No, I mean because of his marriage to Lady Anne Borden, and then the move to Odyssey House. Cleve and Dudley were both ambitious lads, but it never would have occurred to Dudley to marry a title. Not that Cleve received one by the marriage, of course. He might have earned his own were it not for his early death, but, in the meanwhile, Lady Anne's fortune put him in a completely different circle.

"You probably wouldn't understand such things, dear, but marrying her gave him a standing that the English still bow to, even though Lady Anne was not, in herself, someone who could help his career. She was in ill health, as they used to say, almost from the beginning of the marriage."

"How did they ever meet? I really know nothing about her, but it does sound like an unlikely match."

"I don't recall," she said. "We were living in America at the time, but I remember we were quite surprised to receive the wedding announcement, and to learn, when we returned, that they already had a child." The sideways glance she gave Ellie as she spooned up her mulligatawny soup was prim and proper, but left no doubt about what she wished to convey. Then she looked away to concentrate on buttering her bread, and it was clear she would say no more. Which did not mean Ellie was going to forget this hint that the source of some of the problems in the Matthews family might have stemmed from questions about who Pindar's biological father was.

She also did not want to lose the main thread of their conversation. "It must have been hard for your husband when Professor Matthews died. To lose an old friend so suddenly," she said.

"It was, but the business about the coins made it worse."

"How do you mean?"

"Only a few days after Cleve's death, that son of his showed up and began quizzing Dudley about where the coin collection was. His tone was quite unpleasant. Apparently, the family had already discovered that Cleve hid the coins before he left on his trip and did not tell any of them where they were. Dudley thought Pindar suspected he had the coins himself and planned to keep them. As if he would ever do that!"

"Pindar came right out and accused him?"

"No. He pretended to want Dudley's suggestions about where to look and the best methods. What kind of metal detector would recognize gold and so on. But there was an aggressive undercurrent of hostility, which made it clear what he really thought and what he wanted to know. It was most offensive."

"I take it Dudley had no idea what Cleve had done with the coins."

"No, he didn't, but they both had a low opinion of banks and safes."

"Was that the last you heard about it?"

"No. We came home one day, a few weeks later, and found Pindar in the back garden. He claimed he was only checking because he was concerned that we hadn't heard the doorbell. Dudley thought he was lying—that he might have been trying to break in.

"The police wouldn't say where the coins were found on the news today. Only that they were in the possession of someone who had never been informed about what was entrusted to them. And who never discovered it until now.

"I find it quite unbelievable, but apparently that's what happened. I don't think Dudley ever dreamed Cleve could do anything so slipshod. He was very serious about his small collection's historical importance and being a good custodian for it, not an owner."

"Perhaps it was intended only as a temporary measure. He couldn't know he wouldn't be back in a few days. As I understand it."

"True," said Mrs. Carpenter, but, on Dudley's behalf, her expression said she would never approve.

At George Pinkerton's cottage, Ellie found a very subdued George looking pale and depressed. He was still in his robe and slippers, and, while he did accept a cup of tea, he didn't want to eat. He would save his lunch "for later," he told Ellie and slumped at the table, while his dogs looked anxiously from him to the food she'd brought, then flopped at his feet.

He didn't seem to want Ellie to leave, though, so she sat down with a cup of tea herself and waited for him to talk. So much had happened since her last visit, she couldn't guess what was bothering him.

At last, he said, "I haven't been able to take it in. Pen's death. At my age, you know you're going to lose your friends, but this one has hit me very hard. I knew her and Jock when they were first married. They were cheerful, hardworking young people, eager to learn. Jock became a very good manager, and I always thought Pen knew as much as or more about roses than her brother, Geordie.

"I know things were hard for them later. Jock took the tragedies that happened to the Matthews family to heart, as if they reflected on him as estate manager, and when Miss Clio put the house on the market, he retired. Pen stood by him, though he was that difficult toward the end. And you'd think a good woman like that, who was a widow, could live safely in our midst, but instead she ends up murdered in her own home."

He sighed. "I'll speak plainly, Mrs. Kent. It feels like the anarchy is upon us. We've arrived in the future, and it's even uglier than we imagined. Families are gone, and the villages, farms, churches, and schools are going fast."

He looked at Ellie with a challenging expression, as if daring her to contradict him, but she could not think of anything to say. Besides, his words brought back her own shock over Pen's death.

"I hadn't known her long, of course, but I liked her very much too," she said. "And it may not make you feel any better, but I was with her at the hospital when she died. She wasn't alone, and we've adopted her cat, Barney, who seems to be settling in."

Instinctively he reached down and touched the closest dog's head, as if what she said made him think of his own death and how it would affect his beloved dogs.

Ellie debated telling him more, asking him more. But it didn't seem like the right time, so she only added, "There will be a service at Saint Michael's on Tuesday. If you would like to come, I could work out a ride."

He wiped his eyes with his sleeve and sniffed. "I don't do funerals anymore. I have my own ways of saying goodbye."

"All right, then," said Ellie. "Is there anything else I can do for you today?"

"No, I'm set." He chugged down his tea and then looked at her with clearer eyes. "I should have said right off I'm sorry about what happened to you. That shooting. I knew our Lila was bitter. She felt she lost everything when her bloke died, but I never thought she could be such a fool."

"Well, she did apologize, and I believe she didn't mean anything like that to happen."

"A fool's excuse," he said grumpily. "But at least no one was hurt."

"That's right," said Ellie. "And I expect the police will find the shooter is someone she doesn't even know."

"One can only hope."

Ellie smiled. "You know, you once told me hope was free, and it was just what I needed to hear that day, but I'm passing it back to you now." She would have given him a hug, if he were not hunched down, as if he'd pulled back inside a shell. Instead, for her part, she could only hope that he was listening.

Ellie knew her last stop would cheer her up. Maude and Milly Struthers were in their 90s, and she usually saw them at the Little Beecham Library or tootling around in their vintage English Ford. They were only on The Soup Car list because Maude had slipped on an icy path a few weeks before and broken her leg. That left Milly to keep their household going single-handedly, which she did, but they both welcomed the respite of Ellie's visits.

Identical twins, they wore matching dresses and braided each other's snowy hair to crown their heads, but these days Maude's cast made it easy for Ellie to tell them apart. They lived in the isolated farmhouse where they grew up and kept it exactly as their parents had left it, like a living museum, except for the colorful stacks of library books that came and went each week.

Today they greeted her at the door, excited to share their elation over the discovery of the coins, which they had heard about on the radio.

"Imagine that! All those years in Priscilla Worthy's cottage!" said Milly.

Ellie, who was still taking off her coat, looked at her, alarmed. "How did you know that?" she asked. Mullane had promised there would be no mention of—and she hadn't heard anything about—where exactly the collection was found.

"Oh, we have our ways and means," said Maude, with a cackling laugh.

"Don't worry, we won't tell anyone," Milly promised.

"You just told me!"

"Because, dear Mrs. Kent, we know you were at Priscilla's cottage yesterday and that a certain dashing detective joined you there and spoke to you outside afterward. It was obvious to all that the game was afoot."

"And you put that together with the news conference today?"

"Naturally. And we're dying to hear the details." They looked at her expectantly, but she refused to be drawn in. Instead, she served them their lunch, which they liked to eat on trays in the sitting room, where a fire burned cheerfully, and the sagging old armchairs could be drawn close to its warmth.

"Now?" Milly asked, when they were settled and happily eating.

"No," said Ellie. "Not a word until the person responsible for Pen Whittaker's death has been apprehended."

The sisters exchanged looks, and Maude said, "So it *is* all connected." She liked to read noir mysteries, and no horrible death was too shocking for her, but Milly preferred suspense romance, where no elderly ladies are ever frightened to death.

She clutched a red whistle hanging on a cord around her neck. "Ruby was right, then," she said, her face looking a little pale, even though she was sitting close to the fire.

"Ruby?" asked Ellie.

"Ruby Murphy," said Maude, moving aside her soup plate to focus on her chocolate biscuits. "She called today in a state. She said their house had been burgled—a terrible mess—and she claimed it was all Jock's fault: Pen's death and the danger she and Geordie were in too."

"Jock? As in Jock Whittaker, Pen's husband?" The man who George Pinkerton had just told her felt responsible for what happened at Odyssey House?

Milly nodded. "He ruled them all with an iron fist," she said, and there was something about her tone that made Ellie think she was pleased to be able to use that expression. "Everything at Odyssey House had meet his standards, he would say, when all that meant was he wanted everything his own way."

"But he's been dead for years, I thought."

"Plenty of men control their wives from beyond the grave, and Jock was a great one for keeping Pen in her place," said Maude flatly.

"But what does that have to do with her death now?" asked Ellie.

"Ruby wouldn't say, because Geordie was in the background telling her to be quiet and stop dragging up old stories," said Milly.

"Men never do want a woman to live fully and speak her mind," said Maude. The twins' expressions made it obvious they thought they had made a much better bargain by living together.

"Regardless, it sounds as if she did say she thinks Pen's death is linked to some old story that both Jock and Geordie thought best forgotten," said Ellie.

They nodded. "At least, as far as we can tell," said Maude. "Ruby does sometimes get excited, and the things she says come out in a muddle."

"It takes a bit of persistence to get to the truth, but she doesn't mean to lie. She's always been like that. We went to school with her mother, and she was same way."

Maude laughed. "We're so old we remember when Ruby was Pearl."

"She was a pearl?" asked Ellie, thinking this was a rather colorful compliment.

"Not a pearl. Pearl. That was her name. Pearl Woods. It was Geordie, her husband, who upgraded her to a ruby," said Maude, and the twins snickered.

Ellie tried not to show her surprise at this news of yet another PW. Instead, she asked, "Don't you have any idea what this do-not-tell story is about? I can't believe you haven't guessed."

"We do have a theory," they said in unison, with conspiratorial smiles.

Ellie waited expectantly, while Milly tittered nervously. "We think Pen saw a dead man."

"Jock Whittaker?" asked Ellie.

"Nooooo, not Jock," said Millie. "He's dead."

Ellie turned to Maude, but she was pretending to be fascinated by something out the window. Their little smiles showed they were both entertained by this riddle, and Ellie knew the game could go on for a long time, so she stood up.

"I get it. She saw a dead man who isn't dead. Well, 'tis the season . . . Now tell me about the red whistles."

"They're for protection," said Maude, turning back to Ellie.

"You're not connected to the Matthews family, are you?"

"No, but we decided we should be prepared anyway. Want to hear what they sound like?" she said, producing an ear-splitting screech with her whistle. "No one can take one of us without the other being alerted to call nine nine nine."

"That's brilliant, but I doubt you have to worry," said Ellie.

"You mean the crime wave will stop now that the coins have been found?"

"I should hope so." But the sisters exchanged a look that suggested they didn't believe her for a minute.

Ellie had packed up and was about to leave when she turned and asked the sisters, "If you had to guess who it was that Pen thought she saw—or did see—in the newsagent's shop, who would you say it was?"

"We don't know for sure, but we can give you a clue," said Maude. "Before Geordie shut Ruby off, she told us that Pen wouldn't ever have guessed who it was if it weren't for the lamb crisps."

"Lamb crisps?" asked Ellie, at a total loss.

"You know—crisps! Lamb crisps with mint," and that was the last piece of information Ellie could get from them.

At Oak Cottage, she found Corinna and Isabelle weeding and raking the flower beds, readying them for spring. They didn't need her help, so Ellie offered to make tea for everyone and went inside.

She wanted a few minutes alone anyway. Her thoughts had become impossibly scattered, leaping from one issue to another: the still-missing coins, Pindar's parentage, why Jock felt responsible, what Pen said she saw that upset Jock, the person she did see in the newsagent's shop, and the secret behind the murder. It was hard to figure out what to focus on, but at least she could take this opportunity to look at that tea set in the back of the cupboard again. She had the feeling she had seen it before—in the Pindar Matthews crime-scene photos.

The gilded tea pot, sugar bowl, creamer, four saucers, and two cups were still there. Carefully, she moved everything around so she had a good angle, then took some photos with her phone. Maybe Michael-John could help her determine whether the broken china in the photos came from this set or not. What exactly that would mean she wasn't sure, but she still wanted to find out.

When Corinna and Isabelle came in muddy and tired, Ellie was busy making tea in the Brown Betty pot. Corinna was wearing Geordie's old gardening clothes again and sat down on a kitchen chair with Toby at her side, looking very relaxed. Isabelle beamed with pleasure.

Ellie poured the tea then passed the milk, sugar, and biscuits. Corinna took two, gave one to Toby, then said, "I don't know whether I'll even be here long enough to see what comes up out there, but I could dig in the dirt all day. I love the smell of the soil, and the sun on my head."

"I think, with another day's work, everything will be right and tight," said Isabelle.

"Well, that's more than I can say for the house," said Corinna. "Every time I open another box or drawer, more questions arise, and my list of things to sort out gets longer."

"I volunteered to look at every book and see whether anything else from Odyssey House is hidden there," Isabelle told Ellie.

"You don't think the intruder already did that?"

Corinna frowned. "Who knows? If Isabelle doesn't mind doing it, I'm happy to have her company," and they smiled at each other.

"Were you pleased to hear about the discovery of your father's coins?" asked Ellie, and, to her surprise, Corinna shook her head.

"Frankly, I was sure they were long gone, and I would have expected Clio to believe that as well."

Most people would not grumble about finding out their fortune had just increased by half a million pounds, but, Ellie supposed, in this case, there were extenuating circumstances.

"Were you surprised they were hidden in a book? I'd never seen anything like that before."

"That's because you didn't grow up with my mother. She liked to hide pints of Scotch that way. It was pretty funny to be doing my homework and come across a nice pint for inspiration in a book I needed.

"But we all used that trick at different times. With someone like Pindar around, it was essential to hide anything important to you."

Corinna's expression showed she recognized that they were taken aback. Ellie thought about flat out asking her whether she believed Pindar had stolen the coins that were still missing, but, at the last moment she decided that was going too far, and said instead, "I heard from someone that Pindar was a very talented actor. Didn't he ever try to pursue that?"

Corinna laughed bitterly. "Pindar never wanted to do anything that would have involved so much work. So much rejection. I'm sure he did tell people that's what he was going to do—after all, even he couldn't say he was just waiting around for his inheritance—but the only acting he ever did was in a sixth-form production of *King Lear*. Utterly uncharacteristically, we all went to see the play. My parents, Clio, and I were there along with all the other supportive families.

"He was perfectly typecast as the villain. You know, Edmund, who says, 'Now, gods, stand up for bastards!' He did it extremely well too. Even at the time I thought he'd found himself in that role.

"When he was sent down from Oxford, my father pushed him to apply to RADA, and amazingly enough, he was accepted. But he left after a few months—using the excuse that our mother had died—and he never went back. Personally, I've always thought his real calling was to be a bastard. He had a tremendous talent for that from the get-go. People think I should say I'm sorry about the murder, but the truth of the matter is, I'm no more sorry than I would have been if I had killed a fox in my henhouse."

Ellie gulped and Isabelle paled. Even Corinna blushed, but Ellie thought she was relieved to have said what she did out loud.

None of them could think how to continue the conversation after that revelation. Ellie supposed she should say something about the sanctity of human life, but all she could think of was George Pinkerton talking about people taking an eye for an eye literally, and she wondered whether this was Corinna's way of telling them what happened.

With that in mind, Ellie thanked her for being honest with them and hustled Isabelle out the door.

The girl still looked shaken, as they walked home in the gathering dusk. "You know, when I called her Aunty Corinna today, there was a complete change in her face. It was like I'd reached down into the water and pulled up someone who'd already gone down for the third time. But when she said that about Pindar, I realized I know nothing about her at all. It was kind of frightening."

Ellie put her arm around the girl. "I know what you mean . . . but we all have different faces, don't you think? And I expect she's needed to say that—whether it's the truth or not—for a very long time. I like to think it was a sign she trusts us and felt safe with us."

"You really think that?"

"I do. You have to have someone in your life that you can say your worst thoughts to. It may be one of the reasons things turned out the way they did—Corinna had no one like that in her life. She was friends with your mom, but she probably wanted her to believe she was okay. Coping. And she wasn't."

Isabelle started to cry, and Ellie handed her a tissue. "That makes me so sad," she said. "She could have trusted Mum. I'm sure of it. And then maybe none of this would have happened."

"I'm sure she could have too. And I think she knows it. But at the wrong moment, she didn't."

"I guess I can see that. You know, before all that last bit, she asked me to come back tomorrow, and I'm going to do it."

"Good for you, Isabelle. That sounds right to me. But, you know, if you decide you don't want to go, that's fine too."

CHAPTER FOURTEEN

Tuesday, March 20

T he next morning, when Isabelle had left with Hector for Oak Cottage, and Graham had gone to the church to prepare for Pen's funeral, Ellie headed up to her study. She had just sat down at her desk when she heard a little trilling sound, and Barney appeared in the doorway. He paused there and looked around, assessing the options for cat comfort.

The best strategic location, he decided, was the bookcase, and he leapt neatly to the top, settling himself without disturbing any of the framed photos Ellie kept there. She got up and petted him, talking cat talk and encouraging him, until he began to purr. When she went back to her desk, she felt as if she were purring too. She had so often seen him just so on top of the bookcase in Pen's bedroom.

She had hoped her email would include news from Mullane, but there were no messages from him . . . and obviously keeping her informed was not a top priority. Nonetheless, she sent him a note pointing out that she had learned Ruby

Murphy's maiden name was Pearl Woods, making her the third PW who might have signed the book given to Cleve. Hard as it might be to imagine the plump, motherly Ruby as Cleve's secret friend, there was no way of knowing. It was Mullane's problem to sort out whether this was the reason behind the burglary at the Murphys' home or not.

That done, she turned to two interesting new messages.

The first was from "Ramona Blaisdell-Scott" aka Charlotte Worthy. She wrote: *Aunty thought you'd want to see this message, which I have only read today. Catching up on fan mail after the tour has taken forever.*

An email from Clio Matthews was attached. Although it had been sent to the Ramona Blaisdell-Scott fan email address, Clio had written:

> *Dear Miss Worthy,*
>
> *We have never met, but I recently read a book I found in my family's home in Little Beecham—Love at War by Ramona Blaisdell-Scott, whom I have just learned is you! It was inscribed to my father, Cleve Matthews, right before his death, by 'PW,' and that has made me wonder whether that's your signature, and if it means you and he were friends. If I am right, I would love to meet you and learn more about your friendship. If that is okay with you, I will be in touch the next time I am in Little Beecham.*

It was signed Clio Matthews and gave her Oak Cottage and Paris addresses. The message had been sent on February 15th, only a few days before Clio met her death on her way back to the cottage. A chill wind rattled the window panes, like a sign from the beyond, as Ellie reread the message. Then she wrote to Charlotte and thanked her, asking her to let her know whether Clio had sent any further messages.

Ellie let out what felt like a long-held breath, as she contemplated this validation of her view that *Love at War* had triggered the train of thought leading to Clio's new idea about the missing coin collection. As Ellie recalled, Miss Worthy broke her long-standing anonymity in early December, when she offered to have Ramona Blaisdell-Scott sign copies of her books at the village's Christmas coffee morning. When she went off to the US on her book tour in January, it was widely talked about, and Clio might well have heard of this newly discovered local celebrity. That might even have been what inspired her to pick up a book that had been kicking around the family library for more than 15 years. Ellie could not be sure of the exact sequence of events, but they had led Clio from the book to the inscription to the date to the realization that, on his last night in Little Beecham, Cleve Matthews had both received and given a book. That well-established family vehicle for hiding things.

As she considered the possibilities for the identity of PW, Clio might have first thought of Pen Whittaker—or even Ruby, whose original name she undoubtedly knew. But it was hard to imagine a scenario that would have brought either of those women together with Cleve Matthews as equals. Ellie thought Clio, who knew intimately the dynamics among the Murphys, the Whittakers, and her family, would not have found this likely. On the other hand, Priscilla Worthy aka Ramona Blaisdell-Scott was a much more intriguing possibility, who was simultaneously close at hand and not entangled with the family. Unfortunately, Clio never had a chance to meet Miss Worthy, because she and Charlotte were away for so long, and the message was received too late.

Had Clio's theory progressed to the point where she thought her father had hidden the coins in the book he gave to PW? Was this what she told her unknown friend? Had she even considered what her next step might be if she found PW? Ellie could imagine Clio politely asking what book Cleve had given that night in return . . . but where would she go from there? Not to threats, ransacking, and murder, that's for certain.

The person who did that had managed to get into Oak Cottage before Corinna ever arrived, may have found *Love at War*, and, with some ferreting around in the family papers, may have also discovered Pen Whittaker's name and address and guessed she was the PW involved. When that turned out to be a false trail, he must somehow have unearthed the connection to Ruby.

For Clio, the search may have been simply a matter of curiosity—she certainly had not made the recovery of the coins a priority before—but the intruder wanted results. He wanted to get his hands on those coins—and, if they were gone, he wanted the money taken by someone who had never let on that they were in possession of them. Perhaps he saw an opportunity for blackmail.

That would explain the motive for his repeated visits to the cottage, and the rage he felt when Pen denied knowing what he was talking about and could not give him what he wanted: money. Ellie thought he must be very angry now, knowing that he had been on the right trail and the treasure had been sitting there for the taking, but he missed it. And, instead, he had added to his troubles by causing Pen's death.

When she considered the mysterious sighting in the newsagent's shop, Ellie thought Mullane was right—the friend to whom Clio confided had to be a local person who also had some long-ago association with Pen. She hoped the police were exploring any and all connections they might have had, since this was certainly not something she could do.

There was still no email from Mullane, so she put a call in and left a voicemail, then remembered she had become side-tracked and never looked at the other message that had caught her eye earlier: from Janet Shah.

She clicked it open and saw that Vijay had remembered the name of the man he met with Clio in Paris: Edmund. He had described him as a pleasant man, probably French, and he thought they were on affectionate terms. Unfortunately, he hadn't caught the man's surname or any other information about him.

Quickly Ellie downloaded the attached photos from the gallery opening. And there they were. Clio, who bore a striking resemblance to Corinna with her fine-boned features, fair skin, and dark hair and eyes, looked very beautiful in a black sequined jacket and black silk pants, drinking champagne as the guests admired her marionettes and sculpture. Edmund, who stood by her side, was good looking, also with dark eyes, longish dark hair, and a neat beard and mustache. Ellie thought he looked like the quintessential arty and elegant Frenchman, and Clio's expression when she turned toward him was lit with happiness. It was hard to accept that those moments of success were only a bright flash before the end of her life.

Ellie sighed and closed her computer. There were so many aspects of this story that she could do nothing about. The whole notion of solving a mystery implied you could achieve some resolution. Make a difference. Despite her desire to "pick up Louise's flag," as Morag described it, Ellie couldn't see that happening with the tangled fates of the Matthews children. Which did not mean she had any intention of giving up. With a farewell pat to Barney, she picked up the folder of printed-out crime-scene photos and headed over to The Chestnut Tree.

There, she was in luck. There were no customers in the shop, and Michael-John was at his desk playing Solitaire on his computer with Whistler sleeping on his feet.

"No Jeremy today?" she asked, trying not to sound hopeful.

He lifted an eyebrow. "Kidder? No. A man was never more aptly named. He's not here—and I suspect he's off home by now."

"As in gone back to the States?"

"I have no idea. I was never privy to his plans. Definitely a fly-by-night, that one. Did you want to see him for some reason?" His voice had an edge to it.

"No, not especially, but it was sort of a novelty to have another American around."

"Is that what he was?"

"What do you mean?" Ellie could tell Michael-John was not joking.

"I wondered," he said.

"Well, that's easy to do, isn't it? After all, what's an American? Every kind of mongrel. Every of kind immigrant. Why did you think he wasn't?"

"Little things he did made me think he might be a Brit."

"No kidding. Did he eat with his knife and fork in the wrong hands?"

"No kiddering. But let us not waste time talking about him. He turned up. We had some fun. He stole from me, and he's gone. Now I'd much rather have a comfortable coze with you. We haven't done that this age, and I suspect you are at the center of more exciting news. Missing treasure recovered in a Cotswold village."

"You're right that we haven't had a chance to talk, but don't change the subject. Are you saying Jeremy Kidder stole from you?"

"Oh, yes. He made off with a few choice items, but it's my own fault. I knew from the moment he turned up that there was probably something amiss, but I went along with him anyway," he said, with a shrug. "What can I say. Sometimes I'm just in the mood to accept whatever role a bloke is playing. Pretending to have money when you're skint is one of the least original, but he had other endearing qualities."

"Such as being an Englishman pretending to be American in England. That's pretty inventive."

Michael-John gave her a look. "I wouldn't overrate his performance, but, in the end, it doesn't really matter. I have insurance."

"It matters if he might have stolen from other people during his brief sojourn here."

"Are you thinking of Corinna? Jeremy would never waste his energy on that kind of campaign. He was more the spot-and-grab type."

"You don't think the possibility of finding the missing coins would have attracted him?"

"If they were in a case in front of his eyes, I'm sure he would have noticed they were gold and wanted them. But otherwise, not. I would guess Jeremy's knowledge of the Greeks begins and ends with salad. Now tell me what else our local Nancy Drew has been up to."

"Sniffing in circles. In fact, I am beginning to feel like Seamus's description of Toby. Corinna's bloodhound. He says he couldn't find his own dinner at ten paces."

"I don't believe it."

"You should. I keep developing theories and end up back at the start with Corinna's killing Pindar for reasons never divulged. And I don't have a clue who's been harassing her or if he's really involved in anything else that's happened."

"You think that was all the same person?"

"I have no idea, really. The police are investigating."

"That doesn't sound like you. You found the famous missing coins, didn't you? Not that anyone is supposed to know that, but, of course, everyone does. And that means, surely you're only a few steps from solving the murder too."

Ellie laughed. "But which murder? That's what I came to talk to you about."

"I'm going to help solve a murder? This puts a fresh spin on my day. What's up?"

"I need your expert advice on the subject of china. Did Corinna show you her great-grandmother's tea set yet? Porcelain gilded and painted with flowers?"

"The Meissen? She did, briefly. It's too bad she doesn't have the whole set, but even the separate pieces are fine enough to attract interest."

"Okay, so here's the question. Can you tell me whether the same china appears in these photos?" She pulled out her printouts of the crime-scene photos that were in the news.

"Blimey. Whoever took these was not aiming to give us a clear look at the china pattern. There's too much blood all over everything." He wrinkled up his nose, then pulled a magnifying glass out of his desk drawer and studied the photos intently.

"What you think?" asked Ellie, trying not to sound impatient.

"In the wide world of objects, I couldn't swear it was the same pattern from these horrible photos. But given the assumption that they were taken at Odyssey House, I would say it's unlikely that any other china so similar to Lady what's-her-name's could possibly have wound up on the floor in that scene."

Ellie let out the new breath she'd been holding.

"Is that important?" he asked.

"I'm not sure," she admitted. "Something about it bugs me. Maybe it's because when Clio broke one of the cups long ago, her mother wouldn't even throw away the pieces. With that image in my mind, it seems strange to think Corinna would have used that china for every day, you know?

"Also, when I think about it . . . Louise went by the house at ten o'clock, and Corinna seemed to have gone to bed. But based on what that scene shows, she must have gotten up later and gone to work in the library, taking along a cup of tea made in her great-grandmother's gilded china. At some point later, Pindar came home from the pub, they had a fight that turned violent, during which the desk overturned and the cup was broken, and then she killed him, dragged his body to her car wrapped in a tarp, drove to the coast, dumped the body, came back, and went upstairs without a backward glance at the library, stripped off her clothes, and put them in the hamper. Then passed out until Clio arrived later that morning."

"Are you joking?"

"No. It does sound mad, though, doesn't it?"

"It sounds like something you made up."

"Fifteen years in prison says I didn't."

"Crikey. Well, I'm glad she didn't use that beautiful Persian rug to dump the body, but I don't suppose it ever got clean again."

"Michael-John!" said Ellie.

"Sorry. You know what they say. The devil is in the details, and it's your challenge to figure out who the devil is. I'm afraid I'm not much use with that. I have a history of focusing on the wrong things. Blue eyes instead of sticky fingers, for example."

"We all suffer from that disease, I expect. But, regardless, this has been very helpful. Maybe. I'll let you know. For now, I have to run. I have a funeral to attend."

At the vicarage, though, she found Seamus MacDonald and another boy she guessed must be Simon Stephens sitting on the front stoop, waiting for her. Simon was the kind of thin, gangly teen who looked as if he'd grown a foot overnight. He smiled nervously as Seamus introduced him.

"It's nice to meet you at last, Simon," said Ellie. "Has something happened?"

"No. We heard about the coins," said Seamus, sounding downcast. "I knew I was right they were still around. I only wish we'd been the ones to find them." When he looked up at Ellie, his eyes searched her face for signs that she knew what happened.

But she feigned innocence, and said, "Lots of investigations are long shots. It doesn't mean you give up."

"I suppose you're right," he said. "I'm out of business at the moment, though. Mum won't even let me continue the badger research project. As if that could get me into trouble!"

"We were also wondering whether you'd heard anything about the shooter," said Simon.

"I haven't. But that doesn't necessarily mean there hasn't been any progress. You haven't seen that man again, have you?"

"No," said Simon, "and I've been checking as often as I can. At all hours, you know?"

"Is that a wise idea? You know that man has a gun."

"But I'm invisible," said Simon.

"To a badger, maybe. But, you're not Harry Potter, and a man whose life may be at stake will be watching for you every bit as carefully as you might be watching for him."

"Well, the police can't be there, and no one else is looking out," he said, leaving the important words "for Corinna" to Ellie's imagination.

Seamus could sense a criticism coming and jumped in to deflect it. "You have a good point, Guv. But there is another thing we wanted you to know. Remember I told you about Simon seeing the man watching the cottage? Well, I got the days mixed up. The second time was not the Sunday. It was the Saturday. You know, weekend before last."

"Really. That's interesting," said Ellie, trying to calculate whether it made a difference. The Saturday before last was the day she first met Corinna. And Sunday was the day she met Jeremy Kidder. The man who had done his best to inveigle himself into Michael-John's life, stolen from him, and disappeared. He had had an alibi for Sunday, as far as the cottage was concerned, but what had he been up to on Saturday?

"Is it important?" asked Simon. His spotty face flushed.

"It might be. I'm not certain it matters, but it's always good to have the facts straight," she said, and the boys looked gratified. "You've both been a big help, you know. But do be sure to tell the police if you learn anything at all."

"Sure thing, Guv," said Seamus, who gave her a salute as they mounted their bikes and rode off.

Only a small group gathered in the church for Pen Whittaker's funeral. They were elderly people, most of whom Ellie did not know, but she recognized the Murphys; Pen's neighbor, Mrs. Sanders; and the visiting nurse. Graham had asked Mr. Dunn to provide music, and his heartfelt playing made up for their few voices singing.

After the service and burial, Ellie served tea, sandwiches, and cake in the church for those who wanted an opportunity to spend time together. The atmosphere was subdued, and she wondered how she could manage to talk with the Murphys, if they didn't come to the table for tea.

When she saw Geordie begin to shepherd Ruby toward the door, she decided she couldn't wait and left the table unattended to join them. "Mr. Murphy," she said, stepping between them and the exit. "I am so sorry about your sister's passing.

And the break-in at your home. This must have been a terrible time for you both."

Geordie's eyes were red, but he mustered up his dignity and said, "I hope you're not suggesting there is a connection between those events, because there isn't. Crime in our area is on the rise, as it is everywhere."

Ellie was about to say something conciliatory and agreeable, when Ruby began to sob.

"Oh, Geordie, you know that's not the way it was, and I can't bear pretending anymore."

He gripped her around the shoulders as if to force her out the door, but Ruby grabbed Ellie's arm and wouldn't let go.

"They would never believe Pen could be right about anything. And look what happened." Angrily pulling away from her husband, she said, "I blame you both. You and Jock. Instead of listening to her, you left her to this fate."

"Don't be daft, Ruby," said her husband in a hard undertone. "I know you loved Pen, but she was my sister, and I could see her with a clear eye."

"Are you referring to that encounter at the newsagent?" asked Ellie. "Where the man recognized her? Did she tell you whom she thought it was?"

"That has nothing to do with anything," insisted Geordie. "Pen was always imagining she saw people from the past. The week before, it was one of our schoolmates—and before that, my first sweetheart. Both long dead."

"She was certain this was different," said Ruby, "because he knew *her*. And besides she told me about the crisps."

"The crisps?!" said Ellie. "You mean the lamb-flavored crisps?"

Ruby flushed, surprised that Ellie could know about this, but she nodded, before Geordie cut them both off.

"I don't what bollocks you're talking now, but my sister certainly didn't die from eating crisps."

Ellie looked from one to the other as fiercely as she could. "Of course not. But don't you think it might be helpful to the police to tell them everything? What she suspected? Or even imagined?"

Geordie shook his head. "We have told them the truth. That's what they need. She was getting daft. Completely confused. That coroner was off his nut. My sister could have had that stroke any time these past five years. Ask her GP. Watching the telly could have set her off. There was no need to shame her and the family by calling it murder."

Ruby flinched at the word "murder" and dropped her hold on Ellie.

"I don't know what business it is of yours, Mrs. Kent," said Geordie, "but I think I've been as plain as plain can be. Now we just want to go home and mourn our loss, if it's all the same to you."

"Of course," said Ellie. "But one last question. Did Clio ever ask you for Pen's address?"

Ruby looked startled. "Yes, she did. Not long ago. And I left it for her at the cottage. She said something about wanting to keep in touch, which was exactly the kind of thoughtful thing she would do."

Geordie turned from one to the other with a look of baffled anger, then hurried his wife to their car, and drove off.

"I'm certain Ruby Murphy knows the identity of the person Pen saw," said Ellie, as they settled in the sitting room after the funeral. She kicked off her shoes, and Graham stretched out on the sofa. "She wouldn't tell me the name," she continued, "but she did admit that Clio asked for Pen's address, and she left it at the cottage, meaning Corinna's intruder could have found it there."

"That's news," said Graham. He sat up, suddenly paying more attention. "It sounds like some of these threads are beginning to link up. I hope you're keeping in touch with Mullane."

"I am," Ellie promised. "And I'm convinced I was right. The starting point had nothing to do with Corinna's release. It was Clio's idea about what Cleve did with the coins—and the person behind what's happened has been trying to follow some trail based on what little she told him."

"But now the coins have been found."

"Yes, and I am sure that person is fit to be tied to discover he went after the wrong PWs."

"How many PWs did he have to choose from?"

"As far as he knew, Pen Whittaker and Pearl Woods."

"Who in heaven's name is Pearl Woods?"

"You know her as Ruby Murphy, but I learned from Maude and Milly Struthers that her real name is Pearl and her maiden name was Woods."

"Good Lord, you certainly do get around, Ellie. It's no wonder the police can't keep up with you. But I hope you never once imagined that the august professor Cleve Matthews had a romance with his housekeeper, and they kept it a secret by using her maiden name." He could hardly hold back his laughter. "If you had ever known Cleve, believe me, that would be the last theory you'd come up with."

"I know that," said Ellie, feeling a bit indignant. "But the intruder wouldn't have, and anyway, we now know Miss Worthy was the PW, and she is worth the attention of any number of august professors."

"Okay, but you've still lost me. What does this have to do with whatever Pen saw that Jock thought was meaningless. Did it have to do with Cleve? The coin collection?"

"I don't know. Yet."

"If you ask me, the problem is there are too many characters in this plot. It's a kaleidoscope. You twist it to see Corinna's stalker, the prank-playing intruder, the hate-letter writer, the mystery man Pen saw, the one who broke in and terrified her, the shooter, the one who burgled the Murphys . . . I mean, really."

"I know. You can eliminate the letter writer, though. Hermione admitted she has been sending Corinna's hate mail for years. And the rest of those letters were from Lila's cohort."

"That's something anyway. But, please, may we change the subject? Burials always throw me into a kind of netherworld, and it takes me a while to feel like I've returned to planet Earth."

"Speaking of which, how was your discussion of the Resurrection with Isabelle?"

"I have to say, it was exhausting. I never realized what a terrier she could be. Clearly, she takes after Hector more than her mother or me. But I'll tell you more about that later. Let's have our tea now, and I want a shot of whiskey in it tonight."

"Sure thing, but I am going to call Mullane first. He needs to press the Murphys to get that story, even if it turns out to mean nothing."

"Okay, do that. But, afterward, I want you all to myself."

Ellie grinned and kissed him. "Deal."

Warmed by tea with whiskey and a steak and kidney pie with wine, Graham and Ellie ended up stretched out together on the sofa in the sitting room. The room was shadowy, lit only by candles, and there was so little space between them—bodies, hearts, and minds—that Ellie felt merged. A pleasant, no, delicious feeling.

When the doorbell rang, they had to untangle their limbs and straighten their clothes to answer the door. It was after 9 p.m., but there was DI Mullane, and he looked grim.

"I received your messages, and we moved fast, but not fast enough," he said. "Ruby and Geordie Murphy have left town. Disappeared. Even their son claims not to know where they went, but the neighbor said they drove off in their campervan with their dog shortly after returning from Mrs. Whittaker's funeral. Can you tell me anything about the funeral that would explain that?"

"Yes, and it's probably my fault they took off," said Ellie. "I tried to get Ruby to tell me what Pen said about the man she ran into at the newsagent's shop. I'm certain she told Ruby who it was. Or thought it was. And, if Ruby didn't want to tell me, I said she should at least give you the information.

"She didn't get much of a word in, though. Geordie kept insisting that Pen was always mixing people up, and he was sure she never saw anyone. He claimed her stroke was probably brought on by something she saw on television."

"If a telly can bruise your throat, he might be right. Otherwise, that wasn't it."

"No, I guess not."

"I received that other message about Mrs. Murphy and her maiden name. That does suggest there is a pattern to these break-ins."

"Great," said Ellie with a smile and turned to go back inside. But he put out his hand and touched her arm.

"Just remember, Mrs. Kent. You watch yourself. Local or not, there is a desperate and reckless person involved in this who does not want to be identified. And we've seen what he's capable of."

"Righto," she said, thinking this was same advice she gave the boys.

"I'll say one thing for you, though," added Mullane. "I'm increasingly convinced these events do have their origin in what happened in the past."

"You mean, it isn't just about missing treasure. Louise was right that the whole story did not come out back then."

"Don't start gloating yet," he said, and then he turned to leave, but stopped. "I almost forgot. We've pulled a selection of photos from our files, and we're asking everyone who had even a glimpse of the man following Ms. Matthews and so on to come in and take a look. There's very little to go on, but hopefully it will begin to narrow down the scope of our search. Tomorrow morning would be good if you can do it then."

"Sure," said Ellie. "Tomorrow morning."

He nodded curtly, remembered to give her the barest of smiles, and then was gone.

She had no sooner closed the door than the phone in the kitchen rang. Ellie went to answer it and was surprised to hear Corinna's voice. "Could you come over?" she asked.

"Has something happened?"

"I don't know. I thought you might be able to help me decide."

"Of course," said Ellie, who was so flattered she grabbed a sweater, told a surprised Graham where she was going, and stepped out into a starry night.

The air was balmy and, walking up the B road, Ellie felt that spring was finally coming to stay. At the cottage, she found Corinna sitting at the kitchen table with the two gilded tea cups and four saucers in front of her. She looked agitated, and her ashtray was full of cigarette butts.

"What's going on?" asked Ellie, her skin prickling with expectation.

"Michael-John stopped by this afternoon," she said, "and he asked to look at this tea service again. He said he might know someone interested in it."

"That's great. It looks very valuable," she said, thinking Michael-John had certainly not wasted any time in following up on their conversation.

"That's what he told me, but when he asked what happened to the other cups, I remembered something, and it's linked to that tape I played for you."

"Really?" This was not what Ellie expected to hear.

"Clio did break one when we were young, but I broke one too."

Ellie waited for whatever was coming next with her hands clenched in her pockets. She focused on keeping her expression interested, but neutral.

"It happened the night of that fight," Corinna said, tapping the cassette player, which was still on the table. "I've listened to that recording over and over, and I finally remembered the day. It was about a month after my father died. Pindar was furious about not getting a lump-sum inheritance and was fighting hard against the trust. He was so outrageous—insulting to Cleve, me, and everyone else he could think of—that I just lost it. I threw my teacup at him, which only made him laugh, because when I saw what I'd done, I felt as shattered as the cup."

Ellie didn't know what to say. Corinna had finally remembered something, and it couldn't be true.

"Are you sure you broke the cup that night?"

"Absolutely. I was so ashamed, I cleaned everything up myself, and I buried the pieces in the garden."

"You buried them?" That didn't sound like something you could forget. But it didn't fit. There were two cups left, and, if Corinna's memory were correct, there should be only one.

Ellie took a deep breath. "The thing is, Corinna, the crime-scene photos from the night Pindar died also show one of those cups shattered on the floor."

Corinna's expression became confused. "That's impossible. I may have been drunk every night back then, but I wasn't in the habit of flinging around Meissen china. I buried that cup right by the arbor at the entrance to the rose garden."

"But your memory might still be mixing things up. You might have broken some other dish the night of the recorded fight—that's what you can hear on the tape—while your visual memory is from the crime-scene photos."

"I never looked at those photos. Believe me, I didn't need to. I see what you mean, though. How can there be two cups left?"

They both looked at the heavily gilded cups as if willing them to tell their story, and it occurred to Ellie that no one since the time of the murder would have questioned how many cups there should be. Only Pindar and Corinna knew about the one she broke in that earlier fight. And after the murder it would be the last devil in the details to be noticed. Pindar was dead, Clio had fled, and Corinna was under arrest.

"I don't suppose Clio could have bought a replacement sometime later," suggested Ellie.

Corinna shook her head.

"Or your intruder brought one as a present."

Corinna lit a cigarette. "Of the two ideas, I would call that the more likely."

"Really," said Ellie. The stirring of anxiety she felt was the kind that came before inspiration. "Does that mean you've figured out who the intruder is?"

Corinna looked away toward the window and blew out a long stream of smoke. "No. But you've certainly put your finger on something odd. There are too many cups, and only two people who would know that."

"Is that why you asked me to come over?"

Corinna said nothing. She stroked Toby's head absently. "No. Not exactly. I wanted to say something, but now I am not so sure." She picked up the two cups and turned them over. Ellie could see the markings on the bottom of each cup were identical.

"Would it help to listen to the tape again?" Ellie asked.

"No. I know what happened that night. It's the night of the murder that's a blank. Can you imagine what that's like?"

"I can't, and I've tried to. But it must make it a bit easier that you know why you did what you did. And I don't for one second believe you've ever thought it was on a par with killing a fox."

"You'd be wrong about that." She paused, fixing Ellie with a long look, and then put out her cigarette. "I would never for one second put killing a hen or a fox on a par with my own father's death," she said.

Ellie stared. In the circle of light from the converted kerosene lamp, Corinna's eyes were dark and deep, unfathomable not in anger, but sorrow, and Ellie understood what she had been told.

It was after midnight, and Ellie and Graham were in the sitting room, facing each other from opposite ends of the sofa. Two candles were lit, sending shadowy light over their faces. The fire had died down, and Barney sat on the hearthrug, watching the coals flicker and die. Hector and Isabelle had gone to bed.

"Clio was the one who stumbled on the evidence," said Ellie, in a low voice. "That Sunday morning, she'd planned to embroider one of Pindar's shirts as a present for his upcoming birthday, and when she looked into his closet to pick one, she saw something she didn't understand. There was a box with what looked like a pepper grinder, a jar of white powder, a sort of press, some tiny molds, and an empty bottle of Cleve's heart medication.

"She was disturbed enough to fetch Corinna and show her what she'd found. Neither of them could tell what was in the jar, but it was apparent that Pindar had been playing pharmacist. And the goal seemed clear: to tamper with their father's medication in a way that could precipitate his death.

"Corinna was certain this must have been exactly what happened. They left everything in the closet as it was, but Clio was very upset, and Corinna's one thought was to get her away from the house and Pindar. She made her agree to go to Oxford as planned and spend the night with her friends. She also made Clio swear that she would say nothing, act normal, and not worry.

"When Corinna confronted Pindar later that night—as she assumes she did, since she can't remember it—his reaction led to the fight that ended in murder. As she sees it, all she did was avenge Cleve's death in a way that drew the attention and blame to herself and buried the truth she believed was the last thing her father would ever have wanted to come out.

"She told me her only regret came later when she realized that Clio blamed herself, because, if she had kept Pindar's secret—as he would surely have expected her to do—Corinna would never have known what he did, and he would have not died."

Graham's face looked drained of color when he finally spoke. "I can't say I'm surprised to hear that Pindar was capable of killing, but why did Corinna not come to us for help? That breaks my heart more than anything else."

"I don't know," said Ellie. "She must have been in a terribly lonely dark place, because otherwise she would have done that, and she didn't."

CHAPTER FIFTEEN

Wednesday, March 21

In the morning, Ellie went straight to her study. She wanted to think about what to do next. Corinna's story was still her secret, and Ellie would honor that. But she studied the crime-scene photos again, remembering the scenario she described to Michael-John that now seemed so wrong. Impossible.

When the phone rang, she answered on the first ring, expecting it to be Mullane. Instead, she heard Morag's stressed-out voice say, "Can you tell me what the hell Derek is up to?"

DI Mullane was an old hunting buddy of Morag's ex-husband, Oliver, so Morag always called him Derek, but Ellie had to think twice to remember that.

"Why is he demanding that Seamus come to the Chipping Martin Police Station when he should be at school? Is there some sort of emergency that no one told me about?"

"No. No emergency, as far I know," said Ellie, doing her best to convey calm sympathy. "It is important, though. He's trying to identify the person involved with a number of crimes, including that shooting last week. The police think he's local, so they're asking a number of people to look at the photos of past troublemakers they have on file. I've been asked to come in too."

Morag was silent for a moment. "Seamus says he didn't see a thing except a man in black with a gun. Is there more he hasn't been telling me? I mean, I thought all that time he was spending with Simon Stephens was about some school project on badgers, and now I don't know what they were doing, but I hope I've put a stop to it."

"They were definitely observing the badgers," said Ellie, not wanting to tell her anything Seamus should have told her himself. About the treasure hunt, for example. "I expect Simon has also been asked to look at the photos."

"God. Those woods are private property! It seems like no place is safe anymore, but I guess it's important for them to participate and do their civic duty. And you too.

"How are you, by the way? I'm sorry I haven't been in touch. Right when I was ready to close down my interior design business, I was invited to take on an interesting project, so I've been working flat out."

"I'm fine, although it has been a strange couple of weeks."

"I should say. I gather you haven't solved Louise's murder mystery." She sounded more pleased than not, so Ellie said only, "No, you're right about that. I haven't." Then they rang off, with promises to get together soon.

Ellie didn't blame Morag for wanting Seamus not to be pulled further into a murder investigation, but she was also irked by that casual summation of her own efforts. Failure. Before leaving, she decided to look through Louise's research again. Perhaps there was something she had missed. But as carefully as the information was laid out about why what happened could have happened, step-by-step, there was nothing that said it couldn't have happened or may have happened another way.

Then she thought again about the cup Corinna said she buried under the rose arbor. If her memory were true, it should still be there . . . but then how did that explain the broken china in the crime-scene photos? Ellie had no idea, but the next step seemed clear. She sent Seamus a text telling him that she had a job for the High Street Irregulars. Then as clearly as she could, she outlined what he and Simon should do.

Ellie hoped to have a word with Seamus at the police station, but she never saw either of the boys. In fact, the only person she did see was Corinna, who was ashen and clearly angry, as she was escorted into an interview room. Ellie looked frantically for Mullane to ask him what was up, but he was nowhere about, and the young constable who ushered her into a separate room said he knew nothing except that everyone was being asked to look at the photos separately. Then Ellie was left alone with a computer database to review all the people arrested over the past few years for crimes similar in nature to the ones in question. She thought mug shots made everyone look unsavory and was unable to pick out any person who seemed like a possible suspect.

Then she was taken to meet with the constable who was working with Identi-Kit software in an effort to create a composite picture of the man.

"I'm getting the impressions from everyone who had contact with the person, and then I'll do some mergers to see what we get," explained Sheelagh O'Reilly, a young WPC with a pleasant Irish lilt to her voice.

"I only saw him once, you know," said Ellie, "and it was more than a week ago. I was looking out my bedroom window on the second floor, and he was down in the street, so I saw him from a strange angle, and he was standing in the shadows."

"That's fine. Just talk to me about what you saw. Your details might jibe with the memories of others, you see."

Sheelagh took down Ellie's details, then ran the program that combined them with what the other witnesses had seen. The result she came up with was disappointing, but more or less what Ellie suspected: a tall, slenderly built man wearing dark clothes and a hooded jacket.

"I don't see how that can help. It's so generic."

Then Sheelagh showed her the different poses that the other witnesses described. Suddenly, the man became almost animated, and Ellie was reminded of the photos Janet sent.

"Hold on a minute. I want to show you some photos of someone else," said Ellie opening her phone to the pictures of Clio and Edmund at the gallery opening in Paris. He had been dressed in black slacks, a dark turtleneck, and an expensive leather jacket.

"Who is that?" asked Mullane, who walked into the room at that moment.

"Clio Matthews' boyfriend, Edmund, a French art dealer or something. That's all I know about him, but he could be someone Clio confided in about the missing coins. He would be a stranger here, but he would have known where she lived and that she had died. So, he might have thought he could come and take a look himself."

"Perhaps. But why would such a person hang around after Corinna moved in? It's one thing to imagine you might scoop up a valuable collection when no one is looking, and another altogether to hang around harassing people you've never met, who are extremely unlikely to have what you were looking for."

Ellie knew he was right, but said, "Who knows what stories Clio might have told him about the whole Odyssey House setup?"

"I suppose, but I don't buy it."

"Then all you've got is nothing. This generic man in black. Not very helpful."

Mullane shrugged as if he were unfazed, while Ellie kept scrolling back and forth between the photos of Clio and Edmund trying to figure out why she couldn't let this go. Then she recognized what it was.

"Wait a minute. There's another possibility. If Edmund's hair were dyed blond, and he shaved his beard and mustache, put on different glasses and colored contact lenses, I think he might resemble an American who has been visiting this area over the past two weeks."

Mullane looked surprised. "Who is that?"

"His name is Jeremy Kidder. He's from Los Angeles and supposedly has interests in real estate and investing. Antiques. Art. He turned up at The Chestnut Tree and more or less attached himself to Michael-John Parker. I met him a couple of times."

"And is there some way he's connected to Clio or Corinna Matthews?"

"Not that I know of. But yesterday Michael-John mentioned that some things he said made him think Jeremy was really English. Pretending to be American."

"Not French."

"No, but the idea that Clio's boyfriend was French was only an assumption on the part of a Brit who met him in Paris. On top of the fact that his name is Edmund . . . and the way he dresses looks French."

"You think Edmund and Jeremy could be same person?

Why bother with a disguise? No one here would have known Edmund anyway."

"Camouflage? Michael-John said he lifted some things from his shop before he left."

"He's gone? When?"

"Yesterday, the day before. Michael-John thinks he's gone back to America."

"Very helpful, as always, Mrs. Kent." He stood up and told Sheelagh, "See what you can do with those photos following her directions. I want some kind of photos of both men as soon as possible.

"This may come to nothing, but at least it's a lead. A person to pursue rather than a shadowy silhouette. If you have any more interesting theories, let me know," he said to Ellie, and he was gone before she could even say goodbye.

At home, the house was quiet except for the sound of Mrs. Finch's vacuum running upstairs. Isabelle had agreed to do The Soup Car run because Ellie had been unsure how long her business at the police station would take. She hadn't left yet, though. The lunch boxes were still lined up on the table in the kitchen.

Ellie opened the hall door, hoping to find Graham in his study, but she paused when she heard voices.

"That is *not* an answer!" she heard Isabelle say. "And I don't see how you can do your job, if you don't really believe that long list of things in the creed we're always saying!"

She heard Graham start to reply, but Isabelle suddenly stormed out of the study, and Ellie barely had time to let the hall door swing shut and avoid being seen. She waited until the girl had stomped all the way up the stairs to her room before she slipped across the hall.

"Yeow," she said, as she entered the study, where Graham sat at his desk, looking rather shell-shocked. "That was a quite an exit."

He gave her a wan smile. "Even the most intellectual and educated of spiritual seekers can be reduced to childish shrieking by the unanswerable questions of life."

Ellie laughed and gave him a hug. "Do you really believe the creed, chapter and verse? I've wondered myself."

"I tried to tell her I have my own way of thinking about it—and it's rather more Emersonian than the strictest of Anglicans would attest to—but she's entitled to work out her own way."

"Emersonian? As in Jesus wasn't the capital S son of God? Well, I'm glad, even if she's not," and she gave him a kiss. "You're a good man, Charlie Brown. Especially when you don't claim to have all the answers."

"Thank you," he said, kissing her back. "Just don't tell Charles or Mary Bell what I said."

"My lips are sealed."

"So, tell me what's happening with the police investigation," he said.

"You mean you think this Jeremy Kidder and Clio's Edmund are one and the same art thief?" asked Graham when she had filled him in on her morning at the police station.

"There's definitely a resemblance. Look at the photos and what the police did with them," she said, handing him her phone so he could see the doctored photo of Edmund that transformed him into Jeremy. "He could have been playing the role of the mystery man who's been around too. After all, Edmund might well have seen Clio's death as a great opportunity to pick up a bit of the ready."

"Does that mean he was the shooter as well? Why on earth would he want to shoot Corinna? Or you? Or anyone? It sounds as if he were already doing quite well ripping off Michael-John."

Ellie sighed. "I know. You're right. The shooting doesn't fit, although, I must say, every time I saw Jeremy, he seemed very resentful of me and liked to make cracks about my having been involved with solving mysteries."

"Well, hopefully Mullane can track him down quickly. He may be a piece of the puzzle. And, if not, that will quickly become clear too."

After lunch, Ellie walked over to Oak Cottage to see whether Corinna had recovered from her trip to the police station. The car was in the drive, but the door was unlocked, so she went in and poked her head into the kitchen. The Meissen china and cassette player had been put away, but the gold coin necklace lay on the table.

Thinking Corinna and Toby must be in the garden, Ellie was about to go through the back door when she heard footsteps in the hall. Heavier ones than she expected.

She turned, and her surprise at seeing a man standing in the kitchen doorway was equal to his at seeing her.

"Corie," he had started to say, before he realized his mistake. "Oh. It's you. I didn't expect to see you here."

"Ditto," said Ellie. "I thought you were long gone."

Jeremy Kidder grinned. The country gentleman's clothes were gone, and he was dressed in black jeans and a black hoodie that was pulled up over his blond hair. Ellie thought he now looked like one of those over-fit, over-40s from LA who thought dressing like a teenager gave them eternal youth.

Under his arm, he held the Walter Sickert painting that Michael-John had once told her was worth a tidy sum. He had obviously just taken it down from over the fireplace. It wasn't even wrapped.

"I'm leaving soon," he said, making an effort to sound casual, but Ellie could tell from his eyes and the tension in his body that he was feeling anything but. "Just a few loose ends to tie up before I go. Where's Corinna?"

"I don't know," said Ellie. "Did you want to thank her for the painting?"

He laughed. The sound was made harsh by the resentment she recognized. "No, it's not that, but I was hoping to have a word."

"Well, if I were you, I wouldn't hang around too long. The police are looking for you with questions regarding some missing items from The Chestnut Tree. They're also interested in your relationship with Clio Matthews."

A flash of surprise crossed his face at that, but he recovered quickly. "Parker warned me that you were quite the detective," he said, aiming for a disarming smile.

"Not really. Just coincidence," said Ellie. "A vicar's wife has the opportunity to connect dots that other people don't see. You know Michael-John thinks you already went back to America."

"As I will, once I've seen Corinna."

"What do you want with her? It looks as if you've already taken her most valuable possession."

"Hardly. Anyway, we go way back. Corinna and I," he said, which was when Ellie noticed his accent had shifted from American to British.

"Did Clio know that?"

"*Mais non*," he said, suddenly French. "Clio's genius was her ability to see what she wanted to see, not what was in front of her. It was a quite remarkable talent and, in this case, served us both well."

Ellie was about to ask who he really was when the back door opened. Toby entered first, followed by Corinna, carrying a bouquet of wildflowers. It took less than an instant for her to take in the scene: Jeremy and the painting. Ellie looking from one to the other of them.

Jeremy grinned as the color drained from Corinna's face; the flowers floated to the floor, and Toby's hackles rose.

"There you are," he said, with that faked ease. "You know, for a moment I mistook Ellie for you again. There really is quite a strong resemblance. Do you think that was part of the attraction for dear old Father Graham?"

Ellie stepped back against the stove as if his words were bullets. He was still smiling as he admitted that he was the one who shot at Corinna and nearly killed her instead.

Corinna was so white, she looked about to faint.

"You're not really surprised to see me, are you, Corie? Surely my last offering made everything clear," he said, his eyes going to the gold coin necklace on the table. That's when Ellie realized it wasn't the necklace she had found in Louise's box. The coin was carved, not with an owl, but the immortal Pegasus.

"Surely you must have wondered, over the years . . . I know I've thought of you and pictured this moment."

To steady herself, Corinna clutched the back of one of the kitchen chairs, while Toby hugged close to her leg. If she had those powers Graham and his friends once ascribed to her, the man in front of her would have been lucky to get away as a swine.

"Is that why you're here?" she asked. "Has this all been a prelude to your dramatic entrance?"

"Of course. Who could resist the chance to see your face

again? But the fact is I need dosh. A lot of it. You can't live forever off your good looks."

"I think you came here because Clio told you her idea about the coins," Ellie burst in. "You thought you could find them yourself."

"Clio!" said Corinna. If she could possibly have looked more shocked, that did it.

"Yes! He's Edmund, Clio's boyfriend. I've seen the photos."

"Well done, Ellie!" he said with a laugh, but Corinna sat down hard on the chair and covered her face with her hands. When she looked up, her anger was unlike anything Ellie had ever seen before.

"Whoever he's been pretending to be, Ellie . . . and no matter how he has altered his looks . . . that man is no one other than my brother. The long-dead Pindar Matthews."

Now it was Ellie's turn to be aghast, looking at the face that seemed to be three faces at once.

"I've always known you wanted to kill me, in some fashion or another," said Corinna. "But Clio! Why on earth couldn't you have let her be?"

He shrugged. "I only got in touch to see how she was fixed. But she didn't have a sou, except for her allowance from that damned trust. I was going to disappear again, but she seemed to be falling for me . . . her new art-dealer friend, Edmund Danton . . . and I quite enjoyed that. I'd forgotten what it was like to be loved by someone so uncritical. Most women would as soon cut your balls off as say 'Good night.'

"So I started asking her about her life, and once she began to open up, it was incredible what I found out. Not only had she dreamed up her own theory about what Cleve did with his coins, but also, after a couple of bottles of wine, she spilled the sad story of how she caused her brother's death.

"You can't imagine what it was like hearing that. From

Clio. Of all people. For years she'd been carrying this terrible guilt about ruining the lives of her brother and sister, because she discovered evidence that her brother caused their father's death, and, when she told her sister, she went berserk and killed him. Really, it's like one of those Greek plays Cleve was so in love with.

"I pretended to sympathize, but I couldn't believe *she* was the one who betrayed me. My little poppet," he said, with a superficial heartiness that couldn't disguise the chilling lack of empathy in his voice. "I could always tell what *you* were thinking—never anything good when it came to me—but Clio!" He shook his head.

"It was good thing my plan to get rid of Pindar Matthews and break free was ready to roll, because I knew that day the moment had come. It was too bad I couldn't find the rest of the coins first, but it was certainly a stroke of luck—a nice theatrical twist, I thought—to be able turn you into a murderer just when you thought you'd me pegged for one.

"But Clio! I was so sure no matter what I did, she would never grass on me. Of course, once you were involved . . . that was a different story. You did exactly what I expected. Got angry and then legless." He laughed. "I admit I helped that process along a bit, so you wouldn't have any untimely return to consciousness, and, all in all, I have to say my plan was flawless."

"Yes, all right," said Corinna, in a defeated voice. "I see it all now, but why have you come back?"

"I told you. I have to have money," he said.

"Are you saying your own sister never suspected who you were?" Ellie had no brothers or sisters to judge by, but this seemed impossible.

"*Aucune chance!*" he said, and before their eyes, they could see him become the oh-so-charming Frenchman. "I am an excellent actor, you know, and I have more of a knack for languages than Cleve ever gave me credit for. I'd wager you wouldn't have known me either, Corinna, if we weren't standing in this god-awful kitchen."

Corinna scowled and said nothing. She seemed paralyzed by the story that Pindar was so gleefully playing out before their eyes.

"You may be a good actor, but you're a careless murderer," said Ellie. "It must have rankled that Cleve outsmarted you, the way he hid the coins. What was left of them. I suppose he knew you'd already stolen the rest."

Pindar shrugged. "All I've ever wanted is my fair share. Those coins were bought with my mother's family money. Nothing he earned or deserved. And he was so greedy about them. Think how much simpler, how much better, all our lives would have been, if he'd just given them to me. They were my birthright. Mother even said so."

"You've always conveniently forgotten that Mother was our mother too, no matter who your father was," said Corinna. "Did she ever tell you? Or didn't she know? A blackout drinker has so much trouble keeping track of such details."

Now it was finally Pindar's turn to be angry, and Ellie could feel the wave of hatred that passed almost visibly between them.

"You'd know about that, wouldn't you? Graham never knew how lucky he was to find God instead!" he said, turning to Ellie, who couldn't help blushing.

"All water under the dam," said Corinna, standing up. "It's been a pleasure to see you again, but you're too late for the coins. I donated them to the Ashmolean today. If you think that painting is really worth something, then take it and go. There's nothing else to get."

"There's still the trust. I thought a settlement might be in order. After all, think what I'm giving you. Innocence. And with an unexpected, but unimpeachable, witness no less."

Corinna laughed, and it was a horrible sound. "You think I'm going to pay you for that? I've gotten very used to being guilty, you know. And there's a freedom in being as low as you can go."

Ellie, who'd been watching and listening horrified, felt a fresh rush of adrenaline as she saw Corinna's eyes slew over to the knife block on the kitchen counter. These two adversaries could repeat history. This time for real.

"Don't!" she said, stepping forward to get between them, and Pindar's brittle laugh broke the spell.

"You really need to do a better job of keeping out of danger, Ellie. But, in this case, you don't have to worry. Corinna's not a killer."

"But you are," Ellie said, turning on him. "I suppose you thought Pen Whittaker had those coins."

"It was a reasonable theory. I never fell for that holier-than-thou act Jock Whittaker put on. He was perfectly capable of keeping schtum about Cleve giving the coins to him for safe-keeping. It turned out to be a mistake, I admit. But she was another one with a guilty conscience. She admitted she could have saved you, Corie, and she didn't. Didn't have the guts. That's what made her blow a gasket. Not me."

"Really. And she bruised her own throat in the process?" said Ellie. "Even if Michael-John doesn't press charges for what you stole from him, you'll be arrested for Pen's murder. And maybe Clio's too. You didn't happen to be the driver tailgating her in the fog?"

The eyes that now turned toward Ellie glittered, and she realized the laughter was only a ploy to control himself. "She was supposed to return to Paris, and I was only planning to make sure she stayed there, so I could get to the cottage first. I had to get here before she did, so when she changed her plans, I had to change mine."

"That's why you scared her off the cliff?"

"I did no such thing. Anyone will tell you that Clio was the world's worst driver. She always did the wrong thing when the unexpected happened."

"In this case, the unexpected being you."

Pindar's genial mask finally slipped completely, and she saw the implacable and resentful Jeremy again. That's when she noticed that, while he was still holding the painting under his left arm, his right hand had moved into his pocket, where it fastened around a bulge. The gun.

"Even if it had been, it was no more than she deserved for betraying me," he said. "As for you, I still think *you* owe me, Corinna, and I'd like to hear you say so. I could have left without this little reunion, and you would have gone through the rest of your life believing you killed me."

"I don't owe you, and I don't thank you," she said. "I preferred the favor you did me by being dead."

"Well, I'm sorry to have deprived you of your role as Cleve's avenging angel. I'm sure that's kept you warm and *smug* through all these years, while I'm still the bastard dependent on scraps from the table."

"Perhaps this is the only way to end that," he said and pulled out his gun.

Corinna froze, and Toby started baying. Ellie, who wasn't sure whether he meant to shoot himself, Corinna, or all of them, leapt without hesitating and shoved him with all her might. There was a loud bang as the first shot went wild, and the gun flew out of his hand.

Before Pindar could recover himself, Corinna had grabbed the gun from the floor, and turned it on him. Ellie backed away from them both, praying madly that Corinna wouldn't fire, even though she had nothing to lose. She couldn't be tried for killing the man she had already killed.

Just then, they all heard the whoop-whoop of police sirens and the sound of cars pulling into the gravel drive. *Deus ex machina!* Ellie thought and swore to herself that she would never doubt God's existence again.

Corinna's eyes flicked from Pindar to the window and back, then she said, "I'll give you one chance, which is more than you gave either Clio or me. But don't you dare ever approach me again." She waved the gun toward the back door.

"I guess that's my cue," Pindar said coolly, hitching the Sickert up under his arm. Then, with that toothy American smile, he pushed past them and fled.

By the time Graham and the police burst through the front door, Pindar had already sprinted across the garden and reached the woods. He might have gotten clean away too, if Simon Stephens hadn't been watching through his binoculars and seen which way he went. Many hours in those same woods had taught Simon as much as Pindar knew about the fastest ways to navigate through them and where you would come out. He directed the police and, although they failed to catch their quarry, they did reach the edge of the woods in time to see his car and the direction he went.

Two hours later, Ellie, Graham, and Isabelle, Michael-John and Corinna, Morag and the two boys were gathered in the sitting room at the vicarage to wait for news. With a cozy fire and a spread of soup, sandwiches, biscuits, tea, whiskey, and sherry to choose from, they, little by little, shared their parts of the day's events.

"It was Simon who alerted me—although I would have received his message sooner if I hadn't left my mobile in the kitchen while I worked in the garden. Thank goodness, we got there in time," Graham said, nodding to the boy who hovered in a corner, with his binoculars still around his neck. He seemed riveted in place, with eyes only for Corinna, who sat on the sofa next to Michael-John.

"He'd seen you go into the cottage, Ellie, so when he saw a man in black go in after you, he was alarmed and called me."

"But even before that, I'd been on the telephone with Geordie Murphy. He wanted to complain that the police were harassing him and his wife, and did I know how to stop them."

"I asked what the problem was, and, at first, he huffed and puffed about how his sister, Pen, had always been a fantasist, stirring up people with her stories. But eventually he came out with what happened."

"Which was what?" asked Isabelle.

"Louise was right all along," he said, looking from her to Ellie. "Not that she could have known what really took place the night Pindar was supposedly murdered, but her instinct to believe that Corinna was not the killer was spot-on. It's a tragedy that the pieces didn't come together properly back then."

"What do you mean?" asked Ellie, trying not to be impatient.

"It turns out Pen was there at Odyssey House that night too. She'd gone to pick some vegetables in the kitchen garden, thinking the young people wouldn't be around because it was a bank holiday weekend.

"She wasn't supposed to be there, filching lettuce or what-ever, according to Jock's rule of law, so she ducked down when she saw Pindar come out of the house with some kind of rolled-up rug and put it in the trunk of his car, then pick up a large knapsack, and head off into the woods."

"Leaving?" said Ellie. She glanced at Corinna, who was

listening with her head bowed, and Michael-John's arm protectively around her shoulders. "What time was that?"

"Around sunset," said Graham.

"So that was well before Louise got there," said Ellie. "I don't understand how it's important. He could have been going to the pub, knapsack and all."

"He did go to the pub, as we know. But when I called Mullane and reported this conversation, he told me no knapsack was ever found during the original investigation."

"On Pen's side, when she heard the next day that Pindar had been murdered in the library, she told Jock what she'd seen. He dismissed it, saying, as was true, that she couldn't know where he was going or whether he came back, and no one knew exactly what time the murder took place. He insisted that she keep quiet because he didn't want them to become involved in any way, and he was annoyed at her for being there when she shouldn't have been.

"When Corinna confessed, Jock and the Murphys told Pen that proved what she'd seen was meaningless. But she was always bothered by it and worried that she had been wrong to listen to them."

"I don't see why what she saw was significant," said Isabelle.

Corinna looked up then and said, "Because of the tarp. She must have mixed up the cars. Pindar and I had the same type of car and, in the dim light, they would have looked the same color. But the point was, it was my car boot he put the tarp in."

"And that tarp had his blood and salt water on it. It was part of the evidence that led to the belief that his body had been dumped in the Severn," said Seamus, trying not to sound too excited, as they all considered how Pen's information might have changed the outcome of the investigation.

"But if no one was killed, why was there all that blood?" asked Simon, flushing with embarrassment at his boldness.

"Because Pindar created that whole scene," said Ellie. "You can draw your own blood, you know, and store it. Even freeze it." When they all stared at her, she added, "I know that's true. Louise researched it among other things. Four pints are all you need to create a persuasive death scene. Forensic proof that a person died. There's no need for a body."

Seamus's eyes shone. "Wow," he said softly, and Ellie knew he was itching to write this all in the little notebook he always carried. "But, Guv, why did you ask Simon and me to dig up that place by the rose arbor? We didn't find anything at all."

Ellie grinned and glanced at Corinna. "Because that's exactly what I hoped you would find, and it proves another point."

Everyone looked baffled.

"Corinna told me that her great-grandmother's Meissen tea set originally had four cups, but Clio broke one when she was a child. Then Corinna broke one during a fight with Pindar, and she was so ashamed she buried it by the rose arbor. I thought her memory had to be playing tricks on her because she still has two cups, and I knew there was also one in the crime-scene photos."

"I don't get it," said Isabelle. "What was the point?"

"The point is that when I realized there were too many of those cups left, it made me wonder whether there wasn't something odd about those photos. Corinna had played me a recording of an argument she and Pindar had a month or so before the murder, and there were surprising correspondences between the soundtrack—crashing furniture and so on—and the scene of the later murder. I think Pindar used his memory of the way the room looked then to plan the setting of his murder scene. He must have known what Corinna did with that broken cup and decided to include it. A reckless idea, because either of his sisters might have questioned that detail."

Corinna looked up then and said, "Everything Pindar ever did was reckless, but he probably couldn't resist the joke. And he knew we'd be too drunk, in my case, and too terrified, in Clio's, to notice anything like that."

There was an awkward pause before Michael-John said, "It was an incredibly vicious plan. I suppose in the beginning he only imagined he'd steal the whole coin collection and disappear, but one obstacle led to another with increasingly violent consequences. I'm still trying to wrap my head around the fact that this was the person I knew as Jeremy Kidder. I thought he was a charming petty thief. But, in fact, he never even existed."

"Like Clio's friend, Edmund," said Ellie, thinking back to how happy she looked and wondering again how she could not have known her own brother.

"I guess she didn't recognize him because you don't expect the dead to come back, do you?" said Isabelle. "Whether it's fifteen years . . . or three days later," she said, glancing at Graham, "dead is dead."

"Apparently not always," said Graham. "You know, if Pindar had been satisfied with stealing only half of the coins and disappeared before Cleve realized what he had done, none of the rest of these events would have happened. I'm sure Cleve would have somehow covered up the loss to save face, but Pindar wouldn't be satisfied unless he had the whole lot. Even now, all this time later and despite what he'd done."

"And he became increasingly reckless," said Ellie. "Shooting at me—or Corinna—for example, but I still don't know what lamb crisps are or what they had to do with anything."

"Lamb crisps?" asked Seamus, wrinkling up his nose. "Where do they come in?"

"They're potato crisps flavored with lamb and mint. Pindar was mad for them," Corinna said. "He always had packets of them hidden in his room. Not that Clio or I would ever have wanted to pinch them."

"Geordie explained that," said Graham. "Pen told Ruby it was the lamb crisps that made her connect the blond stranger who seemed to recognize her with Pindar Matthews. The expression on his face when he looked at her was unsettling, but it was the fact that he was buying several packets of lamb crisps that made the penny drop. That's why she was frightened because she suddenly knew who he was and that what she had witnessed that night at Odyssey House had been very important indeed."

At that, Corinna stood up, and they all turned toward her. "I can't hear any more about this. I don't even want to know what happens next. Will you walk me home, Michael-John?" she asked, and he immediately got to his feet.

"Of course," he said. "I can't imagine there will be any news tonight anyway."

Morag took the boys home then too, and Ellie, Graham, and Isabelle were clearing up when the doorbell rang. It was DI Mullane, looking haggard with fatigue.

"I've just been to Oak Cottage, and now I thought you should also know that it's over," he said. In a quiet voice, he explained that the police had caught up with Pindar at Heathrow. In the chase across the terminal that followed their sighting him, he had managed to keep well ahead, but when he tried to go down an escalator at speed, carrying that large painting, he lost his footing and fell.

Isabelle sucked in her breath. "On one of those horrible, steep escalators?" she asked, grimacing.

Mullane nodded. "He went head over heels and broke his neck."

Ellie and Graham were stunned. To cover their silence, Mullane kept talking. "We don't have all of the reports in yet, but Matthews had apparently created several identities over the years, and he had at least one ex-wife. It looks as if he came back to Europe when his last lover gave him the push. He really was out of funds."

"I need some whiskey," said Ellie, and the detective welcomed their invitation to come in.

Once they all had drinks, they resettled in the sitting room, where Ellie did her best to tell them all she remembered about her dealings with Jeremy Kidder from their first meeting to the moment when she witnessed him morph into Clio's friend Edmund and then, once Corinna was present, into his real self. Pindar Matthews.

"It was like watching an actor go from one role to another before your eyes. If he had gone into the theater, he might have been very successful."

Mullane cleared his throat. "It appears he found an easier and more lucrative way to make use of his talents."

"Preying on women, you mean," said Ellie.

"On anyone who had some dosh is more like it," said Mullane.

"Can this close the case of Pen Whittaker's death now?" she asked. "He admitted he was there."

Mullane nodded. "I expect so."

"And Clio?" asked Graham.

"I don't think there would be any benefit to re-opening that case. What would be the point? It would be hard on Ms. Matthews, and I expect the priority there is to get her own conviction vacated as soon as possible."

Graham nodded. "That's only her right. And his turning

up like that is probably the only decent thing Pindar ever did in his life."

"Or in his death," said Ellie. "I'm sure Lila and Mrs. Tuttle will be very shocked by this news, but all I can say is I'm glad his story is over."

CHAPTER SIXTEEN

Sunday, April 1 (Easter)

H oly Week turned out to offer ample opportunities for the village to absorb the news that Pindar Matthews, who had not been dead, now was; and that his sister Corinna, who had served 15 years in prison as his murderer, was innocent. Ellie found she didn't mind the long hours sitting in the darkened church with its shrouded crosses. They gave her time to reflect on lives cut short by betrayal, as well as to admit her human need for all they'd been through to have some redeeming purpose. And, who knew? Maybe an afterlife too.

When the weekend came, Mrs. Bell invited her to join the flower committee in decorating the church with armloads of daffodils. Her manner showed this was meant as a generous gesture of forgiveness for the latest round of publicity about the goings-on in Little Beecham, which had in fact attracted a busload of mystery writers and readers who were attending a nearby conference. With equal generosity of spirit, Ellie said yes and discovered that flower arranging was a very meditative and soothing task.

Isabelle was delighted to have a new person in the family to color eggs with, and they stayed up late on Saturday making enough for the entire Easter Egg Hunt in the churchyard to be held after the service the next day.

Easter dawned a glorious day with a cloudless blue sky and warm sun that made you blink and feel your bones were finally warming up. It was the kind of day Ellie remembered from earlier visits to England that had convinced her nothing could be more idyllic than to live there all year round.

She and Isabelle were up very early to hide the Easter eggs around the churchyard, then they all ate Mrs. Finch's hot cross buns before dressing to go to church. A large crowd turned out, including, Ellie suspected, some tourists. The church, bedecked with it bouquets of daffodils, looked beautiful, and everything went smoothly from the singing of the pickup choir to Graham's reflections on how the enduring power of the Easter story came not only from its recounting of the death and resurrection of Jesus, but also from the way it encompassed so much of human experience: recognition and rejection; devotion and betrayal; faith and despair; fear and pain; acceptance and forgiveness; death and hope for the future. A few people in the congregation, who were not regular attendees, even clapped.

At their last rehearsal for the Widor, Mr. Dunn had hinted to Ellie that the service would include a "surprise" for her. A tradition established by Pen Whittaker, which was being taken up by someone new.

It certainly was a surprise when Isabelle, wearing a lilac silk dress, rose from the pew where she and Ellie were sitting and went to the front of the church to sing "I Know That My Redeemer Liveth" from Handel's *Messiah*. Ellie had not even known Isabelle could sing so beautifully, but her clear soprano voice was so simple and sincere, it made her tear up. In that evanescent moment—which she'd read in William James was the essence of spirituality—she even believed the words "and though worms destroy my body, in my flesh shall I see God." A spellbound silence followed.

When Ellie joined Mr. Dunn on the organ bench for the finale, they raced together through the "Toccata" with nary a mistake and were treated to a round of applause before the large congregation fell hungrily on the tea, coffee, and cakes contributed by members of the parish. Then everyone spilled out into the sunshine to watch the children hunt for the Easter eggs, hopping around the churchyard like colorful birds in their spring clothes.

Afterward, Ellie put the finishing touches on the dinner Mrs. Finch had prepared for them, while Graham relaxed with a sherry, and Isabelle popped over to Oak Cottage with an Easter basket she had made for Corinna.

When she returned, Isabelle reported that Michael-John had been there, and he and Corinna were cooking Sunday lunch together. "He said it was good I'd brought candy and eggs, because who knew whether their dinner would ever be ready. That made Corinna laugh, and the weird thing was I recognized the sound. I recognized it from long ago."

Later, as the afternoon light turned from yellow to gold, and the air once again picked up a chill, Ellie went over to the cottage herself to invite Corinna for a walk. She found her as usual sitting with Toby on the back steps overlooking the garden, but she stood, when she saw Ellie, and walked toward her, with a hesitant smile.

Ellie was immediately struck by the way her face had softened and her whole body seemed more fluid, as if the inner tension that radiated from her before had been released. Even Toby seemed less "on alert" loping along beside Hector.

They walked in silence down the drive and out along the B road to the footpath that led through the woods and fields. They didn't mention Pindar, but Corinna told her that Michael-John had offered to take care of whatever she needed help with to sell the cottage, and, as soon as possible, they were going to Paris to clear out Clio's flat and finalize the arrangements for the exhibit she had been planning to have in Trouville.

"That's wonderful," said Ellie. "Michael-John is the perfect partner for that kind of project."

She nodded and fell silent. "He is a good person. Easy to be with. You know, when you've been convicted of murder, everything you are or were or become is subordinate—even invisible —to most people. That's been my identity for so long, I feel naked right now. Blank."

"I can imagine the change will take a while to sink in. For you to find your way back to yourself."

Corinna looked surprised. "But that's not what I want at all," she said. "Pindar set me free from my old self, so now I have the chance to start from scratch. And I am glad I don't have to go through life knowing I took someone else's, so I could start my own."

"Then this is it: ad aspera per astra. Your life ever after."

Ellie was heading home across the churchyard when her eye caught a bright spot of color in the grass: an undiscovered Easter egg nestling at the foot of Louise's grave. It had begun to rain gently, but she set the egg on top of the stone and stood there for a few minutes, remembering the woman she had never known, but who was so much a part of her new life.

She thanked her for the inspiration to try to learn the truth about what happened on that May night so many years ago.

And she added, "Don't forget, Graham finally admitted you were right!"

Then she walked on to the vicarage until she could see through the brightly lit windows, her family—Graham, Isabelle, Hector, and Barney—all together in the sitting room, and she went in to join them.

ACKNOWLEDGMENTS

This book has had a long journey to completion and would still be nothing more than an idea were it not for those who read, listened, and encouraged me: Janet Basu, Jeffrey D. Briggs, Luanne C. Brown, Kathy Chetkovich, Martha Conway, Michelle Dionetti, Marianne Faithfull, Mark Fishman, Jim Mullins, Candace Robb, Sarah Niebuhr Rubin, Victoria Schultz, and Janis Wildy, as well as the Puget Sound Sisters in Crime and the 15th Avenue Marketing Group.

Very special thanks also go to my content experts and advisers: Michael Crowley, Helena Echlin, Catherine Hendricks, Kathleen MacInnis Kichline, D.P. Lyle, Seamus O'Connor, Richard B. Pilgrim, Carol Sanford, Rick Sauvé, Marty Wingate, and Leighton Wingate. Any errors are my own.

Finally, I would also like to thank all the readers who loved the first two Ellie Kent mysteries. I hope you will enjoy this one too!

Book Club Discussion Questions

1. In this book, Ellie Kent tackles a 15-year-old mystery that she is continually told is no mystery. What motivates her to keep trying to find out what really happened?

2. Did you think the village's reaction to the return of Corinna Matthews was appropriate? Justified? Both? Neither?

3. As events in the present become increasingly threatening, Ellie is convinced they prove she's on the right track, but a big obstacle to untangling both the past and present is the silence of the person at the heart of the mystery: Corinna Matthews. Do you agree that she has the right to keep her secret? No matter what?

4. Does Graham understand how Ellie's uncertainty in her new role affects her and her reactions, as well as her determination to prove herself? Does she understand how hard it is for him, having lost his first wife, to have her take so many risks? How well do you think they balance these tensions in their new marriage?

Don't miss these other Ellie Kent mysteries!

Under an English Heaven (Ellie Kent mystery, book 1)

In this first Ellie Kent mystery, Ellie has left behind her college teaching job and life in San Francisco to marry a handsome widowed vicar and live in a Cotswold village. At first, she thinks her biggest challenge will be to gain acceptance from the villagers as a foreigner and "incomer." But, when she discovers a dead man in the churchyard, her outsider status leads to her becoming the prime suspect in his murder. To prove her innocence, Ellie finds she must draw on her research skills to unravel a web of decades-old secrets before more people die—and her new life unravels too.

Available in ebook, paperback, and audiobook editions

What Child Is This? (Ellie Kent mystery, book 2)

American Ellie Kent imagined that spending Christmas in the Cotswolds would be like living in an Advent calendar. But the pleasures of mummers and mince pies, caroling and candlelight are interrupted when a distraught couple asks for her help. Their 20-year-old daughter has been missing for more than two months, and the police search has gone cold. Ellie remembers being a runaway herself and knows she can't refuse. As she learns more about the missing Oxford student, she finds a trail that seems to connect an abandoned baby, a drama club, and a group of girls who identify with Shakespeare's tragic Ophelia. Does that mean there is a Hamlet involved . . . and is he a killer?

Available in ebook, paperback, and audiobook editions

ABOUT THE AUTHOR

Alice K. Boatwright is the author of the Ellie Kent mysteries, which debuted with *Under an English Heaven*, winner of the 2016 Mystery and Mayhem Grand Prize for Best Mystery. The series continues with *What Child Is This?* and *In the Life Ever After*. Alice has also published other fiction, including *Collateral Damage*, three linked novellas about the Vietnam War era; *Sea, Sky, Islands*, a chapbook of stories set in Washington's San Juan Islands; and *Mrs. Potts Finds Thanksgiving*, a holiday parable for ages 8 to 108 that focuses on generosity and community connection. Her career writing about the arts, education, and public health took her around the world, including a decade based in Oxfordshire and Paris. She now lives in the Pacific Northwest.

Author Photo: Maria Aragon

Learn more . . . stay in touch . . . share your experience

If you'd like to learn more about the music and customs described in this book, visit my website at alicekboatwright. com/the-ellie-kent-mysteries and click on the **Sights and Sounds of England/In the Life Ever After**. Enjoy!

For the latest news about Ellie Kent and more, you may sign up for *What's Up?*, my occasional newsletter, at eepurl.com/ cER4Cj

If you enjoyed this Ellie Kent mystery, please tell your friends —and consider posting a review on one of the sites where readers go for ideas about books. Thank you!

www.ingramcontent.com/pod-product-compliance
Lightning Source LLC
Chambersburg PA
CBHW021501240626
47154CB00002B/470